OLIVIA KIDNEY

HOT ON
THE TRAIL

Ellen Potter lives with her husband and son in upstate New York. *Olivia Kidney* was her first children's novel, but Ellen has been writing for children and adults for over a decade and has been published in a number of American journals. She has also published an adult novel.

Ellen is currently working on a new children's novel.

Also by Ellen Potter

OLIVIA KIDNEY
OLIVIA KIDNEY STOPS FOR NO ONE

PISH POSH

OLIVIA KIDNEY

HOT ON THE TRAIL

ELLEN POTTER

ILLUSTRATED BY
NICOLA SLATER

MACMILLAN CHILDREN'S BOOKS

First published 2006 by Macmillan Children's Books

This edition published 2007 by Macmillan Children's Books
a division of Macmillan Publishers Limited
20 New Wharf Road, London N1 9RR
Basingstoke and Oxford
www.panmacmillan.com

Associated companies throughout the world

ISBN: 978-0-330-44142-1

Text copyright © Ellen Potter 2006
Illustrations copyright © Nicola Slater 2006

The right of Ellen Potter and Nicola Slater to be identified
as the author and illustrator of this work has been asserted by them in
accordance with the Copyright, Designs and Patents Act 1988.

1 3 5 7 9 8 6 4 2

A CIP catalogue record for this book is available from
the British Library.

Typeset by Intype Libra Ltd
Printed and bound in Great Britain by Mackays of Chatham plc, Kent

For Jennifer Wielt

Many thanks to Christopher Santiago, who graciously explained the workings and mysteries of the New York City subway system.

CHAPTER ONE

Olivia Kidney had never been much of a morning person. Nor was she the sort of person who rushed gleefully into new situations. In fact, early mornings and new situations always made her feel especially rotten, which is why she chose to take the 7th Avenue IRT subway on Wednesday morning, the first day at her new middle school. She might have taken the bus, but 'bus people' tended to be chirpy, orange-lip-sticked old ladies on their way to the senior centre for a day of creaky aerobics and pasty grilled cheese, or else they were noisy little kids comparing their brand-new backpacks and glow-in-the-dark pens. 'Bus people' were the sort of people who thought that the day was going to be one big, worry-free party, complete with a piñata full of goodies to take home at the end. In other words, they were the sort of people who didn't have a clue.

'Subway people', on the other hand, all looked like

they were on their way to have their wisdom teeth removed, which was exactly how Olivia felt that morning.

All the seats on the train were taken, so she clung to a pole in the centre, trying not to whack people with her knapsack. It wasn't easy, since her knapsack was stuffed so full that it looked like her spine was nine months pregnant. That in itself was just wrong, Olivia felt. *Regular* schools didn't make you carry that much junk on the first day of classes. All over the city, kids were carrying droopy, deflated knapsacks, but because she was going to a *special* school, Olivia had to haul hers around like a pack mule.

Attending the Malcolm Flavius School for the Arts had not been her idea.

'The kids who go to that school are talented, Dad. *Really* talented,' Olivia had objected when her dad insisted she try out for the art programme months ago.

'You're talented, Sweetpea,' her dad had replied. 'You have what they call *raw talent*. All it needs is a little seasoning.'

George Kidney talked in food terms a lot these days. Up until recently he had been a handyman – an appallingly bad handyman. But now he was personal chef to Ansel Plover, the owner of the brownstone they lived in.

'Dad, I couldn't get into that school if I was smothered in barbecue sauce.'

And she was right. She took their art test, and they turned her down flat. But she didn't care. In fact, for the first time in many years, Olivia was looking forward to going to the regular local school, since she would actually know someone there. For most of her life, she'd been forced to switch schools so many times that she never had a chance to make any real friends. Now she had one: Ruben, a whizz of a skateboarder, and a pretty decent guy too. She had met him over the summer and now he was teaching her how to skateboard in Central Park – without too much success, but never mind – and they'd both been excited to be going to the same school, a fact which neither one would be caught dead admitting.

'So that means I'm going to have to put up with your lousy mood swings in school too?' Ruben had said, when they'd found out they were both zoned for Middle School 72.

'Don't worry,' Olivia assured him, 'if we run into each other in the hallway, I'll be sure to completely ignore you.' But after they had parted that day, Olivia walked home trying so hard to suppress her smiles that she had to clap her hand over her mouth a couple of times.

Then, a month ago, she had received a letter from the Malcolm Flavius School for the Arts saying that a

3

spot had opened up and she would be admitted after all. For a solid week she argued about it with her father, but in the end she finally agreed to go, on the condition that if she hated it she could switch to Middle School 72. And she was one hundred per cent sure that she would hate it.

The subway lurched to a halt. Olivia whipped around to check the station, walloping the man standing behind her with her knapsack, which was full of the requisite art supplies: charcoal sticks; a large tin of coloured pencils; some square packages of blue erasers that you could squish, but made your fingers smell bad; a box of pastels; a set of various pencils that looked like normal pencils but which the salesman at the art store assured her, with a smirk, were not; a pad of something called newsprint, which felt like cheap toilet paper, and a regular sketch pad, both of which were too large for her knapsack and poked out of the top.

'Sorry,' Olivia said to the man she'd walloped.

'Yep,' he said gruffly, as though that was exactly the sort of thing he'd expected to happen that morning.

72nd Street. The school was on 65th Street and West End Avenue. Only one more stop to go. Olivia checked her watch. She was early. Good. It would give her a chance to talk with her older brother, Christopher, before school.

A new rush of people shuffled into the carriage and

Olivia turned to back up, smacking the same man with her backpack again.

'Hey, Santa Claus,' he snarled, 'if you hit me with your sack of crap one more time, I'm going to boot you straight back to the North Pole.'

'Sorry,' Olivia said. She slipped the backpack off her shoulders and carried it in her arms, just to be safe.

The train started up again and Olivia stared out the window, pretending to be fascinated by the passing metal beams in the tunnel. In truth, though, she was looking for ghosts. It was a habit, a thing she'd done ever since she was seven and a little girl who lived next door to her told her that there were ghosts in the subways.

'You can see them if you look out the window while you're in the tunnels,' the girl had told Olivia. 'They're little kids. They'll stick their tongues out at you when they float by. Their tongues are black, by the way.'

'I don't believe in ghosts,' Olivia had told the girl. And she didn't when she was seven. Since then, she had discovered that ghosts did indeed exist, but she'd never seen one with a black tongue and, besides, the little girl who told her about them was a chronic liar.

Still, you never know, Olivia reasoned, as she gazed out the window into the murky tunnel. The world is a strange place.

The train slowed, then stopped at the 66th Street Station, where Olivia squeezed her way out of the carriage, taking care to avoid the man whom she'd thwacked with her backpack.

She walked down Broadway to West End Avenue, catching sight of the school before she was even halfway down the block. Considering that it was a school for the arts, it was unbelievably ugly. Constructed as a large and perfectly square chunk of grey-tinted glass, it looked exactly like a gigantic television set. In fact, through the glass you could make out shadowy figures walking around, as though it were tuned to some weird sci-fi channel.

As Olivia approached, she examined the kids milling around on the street outside. They were all artists of some kind or other – dancers, singers, painters, musicians. Quite a few of them seemed anxious to let everyone know exactly what sort of art they practised, like the two whippet-thin girls who were dressed in leotards, short skirts and tights, their hair yanked back into skull-pinching buns. And just in case there was any doubt, they each had a pair of ballet slippers conspicuously slung over their shoulders and one of them carried a pink canvas bag that said 'Dance Diva!'

Olivia rolled her eyes.

There were many kids carrying instrument cases, but for the most part they didn't seem show-offy. In

'You can belch the entire alphabet, if I remember correctly,' Christopher said.

'Oh, you're hysterical today,' Olivia said dryly. 'Anyway, they'll probably kick me out by the end of the day.'

'Then there's nothing to worry about, is there?' Christopher said.

'Nothing except public humiliation.' Olivia sighed.

'Nah. Just think about it, kiddo,' Christopher said. 'For most of the seventh graders, this is the first new school they've been to since kindergarten. They'll be too nervous to pay any attention to you. You, on the other hand, are an old pro at being in new schools. You'll coast right through this.'

'Yeah, maybe,' Olivia said, not entirely convinced. Still, his words managed to take the edge off her nerves. 'So, what have you been up to lately?' she asked, to change the subject. 'Are you working with anyone new?'

According to Christopher, dead people didn't just lounge around all day, doing whatever they wanted. Most of them were assigned to different jobs, which always struck Olivia as very unfair. Christopher's job was to help people who had just died to adjust to the Spirit World. And since he had a lot of patience, he generally was assigned the most difficult spirits.

'I'm in between assignments this week,' Christopher replied. 'The last woman they had me work with refused to believe she was dead. She thought she was dreaming and she kept kicking me in the ankles to see if I was real.'

Suddenly, Olivia was aware of a pair of large, hooded green eyes inches from her own face.

'Jeez!' Olivia cried, drawing back so quickly that she smashed her lower back against the edge of the step behind her.

'Were you sleeping?' The girl in front of her had a low, husky voice, almost like a boy's, and tar-black hair with a too-short fringe. She was wearing a pair of overalls that were obviously hand-sewn, cut out of red velvet.

'What?' Olivia said, confused.

'The school buzzer's been going off. You were just sitting there, staring off into space.'

Olivia heard the buzzer now. It was so loud she was amazed that she could have missed it.

'I thought you might be sleeping,' the girl said.

'With my eyes open?' Olivia shot back incredulously.

'*I* sleep with my eyes open.'

That must be a frightening sight, Olivia thought. The girl's eyes were eerie enough when they were awake. They were large and round and her heavy lids slanted down at an angle, like busted window shades.

'I trained myself to do it,' the girl added.

'Fascinating,' Olivia muttered.

The girl stared at Olivia for a moment. 'Do you mean that? Or are you just being rude to me?' she asked.

Well, what kind of a question is that! Olivia thought, squirming under the girl's stare. Of course she was just being rude. But it was positively indecent to put a person on the spot like that! In her head she could hear her brother softly laughing.

'No, it really is fascinating,' Olivia demurred. What else could she say, after all?

'What's your name?' the girl wanted to know.

When Olivia told her, the girl stared at her for a few seconds, then asked, 'Do you like chicken salad, Olivia?'

'I guess.'

'So do I. Do you want to have lunch with me today?'

'Oh . . . I don't know,' Olivia hedged.

'When will you know?'

'All right, fine, I'll have lunch with you,' Olivia said, just to get rid of her.

The girl smiled. Her eyes didn't crinkle up at all when she smiled, like a normal person. 'My name is Stella. I'll meet you in front of the water fountain on the first floor.'

'Yup.'

'She seems like a nice kid,' Christopher said after

Stella had left. 'And now you know what you'll be doing for lunch.'

'Yeah. Avoiding the water fountain on the first floor. Anyway, I'd better go in.' She hauled her fat knapsack back on to her shoulders. 'And by the way, I was never able to belch past the letter G.'

'Probably a good thing, don't you think?'

'Yeah, probably,' Olivia admitted.

CHAPTER TWO

By the time Olivia walked into her homeroom class, all the other students were already seated. They glanced up at her when she entered, and Olivia automatically braced herself. In the past, when she'd first entered a new school, she had to endure the cold stares of students who already knew each other and who had no room in their tight little cliques for Olivia. But just as Christopher had predicted, most of the kids looked pretty nervous themselves and their stares didn't linger long. Olivia began to relax. This might be a chance at a fresh start. For the first time in her life, she was just another kid in the class. Totally anonymous.

There was one empty desk in the back row, next to a slight red-headed boy who had one arm wrapped around a gargantuan instrument case sitting upright on the floor beside him. It looked like he was on a date with a curvy 200-pound woman. Olivia squeezed past the other desks to get to the back row and turned to take the seat, nearly knocking down the red-haired boy's instrument case with her backpack. He flung his body across the case and clasped his arms around it to rescue his 'date' from a tragic fall, then glanced ruefully at Olivia.

'Sorry,' she said. The boy nodded back, carefully scrutinizing her.

'Art major?' he asked.

'Yeah,' Olivia said, pleased that he could tell. 'How did you know?'

The boy shrugged and said matter-of-factly, 'You're not carrying an instrument, you're too klutzy to be a dancer, and art students are either bizarre-looking or just –' he held his palms out towards her – 'average-ish.'

'Oh.' Olivia slunk down in her seat.

Just then the door opened and a woman walked into the room. She was very thin and had a mass of thick flaxen blonde hair that curtained her face and fell past her hips. When she walked she kept her back slightly arched, as though someone was pushing her from behind and she was resisting. Her slender legs, which were revealed by a lavender, pencil-slim skirt that reached just below her knees, were terribly long, and with each step they extended far out, like she was stepping over puddles. Some of the boys in the class whistled softly.

'Now *she* moves like a dancer,' the red-haired boy said, looking smitten.

'Good morning, children.' The woman turned to them, and there was an audible intake of breath in the classroom. Behind her mane of hair, her face was a mass of sharp bones thinly covered by pale skin with hundreds of hairline wrinkles, like an ancient plaster ceiling. She had to have been at least eighty years old, maybe older. 'My name is Miss Monsoon and I'll be your homeroom teacher. Yes, I hear your whispers, children.' Except for the initial gasp, the room had been perfectly silent, everyone still reeling from the sight of such an ancient face behind the veil of girlish hair. 'I am indeed Miss *Mona* Monsoon, but I want to make one thing perfectly clear. You must try and ignore the fact that I am famous. It is of no consequence. While we are in this classroom, I am just a simple homeroom teacher.'

The boy next to Olivia raised his hand.

'Question?' Miss Monsoon smiled, which made her mouth look like a video deposit slot.

'What exactly are you famous for?' the boy asked.

Miss Monsoon's drawn-on eyebrows rose halfway up her forehead and she demanded, 'Tell me your name, young man.'

'Aidan.'

Miss Monsoon picked up a piece of chalk and wrote 'BRUTE' on the chalkboard and underlined it twice, banging her chalk so hard as she wrote that little bits of it dropped to the floor. Underneath 'BRUTE' she wrote 'Ethan'. Then she turned around and said to Aidan, 'That will stay up on the black-board until you have proved otherwise.'

'I don't care,' Aidan muttered. 'That's not even my name.'

'Now.' Miss Monsoon clapped her hands and swung her blonde mane behind her bony shoulders. 'I welcome you to the Malcolm Flavius School for the Arts! The reason you are here is simple. You are the most talented children in New York City . . .'

Olivia flinched at these words and glanced around at her classmates. They all seemed perfectly comfort-able with the notion.

'. . . and talent, as the old saying goes, will buy you a ham sandwich and a coffee cup full of tears.' She looked around significantly only to find thirty-five blank faces staring back at her.

'Talent, children, is NOTHING! There are two things that are far more important: First of all, you must have PANACHE!'

'Isn't that like a croissant?' one girl asked. 'Except with chocolate in the middle?'

Miss Monsoon thrust out her chin at the girl and said, 'Name?'

'Claire.'

On the board, under the 'BRUTE' column, Miss Monsoon jotted down 'Clara'.

She turned back to the class. 'And the second thing you must do is ignore the BRUTES! You will find that the world is infested with Brutes. They will write horrible things about you in the newspaper. They will throw things at you on stage. Brutes will crush you and grind your tender young souls into the dirt! You must IGNORE THE BRUTES!' She finished her little speech with a pitiful shriek. Then she turned abruptly, and with her odd walk she glided back to the desk, sat down, put on her glasses and pulled a slip of paper out of a Manila envelope.

'Now for attendance.'

She ran through the names quickly, but paused after calling 'Katz, Patricia', frowning down at the paper. She removed her glasses and stared out at the class. 'Will Olivia Kidney please stand,' she said.

For a moment, Olivia just sat there, praying that she had misheard. The other kids looked around, waiting to see who would stand.

'Olivia Kidney? Are you here?' Miss Monsoon asked.

Olivia briefly considered pretending that she wasn't, before she reluctantly got to her feet. All heads in the classroom swung around to look at her. So much for being totally anonymous.

'Miss Kidney, a word of advice,' said Miss

Monsoon. 'You may find it cruel now, but later in life you will thank me.'

Olivia bit down hard on her lower lip. Somehow Miss Monsoon had figured out that Olivia had no business being in the school. But to announce that fact in front of everyone really did seem pretty cruel.

'You must change your last name,' Miss Monsoon continued. '*Kidney* is the name of an internal organ. It is not the name of a *star.*'

This took Olivia so much by surprise that she didn't hear the class's laughter at first. But when she did, she took a deep breath and wilfully ignored it.

'I don't plan on being a star,' Olivia said.

'Oh, but you are halfway there already, Miss Kidney,' Miss Monsoon said. 'You have already mastered one of the two most important rules. You are able to ignore the BRUTES!' She swept her arms across the classroom and the laughter died down. 'All you need now is a healthy dose of PANACHE! You may take your seat, Miss Kidney.'

After attendance, Miss Monsoon distributed their class schedules. Olivia scanned hers quickly till she found Art. Fifth period. Right after lunch. Just the thought of it made her stomach knot up.

The rest of the morning classes were uneventful. The usual handouts and test dates given. Even though no one knew each other, they had already divided themselves into several distinct groups: the musicians, with their instrument cases perched on their laps or on the floor beside them; the weird-looking kids who resembled a flock of exotic birds, with their Crayola-coloured hair (probably art students, Olivia guessed); and the reedy, neat dancers, who moved their seats as far away from the art students as possible, as if they might catch some rare tropical disease from them.

When the lunch bell rang, all the kids filed out into the hallways and flowed in the same general direction, headed for the cafeteria no doubt. Olivia headed that way too, but when she spotted Stella waiting by the water fountain, which happened to be located next to the cafeteria, she did an about-turn. Following several boys who were walking in the opposite direction of everyone else, she travelled down three flights of stairs to the basement, through a long corridor and then into what appeared to be a small auditorium. About a dozen or so of the chairs were occupied by kids who were eating lunch, and up on the stage were three girls in black leotards, stretching their liquorice-whip bodies. Some strange, discordant music was blaring on the sound system – the sort of music that Olivia imagined the CIA played in order to freak out people they were interrogating.

Olivia took a seat near the front, off to the side. Her stomach was so clenched with nervousness about fifth period that she had no appetite. She unzipped her knapsack and peeked at her lunch anyway, just to see what her father had packed: a melted mozzarella and tomato sandwich, a bottle of apple juice, and a generous slice of banana-chocolate-chip cake. Her favourites. She felt her stomach unclenching just a little, enough anyway for a nibble of cake.

The music now sounded like a group of old ladies screeching at each other while sitting in a laundry room with a broken dryer that thumped loudly every five seconds.

The dancers had finished stretching and were leaping and waving their arms and then swooning and collapsing to the ground in some sort of dance routine. It looked fake and silly, but Olivia supposed that it was all very artistic. She looked around the room to check the expressions of the other people and noticed that, except for the dancers, the auditorium was occupied almost entirely by boys. Boys who were all ogling the dancers. Olivia snorted. *Idiots.* For all his faults, she was pretty sure that Ruben wouldn't be caught dead leering at some skinny girls flopping around on stage.

'Eat some lunch, why don't you,' she muttered under her breath to the dancers. 'I can hear your bones clacking together.'

There was no way the dancers could have heard her. Yet right at that moment one of them stopped dancing and stared directly at Olivia. The dancer was very pretty, to be sure. But her prettiness was spoiled by the fact that one eyebrow arched up higher then the other, stamping her with an expression of permanent disdain. She was aiming that disdain right at Olivia now.

'*Quel* disaster!' the dancer announced loudly enough for the other girls to stop dancing and follow their friend's gaze to Olivia. 'It's French, darling,' the pretty dancer said to Olivia. 'It means, what are *you* doing here?'

Olivia gasped as she suddenly realized who the girl was. Renee. Renee, who had lived in the same apartment building as Olivia not too long ago. Renee, who was one of the most unpleasant people Olivia had ever met.

'I'm eating my lunch,' Olivia said a little weakly.

'Ah, the poor girl *ne comprend pas*,' Renee said to her friends pityingly. Her friends looked like they didn't *comprend pas* either, but they rolled their eyes obligingly. Then Renee said to Olivia, in a loud, slow voice, as though Olivia were a dope, 'What I mean is, when did you recover?'

'From what?' Olivia asked.

'Oh for heaven's sake, I'm trying to be nice here . . .' Renee blinked up at the ceiling for a moment as if contemplating how she should put things. Then, in a mock whisper that was loud enough for everyone in the auditorium to hear, she asked, *'When did you recover from your devastating mental illness, darling?'*

The boys in the room had taken their eyes off the dancers and were now staring at Olivia.

'I never had a mental illness,' Olivia retorted, feeling the heat rise to her face.

'Come on, it isn't exactly a secret,' Renee said. 'I mean, are you denying that you had to go to the school psychologist because you were constantly talking to yourself?'

Actually, that was the truth.

'And that you were hearing voices in your head?' Renee asked.

Actually, that wasn't the truth. In fact, Olivia *wanted* to hear voices in her head – well, one voice, really, that of her brother, Christopher. That was before she had learned how to contact him. But she didn't think the explanation would do anything to help her case at the moment.

'And that even your own mother is insane, and lives in a mental institution,' Renee added.

'That's a lie!' Olivia was glad she finally had something she could object to. 'My mother lives in California.'

'I believe there are mental institutions in California too,' Renee said coolly.

There was some laughter from the boys.

'Oh, you and your nutty family were the talk of the

entire apartment building,' Renee continued as Olivia hastily stuffed the remains of her cake back in the lunch bag, gathered up her knapsack, and started to hurry out of the auditorium. 'That was why they had to fire your father. No one wants a janitor whose daughter is stark raving mad. The janitor has keys to everyone's apartment, which means that *you* could have gotten a hold of them and . . . oh, *quel* tragedy! You might have attacked people in their sleep, *mon dieu!*'

'For your information, my father was fired because he flooded six apartments when he was trying to fix someone's bathtub!' The moment the words came out of her mouth, she wished she could take them back. There was a muffled snickering that turned into a roar of laughter. Olivia hitched her knapsack up on her shoulder and hurried out to the sound of Renee's voice advising, 'Don't laugh at her, darlings, she is like a rabid raccoon – *très* dangerous when angry.'

CHAPTER THREE

Art class was on the top floor of the school, down a quiet hallway that smelt of turpentine. The hallway was so hushed that Olivia could hear her own sneakers sucking against the polished black floor. Suck, suck. Suck, suck. What an appropriate way to announce her arrival, she thought.

Studio Five was at the far end of the hall, a cavernous room with tall windows and no desks, just easels with stools set up behind them. To her great dismay, Olivia spotted Stella perched on one of the stools. She quickly averted her eyes in the hopes that Stella wouldn't notice her. No such luck. Stella spotted her right away and began to wave excitedly. Olivia guessed that a person who slept with her eyes open probably wouldn't miss very much when she was wide awake. Still, Olivia pretended not to see her, scanning the room for an out-of-the-way easel behind which she could hide from the teacher's notice.

'Are you pretending not to see me, Olivia?' Stella called out in her raspy voice. Olivia groaned, but turned around and sat down on the stool next to Stella.

'I waited for you by the water fountain at lunch,' Stella said.

'Oh, yeah. Sorry. I guess I just forgot.'

'That's OK. We can have lunch together tomorrow. So, did you hear about our art teacher?' Stella asked.

'What about him?' Olivia said warily.

'He's supposed to be a *fiend*.' Stella's strange heavy-lidded eyes opened wide for a second before the lids descended again. 'If he doesn't like your work, he'll just rip it into tiny pieces and toss it over your head like confetti.'

'Oh, fabulous.'

The classroom door opened and a short, stocky black man entered. He wore a white turtleneck shirt and crisp grey trousers, and all in all had the air of someone who ironed his underwear every morning. He stood in the middle of the room, his arms behind his back and, one by one, stared hard at each and every person in the class. Olivia held her breath when his eyes landed on her and she didn't breathe again until they moved on to the next person.

'Well,' he said finally, 'I can't say I'm impressed with what I see. There are four of you who may have a scrap of talent, but for the most part you are a bunch of poor to middling artists.' He had a very faint accent that hummed a bit on the Ms and skipped over the Rs entirely.

'How can you tell?' one girl objected irately. 'You haven't even seen our work yet.'

The teacher sucked in his cheeks for a moment and lowered his eyes, as if trying to control his temper. Then he looked up at her in such a withering way that the girl put her hand to her lips, as though she were trying to stuff her words back in her mouth.

'I have seen your eyes, mmm,' the teacher said. 'That is sufficient.'

He walked to an easel in the front of the room, scribbled something across the paper tacked to it, and turned the easel to face the class.

'This is my name.' He pointed at the words *Mr Pierre-Louis*. 'You will not pronounce it Mister Pierre-*Looo*-isss.' He made his voice nasally and high, which would have been funny if he were someone else, but as it was no one dared to crack a smile. 'You will address me, instead, as Mister Pierre-*Looo*-*eee*. And I warn you now that I do not respond to foolish questions, false flattery, or tears, of which, no doubt, there will many.'

He handed out a list of homework assignments, as well as two sheets of paper covered with rules and regulations including *Under no circumstances are you to touch Mr Pierre-Louis's clothing*.

'Now,' he clapped his hands, 'take out your sketch-pads and your pencils, and find a face that you can tolerate staring at.'

Stella swivelled around quickly on her stool. 'You and me, right?' she said to Olivia.

It was unavoidable.

'Sure,' Olivia said.

There was some scrambling among the class as people changed stools.

'All right, everyone happy?' Mr Pierre-Louis asked when everyone had settled. 'Good. I want you to face your partner and look at their eyes. Not at their nose or their chin or their lips, do you understand? Eyes only. Stare into their eyes until you figure out what ugly, shameful secret is being concealed. I guarantee everyone has one, mmm. It will be tucked away in the brain's dustiest cupboard, behind the rusty can of corn niblets. Do NOT pick up your pencil and draw until I say so. Understood?'

There was a low murmuring of agreement.

'Excellent. Begin.'

Olivia focused on Stella's eyes, which was a little disconcerting to say the least. Not just because they were so large and droopy-lidded, but because they were staring right back at Olivia's eyes so fixedly. Stella didn't seem the least embarrassed by this exercise. In fact, she looked as though she did this every day.

As the minutes stretched on, Olivia looked away a few times or scratched her nose – anything to give herself a break from those lizard-like eyes. But after a while, she found herself relaxing and beginning to examine Stella's eyes carefully. They were a deep green with a darker green rim around the irises, and the pupils were very small. At first, the hooded eyelids made her look sort of dull and sleepy, but the more Olivia stared, the more she saw that this was not the case at all. In fact, they now struck her as exceptionally alert. What was Stella secretly ashamed of? Olivia stared and stared until her eyes watered, but she couldn't make it out.

She wondered suddenly what Stella might be seeing in her own eyes. Was Stella pawing around in the shadowy recesses of Olivia's mind, finding all her secrets? Lord knew she certainly had plenty of them.

Hastily, Olivia lowered her gaze to escape from Stella's prying stare. That was when she noticed the trail of spittle leaking from the side of Stella's slack mouth. Olivia listened for Stella's breathing. It was slow and regular, like a ticking clock. There was no doubt about it. Stella was sound asleep.

'All right, ladies and gentlemen,' Mr Pierre-Louis announced. 'I believe you've had enough.'

There were audible sighs of relief and stools screeched against the floor.

'Can we start sketching our partners now?' one boy asked. His hair was dyed the colour of a blue raspberry slushy. His right eyebrow sported three little barbell piercings, the rim of his left ear was cluttered with tiny silver balls, and his nose had a ring through the middle of it, much like an ox. Olivia felt sorry for the girl who'd had to stare at *that* face.

'Why on earth would I want you to do that?' Mr Pierre-Louis asked coldly.

'Well, wasn't that the whole point of the exercise? To figure out your partner's shameful secret so you could draw them better?'

'No, I said, "*Stare into their eyes until you figure out what ugly, shameful secret is being concealed.*" The ugly, shameful secret is your own, mmm. You will know what that secret is, because it is the very thing you were hoping your partners would not notice during our little exercise. You, for example –' he pointed to the boy with blue hair – 'I'd venture to guess your secret is that you are as dull as a butter knife, so you poke holes in your face to appear more interesting. We must see ourselves clearly before we can see the world clearly.'

Just then, the period-change buzzer sounded. Olivia felt a terrific surge of relief. Art class was over and she hadn't been asked to draw a single line.

Across from her, Stella blinked, then stirred. She casually wiped away the drool from her chin with the heel of her hand. Looking down, she rubbed at the blobby wet spot on the front of her shirt.

'Oops! I guess I was daydreaming. I do that sometimes. Did I miss anything important?' she asked, without a trace of embarrassment.

Olivia considered for a second, then shook her head. A person who didn't care about drooling in public places wasn't likely to have any secrets she'd be ashamed of.

CHAPTER FOUR

When Olivia returned home that day, she opened the front door to the four-storey, mud-coloured brownstone on West 84th Street only to find two strange men standing in the entrance hallway. They were holding long metal poles with nets on the end of them. At their feet were a dozen or so wooden crates. One of the men was counting a wad of money while the other was saying, in a low voice, '. . . ever see such a weirdo in your life? The guy was practically—'

'Afternoon, young lady.' The man counting money had seen Olivia and quickly interrupted his friend.

Olivia nodded back cagily. She hated when people called her 'young lady'. It was such a phoney way to try and be nice to a kid – as though anybody considered a twelve-year-old girl a 'lady', young or otherwise – and when people said it they almost always meant something else entirely. In this case,

Olivia was pretty sure that 'young lady' meant, 'Shut up, the kid's old enough to guess who we're talking about.'

'He's not a weirdo,' Olivia shot back at them, because in fact she did know who they were talking about. 'He's just eccentric.'

The men looked embarrassed, and the one holding the money quickly shoved it in his pocket while the other set about picking up the crates and carrying them outside.

Olivia dropped her knapsack on the floor and opened the white double doors to the living room. Well, strictly speaking, it was not so much a living room as a lagoon, on top of which living-room furniture floated on little rafts. In fact, the entire ground floor of the brownstone was submerged under water, with the exception of the kitchen. At the edge of the lagoon, tied to moorings that jutted up from the marble walkway, was a fleet of colourful pedalos bobbing lightly on the water.

Floating on his back in the lagoon's water, with his arms and legs splayed wide, was the brownstone's owner, Ansel Plover. He was wearing yellow swimming trunks and had shiny red inflatable rings strapped around his wrists and ankles. Balanced perilously on his stomach was a tall glass with a green umbrella sticking out of it.

'Ansel . . . the snapping turtles!' Olivia cried, scanning the water in case one of them was sneaking up on him. Ansel's mother, the famous psychic Madame Brenda, had stocked the lagoon with them in order to remind her son to take life more seriously. A scheme that hadn't worked very well so far.

'They're gone, thank heavens,' Ansel said, making the glass on his stomach wobble as he spoke. He was a terribly handsome man with thick blond hair and a pouty, lazy, but altogether good-natured expression. 'I called in the Turtle Removal People, or some such whatchamacallit, and the good men have just now cleared them out, every last one of them, and good riddance.'

That must have been what the men in the hallway had in their crates, Olivia thought.

Suddenly, she heard a faint whirring noise. It seemed to be coming from the far end of the living room, where the walls narrowed to form a canal that twisted through the house. In a moment a bright green pedalo emerged from the canal, inside of which was a beefy, rotund man. He was dressed in a smart black three-piece suit and had a towel slung over his left shoulder.

The little boat wobbled violently as the man pedalled. His weight made it sit so low in the water that he looked to be in imminent danger of sinking. Still, he appeared amazingly unruffled, except for a persistent little twitch of his neat black moustache.

'Who's that?' Olivia whispered to Ansel.

'Fellow named Cornwickle,' Ansel whispered back as he pulled himself up out of the water and on to one of the little rafts, on which sat a lawn chair and a nubby glass table beneath a large umbrella. 'Mother sent him this morning. She says I need some proper looking-after.' He sighed. 'I don't like the sound of that, frankly.'

He undid his inflatable rings and idly dropped them into the water, then stretched out in the lawn chair.

'Towel, sir?' Cornwickle said when he reached Ansel. He draped the towel across his forearm and held it out to Ansel while trying to keep the little boat steady by treading backwards and forwards.

'Lovely, thank you, Cornwickle! Excellent timing.' Ansel forced a bright smile at him, took the towel, and began to rub his limbs vigorously. 'Say, Cornwickle, you look like you have a pair of nice strong legs. What do you say to a boat race? Three laps around the living room. Loser gets dunked.'

'I'd rather not, sir.' Cornwickle's moustache shifted to one side then the other, as though it were trying to find a way off his face and as far away from Ansel as possible.

'No,' Ansel said sadly, 'I didn't suppose you would.'

Cornwickle turned his attention to Olivia now. 'Miss Kidney, is it?'

'Yes,' she said. 'But you can call me Olivia.'

'I'm afraid I can't, Miss Kidney. It wouldn't be proper. You have a guest waiting for you in the parlour.'

'Really? Who is it?' Olivia asked.

'A Miss Smithers,' Cornwickle replied.

Olivia frowned. *Miss Smithers?* She didn't know any Miss Smithers.

'Oh, yes!' cried Ansel. 'I forgot to tell you that your friend was here, Olivia. She's a delightful little thing, Miss Smithers. No bigger than my shinbone but awfully smart. She said that she'd always heard I was rather sinister, but that she liked to make up her own mind in such matters. I made her promise to tell me when she decided, and she agreed. I hope she decides quickly. I'll be in a morbid state of suspense until she does.'

'Frannie!' Olivia cried. It had to be. She'd simply forgotten Frannie's last name was Smithers.

Olivia untied the mooring rope of an orange boat, hopped in, and began to pedal quickly across the living room towards the canal. Ansel used to have a fleet of sleek black gondolas instead of pedalos, and his maid Nora would row him around the house while he reclined on a bed of cushions. But Nora had left two months before, and since Ansel felt that rowing was boring, he replaced the gondolas with the little pedalos, each just big enough for one person.

Olivia pedalled into the little canal with its low, vaulted ceiling. She peered into the large kitchen off to the left, which had been built above water level. Inside, Olivia's father was standing over the stove, stirring a large soup pot with his left hand and a saucepan with his right hand. The pungent smell of cooked onions and fresh basil was wafting out of the room.

'Smells good, Dad!' Olivia called as she pedalled past.

'Hi, Olivia!' her dad called back. 'How was schoo—?' But Olivia was in too much of a hurry to stop. She hadn't seen Frannie in months, not since Frannie had left Ms Bender's School for Superior Children, which was right next door to the brownstone. And though, in Olivia's opinion, Frannie was definitely superior, most of the other kids in that school were perfectly average. They were sent to the school to learn how to behave like spoiled wealthy children so that everyone would *think* they were superior. Frannie and her sister were sent to Ms Bender's because their mother was engaged to the very wealthy Claude Vondychomps, and in order to impress him and his father, Frannie's mother had told them that she was a Hungarian countess. In reality, she was a dog groomer from the Bronx. At Ms Bender's school, Frannie and her sister, Stacy, were taught things like how to be rude to waiters and how to ride ponies, but in the end the Vondychomps weren't fooled. Still, Claude married Frannie's mom anyway. As Frannie said, both her mother and Claude were as dumb as a box of rocks, so they made a perfect match.

The canal made a sharp turn past the bathroom, where the toilet and bathtub floated (when the currents were strong, they drifted dangerously into the canal, threatening to collide with the boats). The canal turned yet again, and off to the right was a very pretty parlour, with numerous armchairs that floated dreamily past end tables laden with bouquets of calla lilies. Olivia stopped pedalling and gazed around. The room was perfectly empty.

Oh, I've missed her, Olivia thought unhappily. She must have given up waiting for me and left.

But just as she was about to pedal away, one of the armchairs turned lazily to reveal its occupant – a very small girl with short dark hair, reading a book. The girl looked to be around seven, but the book she was reading was as thick as a dictionary.

'Frannie!' Olivia smiled and pedalled over to her friend. She secured the mooring rope to a ringbolt attached to the leg of one of the armchairs.

'Oh, is that how it's done?' Frannie said, watching. 'My boat just sort of drifted off down the hall a few minutes after I sat down here. I was beginning to wonder how I was going to get back.'

Olivia climbed out of the boat and plopped down in the armchair, which bobbed a little and spun around, so that she was facing away from Frannie. But she shifted her weight and rocked the chair a little until she was facing Frannie again.

'What took you so long to come visit?' Olivia asked.

'Well, what with Mom's marriage to Claude and – Oh!' Frannie had shut her book and shifted to tuck her legs beneath her, which caused the chair to swivel and drift away from Olivia. Olivia reached out just in time to grab the arm of Frannie's chair and spin it back around.

'Stick out your legs out,' she told Frannie. Frannie stuck out her legs, which were short and spindly. Luckily, Olivia's legs were quite a bit longer and she linked her feet around Frannie's ankles. With a little effort, she was able to hold Frannie's chair steady so they could face each other.

'Thank you, that's better,' said Frannie. 'Anyway, what with the marriage and my research, I haven't had a spare minute.'

'What are you researching?' Olivia asked.

'I'm trying to figure out how to make myself grow,' Frannie said.

Although Frannie was the size of a seven-year-old child, she was nearly fifteen – two years older than Olivia.

'Shouldn't you leave that to the doctors?' Olivia asked.

'Doctors!' Frannie said scornfully and folded her tiny arms across her chest. 'I've been going to doctors for years. I've swallowed all sorts of pills and been given loads of injections, and the only thing that's happened is I occasionally get sick to my stomach and once my eyelashes fell out. Otherwise, I haven't grown an inch. I've given up on the doctors. That's why I started doing my own research. And guess what? I think I may be on to something.'

'Really? What is it?'

Frannie picked up her book and held up the cover for Olivia to read: *A Botanical History of the Dreaded Pitta-Pitta Tribe of Papua, New Guinea* by Franklin Steenpister.

'I don't get it,' Olivia said.

'Well, the first three hundred pages are dead boring, to be perfectly honest. It's all Steenpister's journal entries about the plants and flowers in the jungle, and the seeds he's collected for his greenhouse in America. But then, on page three-five-eight, something caught my eye. It turns out that the Pitta-Pittas are only about three feet tall. I mean, for goodness sake, you'd think Steenpister would have mentioned that a little sooner. I bet he's pretty dull in real life.'

'Can I see the pictures?' Olivia asked. To be honest,

she wasn't a big reader, and nothing in the world would have tempted her to pick up a fat book like *A Botanical History of the Dreaded Pitta-Pitta Tribe of New Guinea*. But still, she could see a thin, glossy dark line running down the centre of the closed book – a sure sign of pictures.

Frannie leaned over, her ankles still held securely by Olivia's feet, and held the book out for Olivia. It was a little hard to reach it, since Frannie's arms were so short, and the armchairs twirled around in a circle several times before Olivia managed to take hold of the book.

She turned to the photographs. There weren't many. Most of them were fuzzy black and white shots of plants and trees, and a few of Franklin Steenpister, who was a gaunt, completely bald man with close-set eyes. There was only one photo of the Pitta-Pittas themselves. Steenpister had obviously posed them since they were standing in three neat rows. They certainly did look fierce, Olivia thought, what with the jagged black masks painted across their eyes and white necklaces that looked suspiciously like finger bones. The only thing both the men and the women wore was a twist of leaves around their middles and shrewd expressions on their faces, as though they all knew a really good secret and they weren't telling. But the most unusual thing about the photograph was that at end of the row of tiny Pitta-Pittas was one very tall Pitta-Pitta. He was so tall, the other Pitta-Pittas only reached his hips.

'What's the deal with the tall one?' Olivia asked.

Frannie smiled and pointed a finger at Olivia. 'My question exactly. Look on page four-oh-one. I marked the section with a Post-it.'

Olivia turned to page 401. She saw a little yellow Post-it beside what looked to be a journal entry, and read it out loud:

7 March 1995
Just when I thought I had found out everything there was to know about the dreaded Pitta-Pittas, something astonishing has happened. They sent one of their thirteen-year-old boys, named Blup, into the jungle by himself, without food or water. It seemed unusually cruel, since Blup is one of the tiniest and weakest of the Pitta-Pitta children. They threw stones at him to make him leave, and he was told not to return until two full moons had passed. When I asked them why they had done this, they said that Blup was too weak and they had no need for him. Their brutality seems to have no bounds! I was convinced that Blup would surely die in the jungle. If starvation did not kill him, the poisonous snakes certainly would. Yet, a few days after the second full moon, Blup returned. He was no longer the tiny little boy who had left, but instead had

managed to grow to a height of nearly six feet in the space of two months! The tribe welcomed him back with kicks to his buttocks (that is how the Pitta-Pitta show their affection), and prepared a great feast for him. When I asked Blup how he managed to grow so tall, he grimaced and tried to poke me in the eye.

According to the tribal chief, there is a myth about a mysterious plant in the jungle that makes people grow. This is no myth! For hundreds of years, anthropologists have mentioned instances of miraculous growth among Pygmy tribes in New Guinea, but they have never discovered the secret. I, however, am determined to.

Olivia looked up from the page. 'Well? Does he?'

Frannie shrugged. 'I don't know yet. I haven't finished reading, but I'll bet he does. He seems very, very stubborn. Oh, speaking of stubborn people, the Princepessa Christina Lilli asked me to give you something.' The princepessa was an elderly, exiled princess, who had been one of Olivia's neighbours at her previous apartment building. Frannie unzipped her knapsack, fished around inside it, pulled out a pale blue envelope, and handed it to Olivia. On the front was printed in embossed black script *George and Olivia Kidney.*

Olivia tore open the envelope and took out a pale blue card and read:

Her Royal Highness Princepessa Christina
Lilli and Arthur Vondychomps cordially
invite you to their wedding . . .

Olivia looked up with an expression of both joy and disbelief. 'They're getting married?!' she cried.

'Well, as of an hour ago, they were. But you never know from one minute to the next. Just yesterday, I overheard them fighting about what sort of music to play at the wedding, and the Princepessa said to Mister V (that's what I call him, since Grandpa doesn't really seem right), "You know what? You are still just a thick-headed caveman!" Isn't that awful?'

'Actually, he really is a caveman,' Olivia said. Arthur Vondychomps, Claude's father, had lived in a cave until the age of eleven, when he was taken into the Royal Palace to be raised as a gentleman. The Princepessa Christina Lilli had been a young princess in the palace at the time, and she had treated him abominably, nicknaming him The Thing That I Step On, because that was exactly what she did to him every morning.

'Oh, I know he's a caveman,' Frannie said. 'He's told us all about it. But still, you don't have to go reminding a person of that kind of thing. Then Mister V said, "Christina, you haven't changed a bit since you were a spoiled little girl in the palace, screaming at all your servants like a wild hyena!" Then she turned all purple in the face and said that the wedding was off. But she calls the wedding off nearly every day, and by the end of the evening they had made up.'

Olivia looked back down at the card: . . . to be held on Sunday, 19 September, 3 p.m., at the Vondychomps' mansion. Scrawled on the bottom was the message, *Olivia, you will come see me at the Mansion after school tomorrow, at 4 p.m. sharp – Christina Lilli.*

'Well, I better go,' Frannie said. 'I'm taking three advanced placement classes and I've already got loads of homework, not including my own research.' She detached her legs from Olivia's and then looked anxiously at the boat tethered to Olivia's chair.

'Oh, but how will we do this?' Frannie asked. 'I don't think we'll both fit in the boat . . .'

Just then there was a whirring sound and Cornwickle appeared at the door, pedalling in his dangerously wobbly way. Bumping along behind him was a zebra-striped pedalo, whose mooring rope he was holding.

'I believe you'll be needing a boat now, Miss Smithers,' he said.

'Yeah. Wow! How did you know?' Frannie asked.

Cornwickle raised his fleshy round chin and pursed his lips, which were puffy and red as a radish. 'It's my job to pay attention, Miss Smithers,' he replied. Then he pedalled up to her chair, guiding the zebra-striped boat to her feet, and stood up. Olivia winced as she watched the large man try to find his balance. The boat tipped severely to the right while his arms flailed and his hip flung out to the left. Then the boat dipped so deeply to the left that he had to shimmy his hip quite suddenly to the right.

He looks like a fat hula dancer, Olivia thought. She caught Frannie's eye and nearly laughed out loud, but Frannie shook her head sternly. Finally, Cornwickle managed to crouch a little and regain his balance. His moustache gave one disapproving twitch before he held out his hand to Frannie.

'Miss Smithers, if you'll be so good as to step aboard,' he said, his voice slightly breathless from the exertion. Frannie took his hand and nodded to him in a very respectful way. She stepped into the boat so lightly that it barely made a bobble. Cornwickle sat back down, his boat sinking considerably lower than Frannie's.

'Come visit me soon,' Frannie said to Olivia.

'I'll visit you tomorrow, as a matter of fact,' Olivia

replied. 'The Princepessa asked me to come see her at the Vondychomps' Mansion.'

'You mean she *ordered* you to see her. Did she say why?'

'No.'

'Well, I'm sure she won't try and make you do anything too awful,' Frannie said without conviction before she pedalled out the door, with Cornwickle wobbling behind her.

CHAPTER FIVE

Olivia put off doing her art homework for so long that she completely forgot about it until she was already settled in her huge canopy bed and nearly asleep. When she remembered, she smacked her pillow and groaned. She switched on the little reading lamp beside her bed and groped around in her knapsack until she found the art homework handout: *Draw a portrait (it must be of an actual living person, not from a photograph or your imagination. Trust me, I'll know the difference).*

Olivia considered her options. There was her father, of course. But he was actually convinced that she had talent, and she couldn't bear to see his face when he got a look at what she was really capable of. She might draw Ansel though. He'd probably enjoy having his portrait done. She grabbed her sketchbook and a pencil and wrapped herself in a robe. No sooner had she started down the stairs than she ran into Ansel walking up them, looking uncharacteristically glum.

'Oh, Ansel! Good!' Olivia said. 'How would you like to pose for a portrait?'

'There's nothing I'd like more in the world,' Ansel said. 'But unfortunately, Cornwickle is demanding that we take inventory of my wardrobe. My mother told him that I always dress as if I'm going to the State Fair for a day of cotton candy and teacup rides. What nonsense! In fact, I have two entirely different wardrobes: one for the days when I'm cranky and one for the days when I'm not.' Ansel sighed and opened the door to the second-floor bedrooms. 'I'm afraid this Cornwickle is going to be no fun at all. It's as though Mother knew I was going to get rid of her horrible turtles.'

'She might have,' Olivia said. 'I mean, she is a psychic.'

'It's a curse to have a psychic mother,' Ansel pouted. 'Be thankful yours isn't.'

Olivia supposed he was right, but it was hard to be thankful about anything when it came to her own mother. When she'd lived with them, Monica Kidney was always whizzing about, going to her theatre classes or her transcendental meditation classes or to her acupuncturist, named Earth – just Earth. And when Monica was home, she was often talking on the phone with her friends, one finger plugging her available ear to block out the sounds of her family. To Olivia, her mother always seemed like a loud, hyperactive visitor in their house: a visitor who only stayed because she couldn't think of someplace better to go. That is until two years ago, when she decided that Los Angeles was, in fact, a far better someplace.

'Plus,' Ansel continued petulantly, 'I don't even like cotton candy. Nasty stuff. It always gets wedged in my cuticles.' With that, he entered the second-floor hallway, letting the door slam shut behind him.

Olivia returned to her bedroom and collapsed on her bed, wondering what on earth she was supposed to do now. The chill of autumn had not yet arrived, and a delicious late-summer breeze skimmed her face through the open window. It made the curtains billow out, and Olivia caught a glimpse of movement in the second-floor window of the brownstone across the street. It was the prettiest brownstone on the block, with flowerpots lining the front steps and more flowers spilling out of the cement window boxes. The front door was a beautiful polished mahogany, so slick that it made you want to lick it.

She dragged a chair to the window and pulled back the curtains. The lights on the first floor were on and Olivia saw an elderly lady walk by a window, speaking on the phone. Olivia recognized her as the owner, a neat, sturdy woman who swept the pavement in front of her brownstone each morning. The lights on the second-floor were on too, and a man was standing by one of the windows, staring out. He was an elderly man, with a high forehead and hair as white as a business envelope. He wore a black turtleneck shirt, which appeared very stark against his pale skin and hair.

All right, he'll do, she thought. She grabbed her pencil and sketchbook and sat back down in her chair. Her lamp gave off just enough light to see the sketch pad, yet not enough for the man to catch her watching him. But just as she put her pencil to the paper, the old man walked away from the window.

Great! Just my luck, Olivia thought. But the next moment he returned carrying a chair. He sat down and continued to stare out the window. It struck Olivia as a very sad and lonely sort of thing to do. She wondered if the old man had any children or grandchildren, and decided that he did, and that they were all horrible, piggish types who only visited on holidays in order to get presents from him.

She picked up her pencil again and began to draw.

'Hmmm, I don't know. The mouth doesn't seem right somehow,' a voice said in her ear.

Olivia glanced around to see a frail-looking young woman with a thin face and narrow blue eyes peering over her right shoulder. The woman wasn't flesh and bone, but she wasn't transparent either, the way most people imagine ghosts to be. Instead, she seemed to have a light bulb shining out from inside her body. Her skin was glowing, and the glow pulsed larger and smaller, like a stomach rising and falling with each breath.

'I'm not done yet, Tina,' Olivia said, then went back to her drawing.

She had grown accustomed to these ghostly visits, which had started soon after she'd moved into the brownstone that past summer. As Madame Brenda had explained, Olivia attracted ghosts because she was a Straddler, a person who had one foot in the world of the living and the other foot in the Spirit World. For the most part, Olivia found that ghosts were a lot like living people – some of them were blabbermouths, some of them were shy. And some of them were annoyingly nosy. Like Tina.

'It's the lower lip. It droops too much,' Tina said. She almost always had some kind of advice to give, and Olivia found the best tactic was to ignore her. Eventually Tina began to float around the room in a bored sort of way. She passed through Olivia's closet door and Olivia could hear the hangers shifting on the rod.

'You need to go shopping,' Tina said when she passed out of the closet again. Picking up a tube of lipgloss off of Olivia's dressing table, she removed the cap and started to apply it to her lips.

'Don't do that!' Olivia cried. 'It's totally unhygienic.'

'I have no more germs left on my mouth,' Tina replied, and rolled the gloss across her lips. The effect was peculiar, making Tina's lips look like they were made of pink stained glass. Olivia made a mental note to toss out the gloss after Tina left. True, she probably didn't have any germs left on her lips, but Olivia was not going to use a lipgloss that had been rolled on a dead person's mouth.

'You're too young to be wearing make-up,' Tina advised. 'But you know what you should be wearing?'

'I'm trying to concentrate, OK?' Olivia pleaded.

'A bra. You're starting to grow breasts.'

'Oh, Jeez!' Olivia cried, slapping her pencil down on her sketch pad.

'I'm just trying to be helpful. OK, I see you're busy. I'll leave you alone.' Tina started to fade, like someone was turning the dimmer down on the light inside her body.

Olivia picked her pencil up and started to draw again.

'If you want my advice,' Tina said, her light growing brighter again for a moment, 'you should use the binoculars in your closet to draw that man. You can't see him well enough otherwise. That's just my opinion though. Take it or leave it.' Tina sighed, then dimmed again, and this time she disappeared altogether.

Much as Olivia hated to admit it, Tina was right. She went to her closet and after a few minutes of rummaging (and once again grudgingly admitting that Tina was right – she did need to go shopping), she pulled out the binoculars. She rushed back to the window, relieved to see that the man was still there. She held the binoculars with her left hand, while she sketched with her right, making the old man look especially miserable by sagging his lips. As a finishing touch she added a framed photo on the wall behind him, depicting a sour-looking man, a pinch-faced woman, and two frowning, piggish-looking boys – the old man's family, as Olivia imagined them. When she was done she examined her work and decided that it wasn't too bad. Not great, but not too bad.

She lay back down in bed and checked her alarm clock. 10.45. Any minute now people were going to start arriving at the brownstone, just like they did every night. Sometimes there were only half a dozen, and other times there were twenty or more. It all depended on how many people were scheduled to die within the next few days. Of course, many, many other people who were about to die didn't come to Ansel's brownstone; there were thousands of Exit Academies just like Ansel's all over the world, where people learned how to die while they were dreaming.

Before she moved into the brownstone, Olivia had always assumed that dying was simply a matter of not breathing any more. She had been in the hospital room when Christopher died, and it had all seemed so quick and simple. One minute he was smiling at her and their father and the next minute his eyes closed and he was gone. As horribly uncomplicated as switching off a light. But Olivia had since learned that dying was a complicated business. To do it well, you needed to practise. And to practise, you needed to attend an Exit Academy.

Outside, she heard the first set of footsteps making their way up the brownstone's front stoop. Slow, hesitant footsteps. Sometimes Olivia would rush to the window to see the people coming. Some seemed eager to start their lessons, and practically leapt up the steps and bounded into the brownstone. Those people, Ansel had explained to Olivia, were often the ones who had been sick for a long time. He said that if you saw these people in normal, waking life, they would appear too weak to lift their heads, yet their dream bodies were quite robust and more than ready to leave the earth.

Other visitors, however, were clearly afraid and lingered for a while on the brownstone's steps, or paced back and forth on the pavement, without entering. Those were the people Olivia felt most sorry for. Now, when she heard the slow, cautious steps outside, she resisted looking out the window. Drawing the lonely old man sitting by the window had made her feel a little melancholy, and she didn't want to make herself feel any worse.

She closed her eyes and, right before she drifted off to sleep, she heard the brownstone's front door open and Ansel saying, 'Ah, welcome, I've been expecting you! Now, there's nothing to be afraid of, my love, I'm quite harmless. Except when the bathwater gets chilly too fast . . . then the bubbles start to pop and oh, look out, I'm a beast . . .'

CHAPTER SIX

The following morning, just as Olivia was about to descend the subway stairs, she heard her name being called. Turning, she caught sight of Ansel. He was wearing a dark grey suit with a pale grey tie, trotting across the street against a red light under a drizzle of morning rain, just barely dodging several cars. He took the time to smile charmingly at the drivers, then caught up to Olivia and grabbed her hand.

'Hurry, love, Cornwickle is on my tail!' He pulled her down the subway steps and rushed them to the turnstile. Olivia swiped her school pass and pushed through to the platform, but Ansel stopped short.

'Oh, I forgot about those silly things. I don't suppose I could borrow yours?'

'Can't,' said Olivia. 'The lady in the booth is watching.'

Booth people always seemed to know when someone was thinking about cheating the system, and right then the booth lady was staring right at them, practically daring them to try something.

'Just buy a card from her,' Olivia said.

'I don't have a cent on me. I ran out of the house while Cornwickle was putting on his galoshes. Never mind, I'll manage.'

He turned slowly and smiled at the booth lady, which made her narrow her eyes at him suspiciously. Olivia watched from the platform as he strolled up to her and said something through the booth's circular grille. The booth lady scrunched up her lips disapprovingly, and when Ansel said something else through the grille, she replied with such a scowl that Olivia was glad there was a sheet of glass between her and Ansel. For once, Ansel's infamous charm was failing him. Undeterred, he said something else, then kissed his hand and pressed it up against the glass. Suddenly, a loud buzzer sounded, and Ansel quickly turned and ran to the narrow iron door to the side of the booth. He pushed it open and joined Olivia on the platform.

'What did you say to her?' Olivia said just as the IRT came thundering down the rails.

'I told her that of all the booth ladies in all the world she had the most enchanting fringe. And she said she was sick and tired of creeps like me, and she wished I'd drop dead. And I said that except for the fact that that I had no money for my fare, I would gladly oblige her and throw myself in front of the train to prove my devotion. That was when she buzzed me in. Now, since I'd hate to disappoint the kind lady . . .' The train was approaching the station as Ansel walked rapidly towards the very edge of the platform. 'Mind,' he said, turning back towards Olivia, 'I'd appreciate it if you'd grab me at the very last second—'

Right then the train came roaring in and Ansel began to step over the platform. Several other people on the platform watched, their bleary 7.30 a.m. eyes suddenly bright at the prospect of seeing a man pureed beneath a train, but Olivia lurched forward in time, took hold of Ansel's jacket, and yanked him back. The onlookers seemed a little disappointed, as did the booth lady.

Ansel and Olivia sat down next to each other in the carriage, and Ansel gazed around.

'I'd forgotten how delightful the subway is!' He stretched out his legs but quickly retracted them when a passenger who was standing nearby shot him a filthy look.

'So why are you running from Cornwickle any-way?' Olivia asked, then added to the woman seated next to her, 'That's my armpit, not an umbrella stand.'

The woman grunted then reluctantly shifted the handle of her umbrella away from Olivia.

'Poor Cornwickle,' Ansel sighed. 'He didn't know

what he was in for when he agreed to take this job. I am bound to be a torment him. My mother has hired him to turn me into a respectable headmaster of an Exit Academy, which means attending all the board meetings and reading the newsletters and socializing with the other headmasters, who are all so boring they give me hives. There's a board meeting this morning, and Cornwickle is determined to see me attend it. That's why I'm wearing these grim-looking clothes. Anyway, I've managed to give him the slip. So, love, tell me. How is school coming along?'

'Not great,' Olivia said. 'I don't think I'm as talented as the other kids.'

'Nonsense,' said Ansel. 'You have bony fingers – all great artists have bony fingers.'

'I do NOT have bony fingers,' Olivia protested, holding up her hand as evidence. But on closer examination, she noticed that her fingers were slightly bony. Wonderful! She had no talent, *and* had bony fingers.

'How extraordinary!' Ansel cried suddenly. He was watching the approach of a woman who was tightly swathed in bubble wrap from neck to ankle, with duct tape strapped along the seams. Beneath the bubble wrap she wore a pair of green and white striped pyjamas. Looped around her head was a wire coat hanger and dangling from the wire, attached by pieces of soiled string, were tiny, trial-sized bottles of shampoo and lotion and tubes of toothpaste.

'Now that's something one doesn't get to see every day!' Ansel said.

'You do if you ride the subway,' Olivia replied.

The woman was a subway lunatic. Subway lunatics were a slightly different breed than above-ground lunatics. Above-ground lunatics tended to blend into the messy New York landscape. No one wanted to look at them for fear that they might ask them for money or do something embarrassing. But subway lunatics had a captive audience, so they tended to be performers of one kind or another. They sang, they danced, they wore outrageous outfits. Olivia supposed that, if she were ever to become a lunatic, she'd like to be the subway variety. At least you wouldn't feel like you were invisible.

Still, it was simple good sense to try to avoid eye contact with them if you could help it. Everyone in the car suddenly became deeply engrossed in their newspapers or transfixed by their shoes. But Ansel made the grievous mistake of actually smiling at the woman as she approached. She stopped in her tracks, looking shocked. Then she placed her hand over her heart and squeezed a bubble till it popped.

'Hi,' she said to Ansel.

'Good morning,' Ansel said brightly. 'I was just admiring your hat.'

Olivia groaned and slumped down in her seat. Sometimes it seemed like Ansel didn't have a scrap of common sense. She wondered how he'd managed to get through life at all. He was charming, sure, but that could only get you so far. And charm, Olivia suspected, didn't get you very far at all with subway lunatics.

'It's my fancy-*shmancy* hat,' the woman said. Her eyes were large and a watery green, and despite her yellowish, unhealthy complexion and lips that were loaded up with some mushy violently red lipstick that overshot her lipline, you could see that she had once been a pretty woman.

'Not enough people wear hats any more, don't you agree?' Ansel said amiably, eyeing the dangling bottles as they swayed around her forehead to the rhythm of the train.

'Stop talking to her,' Olivia hissed under her breath.

'I'm sorry, Olivia, love.' Ansel turned to her. 'What did you say?'

'For cripes sake, don't say my name!' she whispered furiously to Ansel.

But it was too late. The lunatic threw up her arms and began to sing, 'Oh, lanky Oh-livia, Oh, lousy Ohhh-livia . . .' The singing continued until the woman sitting next to Ansel reached out and quickly popped a bubble in the subway lunatic's bubble wrap. The lunatic instantly stopped singing and pointed a finger at the woman.

'You popped me,' she accused.

'No I didn't,' the woman lied.

'Yes, you did,' said another woman standing nearby (although subway people are gloomy, mind-your-own-business types, they also hate liars). 'I saw you pop her.'

'Well, maybe I did pop her,' the first woman admitted. 'But in my opinion, if you wear bubble wrap in public places, you're practically begging to get popped.'

'That's ridiculous!' The second woman was livid now. 'She has the right to wear whatever she wants without people like you pinching her bubbles . . .'

And as the argument raged on, gathering input from other passengers, the subway stopped at 72nd Street and the lunatic hurried off the train.

'Is the subway always this invigorating?' Ansel asked, clapping his hands together with delight.

'Some days more than others,' Olivia sighed.

The train had no sooner pulled out of the station than Ansel muttered unhappily, 'Oh, Lord help us.'

The crowd shifted to allow a large man in a bowler hat to pass through.

'Fine morning for a subway ride, sir.'

'Yes. Yes, it is, Cornwickle,' Ansel replied miserably.

'And good morning to you, Miss Kidney.' Cornwickle nodded courteously and Olivia smiled up at him, truly glad to see him. She was beginning to agree with Madame Brenda. Ansel did need some proper looking-after.

'I'm sure it must have slipped your mind, sir,' Cornwickle said, 'but there is a rather important board meeting for Exit Academy headmasters this morning.'

'How did you manage to catch up to us?' Ansel said.

'I jogged up to 96th Street and caught the express train, then hopped on this local at 72nd Street, sir.'

'You *jogged* all the way to 96th Street?' Ansel said, unabashedly eyeing Cornwickle's large body, which was trussed up in a crisply pressed dark grey suit.

'I'm swift as a bunny, sir, when needs be.'

'Really, Cornwickle,' Ansel said, 'I do appreciate your efforts to make me into an upstanding citizen, but you must understand that I am hopelessly wicked.'

'Not hopeless, sir. No one is hopeless.'

'Now listen here, Cornwickle.' Ansel's usually amiable tone turned harsh. 'I am NOT going to waste a perfectly glorious day –' here, Cornwickle raised his eyebrows and glanced down wryly at his dripping umbrella, which had formed a little puddle around his galoshes – 'to sit among a pack of tweedy,

cabbage-faced headmasters, listening to them bab-
ble on and on until I want to set my head on fire. I
intend to take a ferry ride instead.'

'That would be unwise, sir.'

The two men stared at each other, until Ansel
finally pouted, then sniffed, then said, 'Fine. I'll go to
the meeting, Cornwickle. Now hurry on home. I'm
sure you have oodles of butler-type things to do.'

'Actually, sir, your mother has requested that I
accompany you to your meetings.'

'Of course she did,' Ansel muttered.

The train shuddered into the 66th Street station and
Olivia rose, stumbling a little from the herky-jerky
motion. She noted that Cornwickle stood with
admirable steadiness, without even holding on to a
pole. Amazing, really, she thought, when he was so
wobbly in the pedalos.

'I'm a land animal, Miss Kidney,' he said to her,
guessing her thoughts. 'Have a pleasant day at
school.'

'So long, Cornwickle.' She glanced at Ansel, who
looked thoroughly miserable. Ansel was simply not
cut out for misery, she thought. It pinched up his delicate features and even made his jacket sag off his
shoulders in a pathetic sort of way.

'Hey, Ansel,' she said.

'Hmm?' He looked up at her listlessly.

'There's a belly dancer coming up the aisle.' She

nodded towards the far end of the carriage where a red-headed woman in a two-piece dustbin liner was frantically jiggling her hips to music coming from a little cassette player. Ansel's expression immediately brightened, which relieved Olivia greatly as she left the train and wended her way through the morning crowd on the 66th Street platform.

CHAPTER SEVEN

Olivia entered the art class feeling slightly less nervous than she had the day before. At least Mr Pierre-Louis seemed to have contempt for the *entire* class, not just Olivia.

'I waited for you again by the water fountain today,' Stella said.

'Oh, yeah. I guess I just forgot again.' In fact, Olivia had managed to duck behind a girl's cello case and sneak into the cafeteria unseen by Stella.

Stella reached into her back pocket and withdrew a thick marker. Then she grabbed Olivia's hand and wrote on her palm: LUNCH WITH STELLA, FRIDAY.

'I do that for my grandmother sometimes,' Stella said. 'She's forgetful too. Don't worry, it's a special marker. Really hard to wash off.'

'Great. Thanks,' Olivia said dryly.

Mr Pierre-Louis entered the room briskly, clapped his hands, and said, 'Sketchbooks open to your homework assignment, please!' There was a prompt rustling of paper as everyone hurriedly turned to their assignments and placed their sketchbooks on their easels.

Olivia glanced at Stella's sketchbook. It was a beautiful, intricately detailed drawing of an old woman – Stella's grandmother, Olivia guessed. By comparison, Olivia's own drawing looked pathetic. She sat down on her stool and waited for the worst.

Mr Pierre-Louis stopped at the first girl's sketch-book, his hands clasped behind his back. He made a sort of growling sound in his throat, and his eyebrows knitted together. The girl blanched. She looked like she wanted to shut her sketchbook and run out of the room. Mr Pierre-Louis leaned in close to the girl's ear and spoke so quietly that no one could have heard a word of it. The girl nodded her head several times, and though she did not look happy, at least the colour began to come back into her face.

Slowly, Mr Pierre-Louis made his way around the room, examining homework and speaking in hushed tones. From the looks on the students' faces, he wasn't too pleased. After staring for a minute at the homework of the pierced blue-haired boy, he snatched the sketchbook, ripped the boy's homework out of it, and tore it up into small pieces. The bits of paper fluttered down on the boy's head.

'Hey!' the boy protested. 'What do you think you're doing?'

'I might ask you the same question.' Mr Pierre-Louis handed the boy back his sketch pad.

'What do you mean? I did what you told us to do!' the boy said, his voice pitched with outrage. 'A portrait. That was the assignment, wasn't it?'

Mr Pierre-Louis said nothing for a moment, just stared at the boy, who could not meet his eyes for very long. The boy picked off a tiny piece of the paper that had caught on a piercing in his eyebrow.

'Tell me . . . Carl, isn't it?' Mr Pierre-Louis said. The boy seemed reluctant to admit that was his name but he finally nodded.

'Look at my face, Carl.' Mr Pierre-Louis put his face close to Carl's. 'Tell me. Do you see any wrinkles?' He touched the skin on the outside of his eyes. 'Right here?'

Carl nodded.

'Yes, you do,' Mr Pierre-Louis agreed. Then he dipped his chin down so that Carl could see the top of his head. 'And here, Carl? Do you see any grey hairs on my head?'

'A few,' Carl admitted hesitantly.

'Yes, a few.' Mr Pierre-Louis looked up and stared very gravely at Carl, who was fingering the hoop in his nose. 'So why, Carl, are you treating me as though I was born yesterday?'

'I – I don't understand . . .' Carl was blinking very quickly now.

'You didn't draw this from life, did you?'

'Yes, I did,' Carl said defiantly. Mr Pierre-Louis said nothing until finally Carl admitted, 'OK, I didn't.'

'Where, may I ask, did you draw that face from?' Mr Pierre-Louis enquired.

'A comic book,' Carl muttered.

'Do you understand now why I tore up your home-work, Carl?'

Carl sighed. 'Yes.'

Satisfied, Mr Pierre-Louis moved on to the next person, and then the next, and by the time he reached Olivia, her face was damp with sweat and she had a sickish feeling in her gut. She felt him behind her, staring at her sketchbook. The room was so silent that she could hear the soft clicking in her throat as she swallowed. She hoped he couldn't smell her armpits, which were soppy with sweat.

Finally, Mr Pierre-Louis said in her ear, 'The eyes are correct. But other than that, there are so many problems with this drawing that I don't have time to list them all. First and foremost, though, you have decided that he should be a lonely, unhappy old man, so you have forced his lips down into a frown, and added that silly made-up picture behind him. How dare you, Olivia? Yes, there are, indeed, sad and lonely old men who stare out the window at nothing in particular. But this man is not one of them. Look at his eyes. He is watching for something. Or someone. He will watch all night if he has to, mmm. Can you see it now?'

Olivia looked at her drawing. Yes, she had to admit it. Mr Pierre-Louis was right. When she thought back, the old man wasn't staring aimlessly out the window. He did look like he was watching for something.

She would have smiled at the sudden realization, if Mr Pierre-Louis had not abruptly reached out and grabbed her sketchbook. He tore the homework off the spiral coil with a *spliffft!* and proceeded to rip it up over her head into tiny little pieces. Olivia watched as her work fluttered down from between his fingers, landing in her hair and spilling around her feet. She felt a sudden urge to smack Mr Pierre-Louis.

'That's just mean,' she said to him before she could stop herself. She held her breath and felt the hard, angry pulse of her heart punching at her ribcage. The other kids in the class were staring at her, stunned and waiting to see what awful thing would happen next.

Mr Pierre-Louis gazed at her silently for a moment. Then he slowly nodded.

'You're right. That *was* mean,' he said. 'I should not have destroyed it. In fact, now that I have torn it up, I find myself missing the sight of it. Oh how I *long* to see it again and again, every day. Prominently displayed, mmm. You must re-draw that man tonight. In fact, I insist upon it. If you fail to do so, I will give you a D for the first quarter of the semester. You are to hand it in tomorrow and I will hang it there,' he pointed to a spot front and centre on the wall 'so that every day the entire class can admire it, and tremble in the presence of such an exquisite artistic genius.' Mr Pierre-Louis lifted his smooth, round chin and sucked in his cheeks with satisfaction. Then he moved on to Stella, who eyed Olivia pityingly.

Olivia pretended not to notice. She didn't need Stella's pity. She felt sorry enough for herself as she picked bits of homework out of her hair.

CHAPTER EIGHT

The Vondychomps' Mansion stood on a neat, tree-lined street in Gramercy Park, cosseted by a fearsome spiked iron gate. The building was constructed of a pale yellow stone, and its façade was adorned with colourfully painted coils – red, orange, blue, purple – like the poles on a carousel. They ran vertically upward, framing windows that were long and very thin. On either end of the building, between a copper domed roof that glinted in the late-day sun, were turrets, just like in a castle. But these were tipped all around with very threatening-looking iron barbs. All in all, the place was both beautiful and sinister, and for a minute Olivia just stood there, staring at it in awe.

'You're late, Olivia Kidney!' a cantankerous voice shouted at her from behind the gate. The Princepessa Christina Lilli was standing on the top landing of the house's front steps. Her bony arms were crossed against her chest, and she wore a look of extreme vexation on her narrow face, which Olivia knew was a sign that the Princepessa was delighted to see her. She had probably been standing on that landing for some time, Olivia guessed, anxiously waiting for her.

Olivia checked her watch, and replied, 'I'm not late at all. You said four o'clock sharp and I still have three minutes to go.'

'Your watch is slow,' the Princepessa declared firmly.

There was never any point in arguing with the Princepessa, although sometimes Olivia did anyway.

Olivia unlatched the gate and walked up the stone path towards the house. There was a tiny bit of lawn on either side – but even a tiny bit was impressive in New York City – and a few trees the likes of which Olivia had never seen before. They were short and squat with branches that hung limply, dripping with black scimitar-shaped leaves.

'Chop-chop!' the Princepessa cried. 'Don't dilly-dally like a tourist. You're really an exasperating child.'

'Do the Vondychomps really *live* in this place?' Olivia asked, again gazing up at the magnificent building as she ascended the steps.

'It's appalling, isn't it?' the Princepessa said.

'I think it's amazing,' Olivia said.

'Then you'll want to think again. I won't have you

agreeing with Arthur . . . it will only make him more insufferable than he already is.' She opened the front door just as a tall, attractive, well-dressed woman was walking out, holding the leash of a small terrier with long silky hair that swished against the ground as it moved.

'Oh, pardon me, Your Highness!' The woman had a raspy, breathless, high-pitched voice that made her sound like a four-year-old who smoked a pack of cigarettes every day. She made an awkward curtsey then stumbled on her high heels, nearly falling right on the Princepessa, who stepped away just in time. The dog shrieked and leaped away from his mistress's shoes, as if he'd been stepped on many times before.

'Mimi, for heaven's sake!' The Princepessa snapped as she glanced around nervously. 'I have told you a hundred times not to curtsey before me, particularly in public.'

'Oh, Jeez, I'm awfully sorry, Your Highness—' Mimi started.

'And you *must* stop calling me Your Highness! There are certain people – certain enemies of the royal family – who would be most interested to know that I am still alive.'

Olivia couldn't help but roll her eyes behind the Princepessa's back. In Olivia's opinion, the Princepessa was a little bit paranoid. And even if there still were any enemies of the royal Babatavian family, which Olivia sincerely doubted, they were probably shuffling around in walkers, smelling of arthritis cream.

'What would your enemies do to you if they found you?' Mimi asked, her eyes wide and shooting excited glances up and down the street, as though the Princepessa's enemies were lurking behind the spindly trees that lined the street. 'I mean, would they, like . . . torture you or something?'

'Please, Mimi, try not to sound so eager. And don't you make faces at me, Olivia Kidney,' the Princepessa said tartly, 'or I might have to reconsider things.'

'Reconsider what?' Olivia asked, annoyed that the Princepessa had caught her.

'Never mind what. Now stop loitering on the street like a common thug and come inside.'

Olivia followed the Princepessa through the front door and found herself in a large dimly lit room. At first glance, it appeared that the walls were made of tremendous grey blocks of dripping candle wax. But as Olivia's eyes adjusted to the darkness, she could see that the blocks were made of stone – a peculiar sort of stone that was covered with stone dribbles, some of which hung off the wall like dangerously spiked icicles. The only lighting came from oil lamps hanging from the ceiling by slender chains. They cast a dull greenish glow, which only added to the gloom.

Damp, chilly air crept across Olivia's skin, and she was aware of an odd smell permeating the room. At first she couldn't place it, but after a few good sniffs, she realized that it smelt like the snake house at the Bronx Zoo – a musty, vaguely fishy kind of smell.

'Are there snakes in here?' she asked the Princepessa nervously.

'Snakes?' the Princepessa said. 'Of course there are no snakes in here.'

'But that smell . . .' Olivia said, wrinkling her nose. The Princepessa sniffed the air.

'Snake oil,' The Princepessa declared. 'Arthur burns it in the lamps. It's what we used to do in the palace back in Babatavia. Ridiculous man! He built this house for me, you know.'

'How can that be?' Olivia said. 'You only just reconnected with him two months ago.'

Despite the Princepessa's appalling behaviour towards Arthur when they were young (in truth, she treated him like a pet dog, and the Princepessa had never been much of an animal lover), he had fallen in love with her. By the time she realized that she loved him back (with every cell in her spoiled young heart), the two of them had been tragically separated. It was Olivia who had brought them together again, over fifty years later.

'Oh, the foolish man has been pining away for me all this time,' the Princepessa snorted. Olivia opened her mouth to remind the Princepessa that she had been just as foolish, since she went to a certain Babatavian restaurant every night for years and years in the hopes that Arthur might show up there one day. But the Princepessa continued, 'For the longest time, Arthur tried to find me. He returned to Babatavia years after he left, but by then I had fled from the Revolution. The people in Babatavia told him that I'd been taken to a prison in Refnastova. But he didn't believe them.'

'Why not?' Olivia asked.

The Princepessa pressed her lips together and batted her eyelids a few times. Olivia knew that look. It was the look she gave when someone had offended her.

'He said he refused to believe them because . . .' the Princepessa shot Olivia a sidelong glance, as if to decide whether or not to tell her. '. . . because he felt I was such a nasty, unpleasant girl that my captors would have either killed me on the way to the prison or let me go just to get rid of me.'

Olivia laughed out loud, and the Princepessa gave her a sour look.

'Well, come on, that's pretty funny,' Olivia said.

The Princepessa lifted her chin and batted her eyelids even faster. 'He was wrong on both counts, of course, since I escaped. Arthur searched for me in all the royal households in Europe and Asia, hoping that one of them had hidden me. But he didn't find me, of course. In the end he moved to New York City, exactly as I had done. He built this house, which is a duplicate of the very palace in which I had grown up – far smaller, of course, and lacking several things, like the pride of white tigers in the courtyard. But very nearly the same. Arthur hoped that, should I still be alive, I might one day stumble upon his house and naturally enquire about it. I did, once, years ago. I knocked and a small boy with a dull look in his eyes opened the door. I asked him who built the house and he said, "The house builders." "Are your parents Babatavian?" I asked him, and he said, "I have a hermit crab named Kenny." Clearly the child is an imbecile, I thought, and I left and never came back.'

'Oh,' Olivia realized, 'that must have been Claude! The man who Frannie's mother married.'

'Yes, it was *Claude*.' The Princepessa drawled out the name as if she had uttered in it exasperation hundreds of times. 'And he hasn't improved with age, I've discovered. He's still a bobble-headed nitwit, but at least he's found his match in Mimi. Between the two of them, they have just enough brains to operate a can opener.'

'So that woman with the dog is Frannie's mother?' Olivia asked.

'I wouldn't admit it if I were Frannie, but yes, poor girl, that woman is her flesh and blood. Arthur seems to think Frannie is clever. But, I ask you, if she were so clever, why on earth would she tolerate being so preposterously small?'

'The smallest Ipsback tree casts the largest shadow,' said a deep voice which seemed to come from the very bowels of the house. In a moment a very imposing-looking man in black trousers and a white dress shirt descended the stone staircase. His hair was silky black, but he had the hardened, creased face of a man in his sixties. Olivia thought he was the most royal-looking individual she'd ever seen, including the Princepessa.

'It's an old Babatavian saying,' the man explained to Olivia as he walked towards them in an elegant, gliding fashion.

'Well, I never heard it,' said the Princepessa.

'You never heard it, my beloved, because you were sealed up in your palace, like a pickle in a jar.' He extended his hand to Olivia. 'Arthur Vondychomps.'

'I'm Olivia,' she said and put out her hand for Arthur to shake. But instead he bent over and kissed it in a way that was not at all disgusting.

'Enchanted, Olivia,' he said gallantly.

'Pompous beast!' the Princepessa sniped. But when he kissed her hand as well, her lips quivered for a moment then lifted up into a smile.

'Anyway, Frannie is delightful whatever size she is,' Arthur said.

Olivia looked at the Princepessa. 'Aren't you going to disagree with him?' she asked.

'Of course not! Arthur is perfectly correct,' the Princepessa said, laying an affectionate hand on Arthur's forearm. Then to Arthur, 'I told you the girl was brazen.'

Olivia sighed. It seemed that the Princepessa simply needed to contradict someone at every pass, and Olivia would do just as nicely as Arthur.

'I once fell madly in love with a brazen girl,' Arthur said. He bowed slowly and significantly to the Princepessa. 'And I've had a life full of troubles ever since,' he added. Then he glided gracefully off towards the vaulted stone passage behind the stairs.

The Princepessa sniffed scornfully in his direction before she turned and started for the stairs.

'This way,' she said.

The stairs were made of thick, rough-hewn slabs of stone, and the drippy stone walls closed in tightly on either side, like a vertical tunnel. It had a cold, creepy feeling, made worse by the smattering of wall sconces, which gave off the dim, greenish snake-oil light. Frannie must think twice before raiding the refrigerator at night, Olivia thought.

'Where's Frannie anyway?' Olivia asked.

'Being measured,' the Princepessa answered.

'Oh! Did she grow?' Olivia asked excitedly. Maybe she had discovered the secret of the Pitta-Pitta tribe.

'Of course not,' the Princepessa said. She stopped on the stairs and turned to Olivia sharply. 'Why? Does she have plans to grow?'

'Maybe,' Olivia hedged.

'Well, she'll have to hold off until after the wedding,' the Princepessa said, and continued on.

At the top of the stairs they walked down a hallway and stopped in front of a bullet-shaped door made of beaten copper. With some effort, the Princepessa pulled it open. Inside, Frannie and her older sister Stacy were standing in the midst of a frothy tumble of bright orange silk while an immensely fat woman fussed over them with a measuring tape. The two girls turned eagerly, as if hoping for a reason to escape.

'Standing still, girlies, for heaven's sake,' the fat seamstress commanded the two girls in a thick, guttural accent. 'Really, Your Highness,' the woman shook her head at the Princepessa, 'I am to having the most difficult time fitting this two girlies for their gowns! That one –' the seamstress swept a plump hand accusingly towards Stacy – 'she shlumpening her shoulders.'

Stacy, who was wearing a grey sweatshirt that had seen better days and a pair of baggy brown pants, scowled at the seamstress and dug her hands into her pants pockets, shlumpening her shoulders even more.

'And this littling-bittling one . . .' she pointed at Frannie, 'won't putting down her book so I can measure her arms. What does such a smallish child need for such a biggin book, I ask you?'

Frannie was holding the book with the cover pressed against her chest, but Olivia recognized it as the book on the Pitta-Pitta tribe.

'Oh, never mind,' the Princepessa told the seamstress. 'They can be fitted for their gowns later. We must prepare the Royal Imposter, pronto. Here's the girl.' She gave Olivia a little push towards the seamstress.

At this, Stacy and Frannie scrambled to the door, trampling over the carpet of silk material despite the seamstress's angry protests.

'Watch out for the pins,' Frannie whispered to Olivia. She lifted her shirtsleeve to flash a shoulder speckled with tiny red pinpricks. 'I was beginning to feel like a cork board. Hey, I found out some interesting stuff about the Pitta-Pittas. I'll tell you after she's finished with you.'

'Finished doing what?' Olivia asked nervously. But before she could answer, the Princepessa hustled Frannie out the door.

'I must be going as well,' the Princepessa said. 'Arthur's sister and niece will be arriving any moment, straight from Babatavia. And since I don't imagine they have showers in caves, they're sure to be a filthy, barbaric pair. I'm going to have them scrubbed and de-wormed, thank you very much.' With that, she departed, letting the copper door slam shut behind her.

Olivia looked over at the seamstress, who was stroking her measuring tape with her thick fingers.

'Now we getsing started!' For a large woman, the seamstress moved very quickly, and before Olivia knew it, the measuring tape was coiled around her waist like a lasso.

'What is a Royal Imposter?' Olivia asked

The seamstress pulled a nubby pencil out from behind her ear and jotted down some measurements on the notepad that hung around her neck.

'You.' The seamstress pointed her pencil at Olivia. 'You is the Royal Imposter.'

'Yes, but what does a Royal Imposter do?' Olivia asked.

'She dress exactly like Princepessa bride, like so.' The seamstress held up a bolt of the most delicate silvery material. She put it against Olivia's body and let it drape down over her.

'Wow! That's pretty,' Olivia couldn't help saying.

'Yes, exactly pretty. Then she walkin down the aisle with the Princepessa.'

'Really?' Olivia had never been to a wedding, much less been part of the ceremony.

The seamstress placed her measuring tape against Olivia's shoulder and began to measure her arm.

'Yes, she do. She look the same like Princepessa. And with veil over face, no one in room knows who is Princepessa and who is Royal Imposter. So when assassins come, they will confuse, you see. They not know which lady to kill.'

'Assassins?' Olivia turned to look at the seamstress, who took a pin out of her apron and poked Olivia's arm with it. 'Ow! You poked me!'

'Keep still.'

'What do you mean, assassins?' Olivia said, trying to keep her body still while eyeing the seamstress.

'Oh, ssst, nothing to worry.' The seamstress shook her head. 'It is old custom. Used to be many such kind assassins in old days. No one knew who was assassin and who was friend. Sometime, assassin was even part of royal family. There was assassin at the Princepessa Christina Lilli's grandmother's wedding. The assassin throwing big butcher knife at the bride. And who do you think assassin was?' The seamstress snapped her tape measure against the wall for emphasis.

'Who?' Olivia asked, trying to keep an eye on the apron full of pins as well as the whip-like tape measure.

'The bride's own little sister! Thirteen years old!'

'Wow! Did she kill the bride?' Olivia asked.

'How you asking such silly kind of question? If she kill bride, there be no Princepessa Christina Lilli, huh?' The seamstress let out a deep, explosive laugh and shook her head at Olivia with amusement. 'No, no, she not kill bride. The knife hit imposter instead.'

'Holy cow!' Olivia said.

'Not to worry, not to worry. Imposter lived. The knife only land on her foot. Baby toe gone, but who miss baby toe?' The seamstress smiled. She had a very lovely, delicate smile, in fact, with a set of brilliant white teeth. Olivia wondered how a smile like that could lurk inside such a brute. But people were sometimes surprising in that way, she concluded. They had stray bits and pieces in them that didn't always fit. That's why it was so hard to really and truly hate someone – there was always some stray bit that was sort of likeable. But the seamstress's likeability, it turned out, was short-lived as she abruptly whipped her measuring tape around Olivia's head and pulled it so tight that Olivia cried out. In response, the seamstress poked her in the leg with a pin.

'Not move!' she commanded. For the rest of the time, Olivia submitted meekly to the woman. After several minutes, the seamstress rolled up her tape measure and plunked it into her apron pocket. Then she stared at Olivia with her tiny green eyes, assessing her.

'You are same height as Her Highness – good. Your

head not as biggin as Her Highness's head.' (Here, she muttered something in her language and chuckled snidely to herself. Olivia wondered if it was some nasty remark about the Princepessa's snobbishness. And though Olivia was the first to admit that the Princepessa was a horrible snob, she didn't like the seamstress laughing at her friend.) 'You are skinny like Her Highness, but we'll have to pad the booblies.' The seamstress pointed at Olivia's chest, which made Olivia go crimson. The seamstress noted it, and, satisfied that she had administered her final dose of humiliation, she stepped back and nodded. 'OK, girlie, you done.'

CHAPTER NINE

Olivia bolted for the door. Frannie was waiting for her outside, sitting on the floor with her head buried in her book.

'How many times did she stick you with her pin?' Frannie asked.

'Four,' Olivia replied. 'She's a total menace.'

'I know it. But she must be a really good seamstress. Mister V had her flown here all the way from Yurkistan. She's been sleeping in the room next to mine and she makes the most awful sounds at night. I think she might be laughing. It gives me goose pimples.'

'Did you know that I'm supposed to be the Royal Imposter?' Olivia asked.

'Yeah, that was another thing the Princepessa and Mister V were arguing about. He thought it was silly to have a Royal Imposter since the royal family is no longer in power. Oh, they had a walloping loud fight over that one!'

'I guess the Princepessa won.'

'She almost always does. But I wouldn't worry about all that assassin stuff. I don't think anyone cares enough any more to try to assassinate her, except maybe the wedding caterers. She's driving them crazy.' Frannie stood up. 'Come on, let's go to my room.'

Olivia followed Frannie down the hall. They walked past several doors that were all made of the same beaten copper, finally stopping in front of a large gaping hole in the wall. It was no higher than Olivia's thigh, and it looked as if some giant rodent had burrowed right through the stone. Just as Olivia was beginning to wonder why on earth Arthur didn't fix such a hole, Frannie dropped to all fours.

'This way,' she said, and crawled into the hole.

Crouching down, Olivia peered inside, but it was too dark to see anything. She looked up and down the hallway. There was just something ridiculous about a twelve-year-old crawling around on the floor. But since no one was in sight, she dropped to her hands and knees and crawled through the hole. In the inky darkness she could hear a rhythmic clack-clack-clack sound. Suddenly, there was a flicker of light near the ground.

'Frannie?' Olivia whispered.

'Hang on,' came Frannie's voice, 'I've nearly got

this thing going . . . it still takes me a little while to . . . OK, here we go.'

The flicker of light spread and elongated, and now Olivia could see that it was actually a campfire sheltered within a circle of stone, with wisps of smoke spiralling up through a hole in the ceiling. Frannie knelt beside the fire, holding two stones and looking very pleased with herself.

'I could use a match, of course, but that would seem like cheating,' Frannie said, clacking the stones together quickly and making them spark.

Now Olivia could see Frannie's room more clearly. Well, 'room' was a bit of a stretch. The walls and the ceiling were made of the same drippy stone as the rest of the mansion, but it was not cut into blocks. This stone was rough and natural, and it gave off a cool, clean odour, much more pleasant than the scent of snake oil. The curved ceiling was so low that Olivia had to duck so as not to hit her head. The floor was soft, however, and when she looked down she could see that it was made of packed earth.

'Frannie,' – Olivia looked at her friend, whose tiny peaked face was watching Olivia's for a reaction – 'this is a cave.'

'Isn't it wonderful?' Frannie said. She picked up a long stick and poked it at the wood, encouraging the flames to grow higher. 'Arthur said he used to sleep in it when he got homesick. I guess you can take the caveboy out of the cave, but you can't take cave out of the caveboy. When we first moved in here, Arthur put me in one of the regular bedrooms. It was really nice and all, but frankly I prefer sleeping in a cave. It's so cosy, and it's just the right size for me. Besides, the Princepessa hates it and won't come in. I mean, I like her fine, but she can be a little irritating, you know what I mean? Oh, and look.' She pointed at one of the walls. Olivia could see that it was painted with many different animals – some running, some grazing on hills, and others lying dead with spears piercing their sides. All of the animals, even the dead ones, had huge, silly grins painted on them.

'It's one of the walls from the actual cave where Arthur lived as a child. He had it flown here specially. Arthur's great-great-great (and about a dozen more 'greats') grandfather painted that. He gave all the animals big smiles so they wouldn't scare the little cave children. Clever, huh?'

The fire was stoked high and Olivia could see the room quite clearly now. In one corner, piled comfortably, were animal pelts. Frannie's bed, Olivia guessed, since there was a stack of books beside it. All the books were open and fanned out to the page where she had left off reading, then piled one on top of the other. From the look of it, Frannie was reading nine books all at once. Besides the books, the only other allowance for modern convenience was a dresser and, taped up on the cave walls, various posters. They weren't your typical teenager's posters, however. They were mostly photos of old, serious-looking men in clothes from the 1800s.

'That's Emerson,' Frannie said, seeing that Olivia was looking at the posters. 'He was a great philosopher. And that one's Thoreau, and that one there is William James. They're my heroes. I know they look old and crotchety, but they were into all kinds of interesting things. William James was even hunting ghosts for a while. Ridiculous, I know, but he was brilliant in every other way.'

She looked at William James's portrait. Beneath the stodgy face, she thought she could see a sharp, searching expression in his eyes.

'So,' Frannie said, putting the stones down now that the fire was burning well. 'Here's what I found out from the book on the Pitta-Pittas. Franklin Steenpister was very interested to find out how Blup, the Pitta-Pitta boy who suddenly grew three feet, had managed to do it. But Blup refused to tell him what he had eaten to make him grow. And I guess you can't really blame him. Since he was the tallest member of the tribe, all the Pitta-Pitta girls were head over heels for him. He didn't want his secret to get out to the other Pitta-Pitta boys – or the men too – who were all afraid of him now.

'But Steenpister finally discovered Blup's weakness.

He liked shoes. Strange, huh? He used to make his own shoes out of leaves coated with the vomit of a parrot, which sounds awful, but apparently made the shoes waterproof. Anyway, Steenpister made a deal with Blup. He said that if Blup told him what he had eaten to make himself grow, he would give Blup a pair of his own shoes.'

'Did Blup tell him?' Olivia asked.

Frannie shrugged. 'Not according to the book. It says that Steenpister became ill soon after, poisoned by the Pitta-Pittas probably, and returned to America, where he died.'

'I'm sorry, Frannie,' Olivia said. She couldn't imagine what it must be like to be fourteen and still look as though you were in second grade.

'Boy, you give up easily, don't you?' Frannie said.

'But you said Franklin Steenpister never found out what the plant was.' Olivia admired her little friend's steeliness, but now she wondered if Frannie was just being dumb, which really bothered her. She hated to see people whom she admired being dumb.

'I said the *book* claims he never found out. But I think Steenpister actually did discover what it was. That's why the Pitta-Pittas poisoned him. *And* I think he brought the plant back from New Guinea to add it to his collection before he died,' Frannie said. 'According to the book's preface, lots of scientists believe the same thing. The only problem is, Steenpister's son owns the collection now and he won't talk to the scientists about it. If you ask me, the son sounds like a real curmudgeon, but I'll find out for sure on Saturday.'

'Why? What's Saturday?'

'That's when I'm going to have a talk with him. Doctor. J. P. Steenpister. He works at the Museum of Natural History. It says so in the preface.'

'Oh, come on, Frannie,' Olivia said. 'Why would he talk to you when he won't talk to the scientists?'

'Because I'll be bringing something that will interest him very much,' Frannie said mysteriously. And since she refused to reveal what that thing was, no matter how much Olivia asked, Olivia offered to go with her just out of curiosity. Which, she realized later, was exactly what Frannie had wanted.

'But, honestly, Frannie,' Olivia warned, 'I wouldn't get my hopes up or anything.'

'Of course my hopes are up!' Frannie cried. 'They're way up! I mean, what if Thomas Edison never got his hopes up? We'd still be sitting in the dark.'

'We *are* sitting in the dark,' Olivia pointed out.

'By choice!' Frannie jabbed her finger in the air.

'I'd better get going.' Olivia stood up, cracking her head against the low ceiling. 'Ow!' She clutched her head for a moment, then brushed the dirt off the back of her pants. 'I have to go home and draw some old dude who sits by his window.'

'*Dude?*' Frannie made a face. 'You aren't going to become one of those artsy types, are you?'

'Hardly. I don't have enough talent to be a "type."'

'On the contrary. It's the "types" who usually *don't* have talent. I guarantee you that Rembrandt didn't walk around with green hair. Anyway, I'll meet you at the museum Saturday at two-thirty, right under Teddy.'

'Teddy?'

'Teddy. As in Roosevelt. Oh, never mind.' Frannie shook her head in dismay when Olivia still looked confused. 'Just look for the chubby dude on the horse.'

That evening, Olivia sat in her room, her sketch pad, pencil and binoculars poised on her lap, staring out her window at the old man's apartment. The lights were off. Either he was sleeping or he simply wasn't home. After twenty minutes of watching and waiting, she tossed the sketch pad and binoculars on the floor.

Well, I can't *force* the guy to come to the window, she thought crankily. She crept into bed and switched off her reading lamp. But as soon as she closed her eyes, thoughts of Mr Pierre-Louis snaked into her brain. She threw off her covers and went back to the window to check one more time. There he was, sitting in the same spot as he had the night before, gazing out the window.

Quickly, before he went away, she flipped on the reading lamp, grabbed her binoculars, sketch pad and pencil off the floor, and took a seat in front of the window. She carefully scrutinized the old man through the binoculars before she started drawing. His expression looked keen, not sad and lonely at all. His white hair was carefully combed, as though he took some care with his appearance. His mouth was not turned down, as she had originally drawn it, but had a firm and determined set. And his eyes looked steady, penetrating almost, as they gazed out the window.

She started to sketch him, her pencil scratching at the paper with more confidence than the day before. All of a sudden, the old man buried his head in his hands. He stayed that way for some time before he finally stood and disappeared from sight. A moment later the light in his apartment went off.

Olivia looked down at her sketch pad. Her drawing wasn't even close to finished. All she'd be able to show Mr Pierre-Louis tomorrow was a half a face. And not a very good half at that.

CHAPTER TEN

The next day in homeroom, Miss Monsoon rushed in breathlessly after everyone was seated. She was wearing a pair of large dark sunglasses and a long flowered scarf that was wrapped around her head and neck. The end of it trailed behind her and got caught in the closing door as she entered. She made a soft gurgling sound as the scarf tightened around her throat. With a wave of her hand, she gestured for a boy in the first row to open the door and release her. He jumped up and opened the door. Without stopping to thank him, Miss Monsoon hurried to the windows and pulled down the shades, one by one in frantic little snaps, until the room was quite dark. Afterwards, she collapsed in her chair, her hand pressed to her chest. She tipped her head back and closed her eyes. The class watched her in shocked silence for a minute.

'Excuse me, but are you, like, having a stroke or something?' a girl in the front row asked.

'Brutes!' Miss Monsoon cried suddenly, causing the girl to draw back in her seat. 'Will they never let me be?!' She began to unwrap the scarf from her head. 'After all these years, they're still stalking me, asking me their sneaky questions about that tragic night. Just to watch me squirm.' Her long blonde hair fell out from under the scarf, but it was puffed up in wild hanks. She removed her sunglasses and stared out at the class with mild surprise, as though she were noticing them for the first time.

'I'm sorry, children,' she said, pressing her palms together in front of her chest. 'I've frightened you. It's the swarming throng of reporters and photographers outside . . . I'm afraid they will never cease to plague me.'

One of the kids rushed to the window to peek outside, but Miss Monsoon flapped her hands wildly and shrieked, 'Get away from the window, child! They are just waiting out there – the vultures that they are – with their cameras and their telepathic lenses –' some of the kids giggled at this – 'to get a shot of me. I refuse to give them the satisfaction! But enough! Whatever the world thinks of me, I am first and foremost a homeroom teacher.' Miss Monsoon stood up, grabbed her register, and began to call out their names.

Aidan leaned over to Olivia and whispered, 'Did you see any photographers outside the school this morning?'

Olivia shook her head.

'Me neither,' he said, and tapped his finger against his head, waggling his eyebrows. 'Fruit loops.'

All day long, Olivia counted down the hours until art class – and her official public humiliation. During the morning classes time seemed to drag along, which only stirred up her anxiety. She wished that she could just skip the first four periods and go straight to art to get the whole miserable affair over with. But as the morning began to creep up towards the afternoon, Olivia wished she were back in first period again.

'Maybe Mister Pierre-Louis will forget about the whole thing,' Olivia said, mostly to herself but also to Stella, who sat across from her in the cafeteria. Olivia had been unable to wash the marker off her hand that morning, no matter how hard she scrubbed.

'Are you going to eat that sandwich?' Stella asked, watching as Olivia absently stabbed holes in the bread with her finger.

'Why?'

'Because I'll eat it if you don't.'

'But I stuck my finger in it,' Olivia said.

'I don't care.' Stella had already devoured her own cafeteria lunch, some of the contents of which were now caught in her hair. Eating with Stella could really ruin a person's appetite.

'Have it.' Olivia pushed her sandwich towards Stella, who immediately tucked into it.

'Hethnottpith,' Stella said suddenly, her mouth crammed with sandwich.

'What?'

Stella chewed vigorously, her head nodding with each chew as if to help it along, then swallowed.

'I said, he's not the type to forget. Mister Pierre-Louis, I mean. I bet he's probably even looking forward to it.'

Olivia groaned. Stella was probably right. She opened her knapsack and looked at her sketch of the old man. His head was shaped like a sweet potato and was floating without a neck in the middle of the page. Olivia shook her head in dismay.

She turned the drawing around for Stella to see.

'Is this as bad as I think it is?' Olivia asked her. Stella stared at it. She had finished the sandwich, but there was a blob of cheese stuck to her cheek. She stared for such a long time that Olivia began to squirm, waiting for the verdict.

'Well?' Olivia said finally. Then she noticed a thin stream of drool trickling down the side of Stella's mouth. She was fast asleep.

The sound of the fifth-period bell clawed through Olivia's brain. She nudged Stella awake and, gathering up as much bravado as she could, she walked up the stairs with her spine straight and her eyes coolly focused on the space directly in front of her. If she was going to be humiliated, at least she could pretend it didn't matter. But when she reached the second floor, her courage started to go limp, then crumpled altogether.

'I have to go to the bathroom,' she told Stella as they approached Studio Five. 'I'll see you inside.' She turned back a second later and said, 'Wait.' With her face screwed up in distaste, she hastily picked a bit of canned peach out of Stella's fringe, flicked a hunk of pizza crust off the top of her head, and poked at the piece of cheese on her cheek until it fell off.

'Thanks,' Stella said brightly, as Olivia hurried back down the hallway.

Cutting Mr Pierre-Louis's class was the act of a coward. Plus, it would probably only make things worse. *Plus,* cutting a class on the third day of a new school was probably one of the dumbest things a person could do. Olivia knew all this, yet she did it anyway.

She walked back down the stairs to the ground floor, then up again to the first, where she walked through the hallway aimlessly, not entirely sure where you were supposed to go when you cut a class. As the last few malingerers filed into their classrooms, Olivia found herself in an empty hallway. In her previous school, when Olivia had to go to see the school therapist during homeroom, the hallway was always eerily silent. Every so often there was the muffled voice of a particularly loud teacher, but generally the hallway had an echoing, scary-movie sort of feel. Olivia used to walk faster and faster, imagining that someone was following her, until she frightened herself into an all-out sprint to the therapist's office.

But in the Malcolm Flavius School for the Arts all different sort of noises bounced up and down the hallway – the powerful voices of a gospel choir, the lazy strings of someone's violin. It was all very pleasant and she stopped to listen. It reminded her of when she first tried to contact Christopher in the Spirit World. Back then, before she became skilful at connecting with him, she'd hear bits and pieces of other conversations, voices in the distance, not connected to each other yet all in all creating a dizzyingly beautiful chorus. It had made Olivia feel like the world was not quite as lonely a place as she sometimes imagined it to be. That there were spirits riding the air molecules all around her.

Suddenly she heard the hurried padding of several soft-soled shoes coming down the hall, and she ducked into the girls' bathroom. Checking her watch, she saw that she had thirty more minutes to kill. The safest place to kill them was probably inside the girls' bathroom.

She washed her hands three times. Then she examined her skin in the mirror, squeezed a few especially painful blackheads along the rim of her nostrils, noted with amazement that there was a tiny chip in her right incisor (probably from a skateboarding tumble), and just when she was thoroughly bored, the bathroom door opened and Renee and two of her dancer friends walked in. They were all dressed in black unitards and wearing white dancing slippers. They had obviously just been dancing, because they were all coated with a sheen of sweat. Even their scraped-back hair was wet around the roots.

'*Quel* surprise!' Renee cried. 'But you're on the wrong floor, darling. The school psychologist is on the *ground* floor. I can escort you, if you like.' She put an arm around Olivia's shoulder and grinned at her friends, who were splashing water on their sweaty faces.

'Only if I can escort you to the drug store first and buy you some deodorant. My treat,' Olivia replied, shaking Renee's arm off of her shoulder. Honestly, the girl smelt like a water buffalo.

The other girls snorted at this, although frankly they didn't smell too great either.

Renee's beautiful eyes widened at her fellow dancers. Her creamy white skin had turned a patchy purple and her one eyebrow lifted a little higher than usual. Immediately, her friends stopped laughing –

clearly they had felt Renee's wrath before and were not anxious to repeat the experience.

'I'm glad you find her so amusing,' Renee said to her friends. 'I hear she was a real hoot at the mental hospital.'

Renee swivelled on her dance slippers and headed for the door.

'Oh, come on, Renee,' one of her friends pleaded. 'We didn't mean anything. It was just kind of funny.'

'So are those revolting press-on nails you're wearing, darling,' Renee said, 'but you don't hear me tittering like a ninny. Ta-ta, girls. Enjoy your new friend.' She bounded off, leaving behind an odour reminiscent of day-old Indian food.

The girls glared at Olivia as though it were her fault Renee was angry with them. Olivia did her best to ignore them by turning on the sink tap full blast and smacking the soap dispenser with her palm.

'Are they really revolting?' the one dancer asked her friend, spreading her fingers out and waving ten brick-red talons.

'A little,' the other girl admitted. While the girls finished patting off their wet faces with paper towels, Olivia pretended to be absorbed by a particularly vigorous hand washing. Cutting class seemed to be one of the more hygienic forms of criminal behaviour.

A few minutes after the two dancers left, the

bathroom door squealed open again. This time Olivia rushed into one of the stalls and latched the door shut. The seat looked pretty clean, but she tore off two long pieces of toilet paper anyway before she sat down, waiting for the person to leave. In a minute she heard an awkward clickety-clickety sound of heels on the tiled floor. They stopped suddenly and there was a pause before a woman's voice said, 'Olivia?'

Olivia didn't answer at first, on the off-chance that perhaps she meant another Olivia who also hung around the first floor girls' bathroom.

'Olivia Kidney? Is that you in there?'

'Who are *you*?' Olivia asked before admitting to anything.

'I'm Gwen, one of the school counsellors. A student told me that you were in here, having a . . . well, she described it as a "psycho attack", but I'm sure that's not what she meant.'

'No, that was exactly what she meant,' Olivia said. Renee must have chafed her thighs sprinting down to the counsellor's office to snitch her out.

'Really?' the woman suddenly sounded alarmed and her shoes clickety-clicketied closer to the bathroom door. 'Are you OK in there?'

'Yes, of course I'm OK. That girl just hates me.'

'Well, how about coming out anyway . . . unless you're . . . you know, busy.'

'Jeez, no, I'm not *busy*! Just . . . can you just leave

me alone?' Olivia sunk her head into her hands. This was going from bad to worse! It probably would have been easier to go to Mr Pierre-Louis's class.

There was silence, and then the awkward clickety-clickety sound. But instead of leaving, Gwen had simply entered the stall next to Olivia's. In a moment, Olivia heard the sound of toilet paper tearing – obviously Gwen had about as much faith in the cleanliness of the school toilet seats as Olivia did.

'Look, Olivia,' Gwen said, 'you're obviously supposed to be in class now. So either you're cutting or there's something the matter. Either way, I can't just leave you here. So why don't you just tell me what's going on.'

Olivia ducked her head slightly and peeked under the stall divider. She could see a pair of black, pinchy-toed pumps.

'What would you do if I was cutting?' Olivia asked.

'Well, generally we call your parents.'

That would be awful, Olivia thought. Her father had spent last school year worried out of his mind because of what the school therapist was telling him. She just couldn't do that to him again, especially now when he seemed so happy with life again.

'And if I wasn't cutting? If I was hiding in here because I had some personal problem, and I spoke to you about it . . . would you call my parents then too?'

'Absolutely not.' Gwen wedged her left shoe off

with the toe of the other and Olivia saw a hand come down and rub the stockinged foot. 'Whatever you tell me is totally confidential.'

Well, that was that. It looked like she was going to have to bite the bullet and talk to yet another school therapist. At least she had experience in this. She knew what sort of problems got them really worked up, and she knew what to say to make them feel like they were really helping her. She bit at the knuckle of her thumb, trying to think up a good problem, but was temporarily sidetracked by Gwen's right shoe suddenly shooting across the floor and into her stall.

'Ooops, sorry,' Gwen said, giggling. She reached under the stall to fetch it back, and replaced it on her foot.

'Those shoes look really uncomfortable,' Olivia said.

'They're killing me.'

'Why do you wear them if they're so uncomfortable?' Olivia asked.

Gwen's toes jumped a bit under the shiny leather, as if they were wondering the same thing. There was a short pause before Gwen said, 'What sort of things make *you* uncomfortable, Olivia?' Her voice took on the same sort of casually nosy tone that Olivia's old school therapist used to have.

'Do they teach you to answer questions with questions in therapist school?' Olivia asked. 'Because it's pretty rude.'

'OK, I guess you have a point,' Gwen said. That annoying nosy tone had left her voice. 'I'm wearing these shoes because when I saw them in the store I thought they looked very professional. And since I just started this job, I wanted to make a good impression.'

'Do you really think anyone is going to notice your shoes?' Olivia asked.

'You did.'

'Yeah, but how many people do you talk to while sitting on a toilet?' Olivia said.

'You're my first,' Gwen admitted. She worked her left shoe off her foot and then her right, flexing her toes. 'Which reminds me. You still haven't told me why you're here.'

Olivia searched her brain for a really good problem, but before she found one, the sixth-period bell rang.

'Do you have a piece of paper?' Gwen asked Olivia. 'And a pen?'

Olivia opened her knapsack and pulled out her notebook, then ripped out a piece of paper. She passed it to Gwen under the stall, along with a green felt-tip pen. She heard some quick scratching after which Gwen passed the paper and pen back under the stall. On the top of the paper was the date and beneath that was written: *Olivia Kidney was unable to attend fifth-period class today due to a headache.* It was signed *Ms Riley.*

'You can give this to your fifth-period teacher on Monday,' Gwen said.

'What's the catch?' Olivia asked.

'The catch is you have lunch with me on Monday, and we'll talk some more then,' Gwen said, hastily stuffing her feet back into her shoes. 'I'm in Room 114.'

Well, so much for a fresh start. Olivia had landed right back in the school therapist's office. How on earth was she supposed to shed her past when there was a bloodhound in a unitard following her?

Olivia heard the door latch flip open and then the retreating clickety-clickety – with one interrupted clickety followed by a yelp of 'Ouch! Damn it!' – before the bathroom door closed again.

CHAPTER ELEVEN

Friday was the unofficial day that Olivia and Ruben hung out together as unofficial friends. Neither one of them had ever said, 'I'll meet you at the band shell on Friday,' but they always did. And though Ruben was a master at skateboarding while Olivia, when she wasn't in a heap on the pavement, only managed to turn the skateboard into an atomic warhead, he nevertheless seemed to prefer her company to the other more-skilled skateboarders. Still, they bickered almost constantly. Once one of the other skateboarders who overhead them fighting said snidely, 'Why don't you two just get married?' That was enough to make them stop bickering for the rest of the day, but the following week they started right up again.

As Olivia headed home she felt especially eager to see him. Maybe it was because she'd felt troubled all afternoon – a restless, anxious feeling. Like something bad was about to happen. A few hours of squabbling with Ruben would definitely take her mind off things.

Parked outside her brownstone were three long limousines, and standing awkwardly in front of them were a dozen or so boys and girls dressed in school uniforms – plaid skirts and white shirts for the girls, and black trousers, white shirts and ties for the boys. They were new students from Ms Bender's School for Superior Children.

'OK, children, listen up!' cried a tall blonde woman with a severe pageboy haircut. She was holding a paper bag in each hand. 'This will be your first ride in a limousine. I expect you all to act like sophisticated young ladies and gentlemen. That means you are NOT to make conversation with the driver. Think of your driver as a draught horse that hauls you from one place to another. You MAY, however, kick the back of his seat. It sometimes makes them go faster.' She extended her arms, holding out the paper bags. 'Now, in one bag there are rubber bands and in the other there are macadamia nuts. You are all to take a handful of each, and when you see what you consider poorly dressed people on the street, you will shoot a macadamia nut at them. If you are correct and they are indeed poorly dressed, *and* if you hit them, I will award that student with an extra dessert at dinner.'

'Can't we just point them out?' one girl with blue braces asked. 'Why do we have to shoot at them.'

'Because you must believe that you are *entitled* to shoot at them!'

'But what if it hits them in the eye?' she asked.

'It doesn't matter. They have nothing nice to look at anyway, I assure you,' Ms Bender said.

Olivia shook her head as she walked up the stairs. 'What an idiot,' she muttered as she opened the front door. Ansel never locked it, which Olivia hated, but he insisted that the most interesting people just walked right in without waiting for him to open the door. If that hadn't been exactly what Olivia and her father had done when they first arrived at the brownstone, Olivia would probably have argued her point about robbers and murderers more vehemently.

As soon as she stepped inside, she heard a silky female voice coming from the lagoon. A very familiar voice. Olivia instantly stiffened and stopped dead in her tracks. The huge white doors to the lagoon were open – not wide open, but just enough to make Olivia wonder if she had been seen yet. If she hadn't, perhaps she could simply turn around and slip back outside. She started to back up quietly, then stopped.

This is probably a very unnatural reaction to seeing your own mother for the first time in two years, she thought.

Taking a deep breath, she cautiously approached

the doors and peered through the opening. Sitting on a couch that floated in the middle of the lagoon, looking remarkably like a grasshopper, was Monica Kidney. She wore a straight olive-green tunic made of some stiff material. It was split in the back and fanned out on either side of her rear end, like a pair of insect wings. Pale green tights covered her skinny, twitchy legs, and on her feet she wore pointed brown shoes. Perched on her head was a brown hat shaped like an American football cut in half, lengthwise.

'You know me, I always listen to my inner voice, George,' she was saying to Olivia's father, who was sitting in a chair, his normally genial face now tight with apprehension. '"Monica," my inner voice said to me a few days ago, "pack your bags! Your daughter needs you."'

'But Olivia is fine,' George objected weakly.

'She may *seem* fine, George, but she's not.'

'She'd tell me if there was a problem,' George said.

'Oh please! What eleven-year-old girl confides in her father?'

'She's twelve,' George corrected.

'I think I can remember how old my own daughter is, thank you. Especially since it was my body she nearly ripped to shreds during childbirth, not yours.'

That made Olivia positively cringe.

'I'm twelve,' Olivia said as stepped into the room.

Monica Kidney turned and stared at Olivia blankly

for a moment. Olivia realized, with astonishment, that her mother didn't even recognize her.

'Hi, *Mom*,' she added.

'Oh, Olivia!' Monica Kidney jumped to her feet, beaming, but quickly sat down again when the couch's little raft bobbled. 'Ooo, how dare you get so tall! Look at you. I would never have recognized you!' She quickly realized that this was not the right sort of thing for a mother to say, especially because it was pretty much the truth. 'I mean, of course I would *recognize* you, but oh, you've turned out better than I expected. You were such a scrawny, puny thing the last time I saw you—'

'Monica!' George yelled. It was so rare to see George Kidney angry that both Monica and Olivia jumped a bit.

'I only meant that she looked . . . unfinished. And now she's . . . *finished*! How do *I* look to *you*, Olivia?' She spread her arms wide to give Olivia a better view. 'What do you say? Does Los Angeles agree with me?'

When Olivia was younger, her mother would ask her if she was the prettiest mother of all the mothers she'd ever known. Monica would cup her own face in her hands, smile, and bat her eyelashes as if she were kidding around. But Olivia knew she expected an answer, and the answer was always 'Yes'. It wasn't a lie either. Olivia really did think her mother was stupendously pretty. She had beautiful long, dark curly hair that swished from side to side when she walked. She had huge dark brown eyes and a puckery mouth that was always painted fire-engine red.

But when she looked at her mother now, she noticed that her nose was actually sort of blobby and her chin was way too pointy and either Los Angeles did not agree with Monica Kidney, or she really wasn't quite so pretty as Olivia remembered.

'You're tanner, I guess,' Olivia said.

Monica burst out laughing – a very loud, theatrical laugh that seemed like something she'd learned in Los Angeles. 'Aren't you funny! So dry. *Sooo* New York. I love it! Now come sit next to Mom and let's have a little girl-to-girl chat. Shoo, George.' She shoved George's chair so hard with her foot that it spun around and drifted towards the opposite side of the lagoon. 'No boys allowed.'

'Can't. Sorry.' Olivia untied a pedalo from its moorings.

'What do you mean, "*can't, sorry*"?' Monica cried after Olivia as she scrambled into the boat and frantically pedalled off towards the canal. 'Olivia! Come back here! George, make her come back!' Her voice was hardening up and becoming brittle, like boiled sugar.

'If she doesn't want to chat with you girl-to-girl, I

can't make her do it, Monica,' Olivia heard her father reply with thinly concealed pleasure. He had managed to spin his chair around so that he was once again facing his ex-wife.

Then came a terrific uproar from Monica. Olivia remembered that sound. It was the tone of voice her mother used to use right before she broke down in tears and locked herself in her bedroom. In the old days, Olivia would do anything to get her mother to come out of the bedroom – apologize, cajole, promise to be good. But now the sound of Monica having a fit only made Olivia pedal faster down the winding, narrow corridor.

By the time she reached the wrought-iron spiral staircase rising out of the water, all she could hear was a faint, muffled wailing. Poor dad, she thought, as she tied her boat to one of the wooden moorings that jutted out of the water and then nimbly hopped from the boat to the staircase.

Up in her bedroom she grabbed her skateboard out of the closet and started downstairs again, but stopped on second thought. She went into the bathroom and brushed her teeth, combed her hair, then examined her face. No zits – excellent. A few weeks ago a particularly repulsive and painful one had sprouted right under her lower lip (it grew so large and stayed on her face so long that Ruben had named it Fred). She made a mental note to herself to try and remember to use the clay face mask that Ansel's mother, Madame Brenda, had brought her from Paris.

She smiled at herself in the mirror. Nice smile. She tipped up her face to check if there were any dry bits in her nostrils. (Once, Ruben waved hello at her face, and when she asked him why, he said that the thing hanging out of her left nostril was waving back at him.)

Downstairs she found her father still sitting in his armchair, which was drifting rather erratically from Monica's wake. His elbows rested on his knees and his head was buried in the palms of his hands.

'Is she gone?' Olivia whispered.

'Yep,' George said in an exhausted voice.

'Are you OK?' Olivia asked.

George lifted his head and wearily ran his fingers through his wild sandy hair.

'She's a handful,' he said.

'Maybe if we ignore her, she'll go away,' Olivia suggested.

George shook his head. 'Nah. It'll just make her mad.' Then he sat up straighter and collected himself. 'Anyway,' he said, attempting to sound more upbeat, 'you two probably should spend some time together. Maybe she's right about the girl thing. I suppose there are things that a twelve-year-old girl only wants to tell to her mother.'

'Not when the mother is wearing a football on her head.'

'Oh, that.' George shook his head. 'She's designing clothes now, she says. Inspired by insects. Go figure.'

CHAPTER TWELVE

The band shell pavilion in Central Park was teeming with people on the move – walkers, runners, skateboarders, bicyclists, rollerbladers. It seemed that the only people who were stationary were some old people sitting on benches and three teenage girls. The girls had planted themselves on a bench in front of where the skateboarders had set up their ramps and were doing their best to pretend they had sat there accidentally, which was especially ridiculous, Olivia thought, since the same three girls – or 'The Groupies,' as Olivia called them – sat at the same bench every day to stare at the skateboarding boys. At the moment they were all chewing gum – amazingly to the same rhythm – and snatching sidelong glances at a dark-haired boy in a brown suede hat, who was flying down one of the ramps. When he reached the bottom, he flipped his skateboard up so it did a backflip in mid-air and he hopped back on it. He managed to do this in such an casual, unfussy way that The Groupies' gum-chewing didn't miss a beat. But Olivia knew how hard the manoeuvre was. She'd tried it herself a few times, and had the scrapes and bruises to prove it.

The dark-haired boy skated up to Olivia, which made The Groupies turn their heads to her simultaneously.

'Hey,' Ruben said happily. He stopped smiling and gazed at her intently. 'What's wrong?'

'Nothing,' Olivia replied.

'Fine, don't tell me. All right, let's start working on your kickflip.' He headed off towards a stretch of pavement near the ramps, but Olivia said, 'No, not here.'

'Don't worry,' Ruben said. He nodded towards the other skateboarders. 'They all know you stink.'

'Not *them*,' Olivia said. 'The Groupies. I don't need them shooting daggers at me with their eyes.'

'Who are The Groupies?' Ruben asked, looking around.

'Those girls. On the bench there,' Olivia said quietly. 'The ones who are always here, ogling you.'

'Really? I never noticed.' Ruben glanced at them for a second, during which The Groupies' gum-chewing instantly ceased. Their eyes grew wide.

'Dopes,' Ruben said, to Olivia's delight.

They headed down towards the band shell, a huge

stone stage with a shell-shaped stone awning rising up from the back of it. Just past that, the pavilion grew a little quieter. A long row of trees shaded a length of benches that were mostly unoccupied on this already shady day.

'All right,' said Ruben, 'let's see what you got.'

Olivia put down her skateboard and rolled off. At the last minute she chickened out and jumped off the board, then had to chase it down as it rolled away.

Ruben watched her walk back, skateboard under her arm. He tugged at the brim of his hat and looked decidedly disgusted.

'Don't say anything!' Olivia pointed a warning finger at him.

'But you didn't even try,' he complained. 'You just flopped off.'

'I didn't flop. I stepped off,' Olivia said.

'You flopped like a pancake. That's not like you. Usually you at least *try* to do the trick before you land on your butt.'

'Gee, I'm sorry I failed to amuse you by injuring myself, Ruben.' She could feel her temper rearing up. She bent down and snatched up a long twig. 'Here. I can stick this in my eye. That should be entertaining.'

'No,' Ruben said, picking up an even longer stick. 'Use this one instead. With any luck it will reach all the way into your brain and you can scrape out whatever it is that's making you so crabby today.'

Olivia gave him a filthy look, which made him clutch at his heart, miming devastation.

If she'd been in the mood to be perfectly honest, she would have admitted that seeing her mother had put her in a bad temper. But when she was in a bad temper, she was never in the mood to be perfectly honest. Instead, she turned her back to Ruben and for a while the two of them skated around without saying a word to each other. Still, she was reasonably certain he wouldn't leave and go back to his skateboarding buddies. That was one good thing about Ruben – he didn't get insulted when Olivia was prickly. In fact, she suspected that he sort of enjoyed it.

They'd been skating for about ten minutes when Olivia noticed The Groupies had abandoned their bench near the ramps and were now approaching, casually swivelling their heads this way and that as though they had no particular destination in mind. Their legs, which were all wrapped in jeans so tight you could see the tubes of lipgloss in their pockets, scissored across the pavement in unison. They all sat down on a bench right in front of where Ruben was skating and proceeded to pretend that they were bored out of their minds.

'Ever hear of stalking?' Olivia said to them as she skated over, furious. 'It's illegal, you know.'

'So is skateboarding in the park,' one of the girls replied.

It was true. And the fact that the girl wasn't a complete moron made Olivia even angrier. On any other day, Olivia might have left it at that, but today she was feeling especially fierce. She was on the brink of mentioning 'restraining orders' when Ruben casually threw his arm over her shoulder, as if he'd done that a hundred times before, instead of never.

'Ready to go, sweetie?' he said loud enough for The Groupies to hear.

Sweetie! Olivia whirled around to stare at him. He managed to keep his hand on her shoulder. In fact, he was holding it a little too firmly, as though he were afraid she might try and hit him. He widened his eyes and tipped his head slightly towards The Groupies. Olivia looked. They had all stopped chewing their gum and were now staring at Olivia – her shoulder, in particular – with a mix of outrage and envy.

Olivia smiled at Ruben. 'Absolutely,' she replied.

Ruben let go and sped off on his board while Olivia followed, her temper suddenly defused. It hadn't been awful, Ruben's hand on her shoulder. In fact, she mused as she skated along, it had felt sort of nice. But then she reminded herself that he had simply done it for the benefit of The Groupies.

Finally, Ruben stopped, flipped his skateboard up so that it somersaulted twice in the air, then caught it niftily and tucked it under his arm.

'You've had enough for today, Jezebel,' he said to the board.

Olivia was glad to hear him calling the board by the name that Christopher had given her years ago. Jezebel had once belonged to Christopher, who had been a terrific skateboarder when he was alive. Not quite as terrific as Ruben was – an admission that Olivia had only recently been able to bring herself to make – but pretty terrific nonetheless. Olivia had kept the board after Christopher died, intending to one day ride her like a pro. It wasn't long before she realized that that was never going to happen, so she passed Jezebel on to Ruben. She didn't regret it either. When she saw Ruben flying around on Jezebel, as if she were a living, breathing creature that willingly did Ruben's bidding, Olivia knew she'd made the right choice. Besides, Jezebel seemed to contain a fragment of Christopher, and Olivia liked the idea of sharing that fragment with Ruben.

Olivia and Ruben walked now, side by side, across the busy bike path, dodging speeding cyclists and packs of joggers. They meandered down to the little boat pond where small kids and grown men sailed remote-controlled model boats. The grown men were all hunkered down, their faces bunched up like fists, as they carefully worked their remotes, while the kids whizzed their boats around the water recklessly, screaming and laughing.

Past the boat pond was the tremendous bronze statue of Alice in Wonderland, and it was here that Ruben and Olivia finally stopped.

Years ago, the same girl who had told Olivia about ghosts in the tunnels also told her that Cheshire Cat in the statue winks at people.

'Go there at noon on Saturday and watch his eyes,' the girl had told her. 'He'll wink right at you.'

So Olivia did. She went to the park with Christopher and made him wait until noon. And sure enough the Cheshire Cat winked at her.

'It's just a trick of the light,' Christopher had explained. 'See, all the kids grab the cat's face when they climb to the top, so it's rubbed smooth. The noon light must catch the cat's eye in a funny way to make it look like it's winking.'

But she had been so sure that the cat had winked, and so hurt that Christopher didn't believe her, that she started to cry. He had picked her up and hugged her.

'You know,' he'd said, 'I always hated the Cheshire Cat. I wouldn't put it past him to wink at little kids, just to freak them out.'

Now Olivia and Ruben climbed on top of the giant mushroom and sat in Alice's tremendous lap. Olivia couldn't help but stroke Alice's cold, buttery skin as she leaned back against the outstretched arm. Ruben rested against the other arm and for a few moments they sat in silence, staring up at the deepening sky. By Olivia's feet, the White Rabbit stared at his pocket watch.

'I was thinking,' Ruben said suddenly. 'We should do something sometime.'

'We're doing something now,' Olivia said.

'No, I mean, like we should go see a movie or something,' Ruben said.

'I don't like movies.'

'How can you not like movies?' Ruben frowned at her.

'Because they get you all worked up and emotional, and it's all fake. And then you wind up feeling like a big sucker.'

'Fine. We could do something else. Whatever you want. How about this Saturday?'

'I can't. I've got . . . this thing I do every Saturday.'

'What thing?' Ruben asked.

Olivia wasn't very opposed to lying in general. It was lying to Ruben in particular that really bugged her. Yet she couldn't exactly tell him the truth about Saturday either – that she always spent it with Christopher. Instead, she said, 'I saw my mother today.'

She hadn't meant to say anything about Monica. The words just slipped out, the way a string of saliva can slip out between your lips and you are so surprised that you can't suck it back in time. She glanced across Alice's lap to check Ruben's expression. He was holding Alice's hand, which was the size of his face, and gazing above the park's trees to the puzzle-piece stretch of buildings along 57th Street.

'Is that why you're in such a crap mood?' he asked.

Olivia was about to object, but didn't. Why bother? She nodded.

'What's she doing here? Doesn't she live in California or something?' Ruben asked, his voice dullish and sullen.

'She wants to get to know me better!' Olivia wailed.

'Good luck to her,' Ruben said.

'What's that supposed to mean?'

'It means you have nothing to worry about, because she won't get to know you better, because you won't let her, because you won't let anybody.' The toe of his sneaker was kicking at the brim of the Mad Hatter's hat.

'That's not true!' Olivia cried. Over her right shoulder she caught a glimpse of the Cheshire Cat grinning at her mockingly.

'Oh, yeah?' Ruben said. 'So tell me who knows Olivia Kidney? I mean really, *really*.'

'My brother knows me really, *really*,' Olivia replied.

'Your brother who's been dead for a year?' Ruben asked, his eyebrows raised.

'That's right,' she said combatively. It was the truth and she wasn't going to back down just because Ruben didn't know that she still spoke to Christopher.

And that was the problem, Olivia thought. She had so many secrets – that she could talk to her brother, that she could see spirits, that she lived in an Exit Academy. If she told Ruben these things, he'd just think she was crazy. Just a half-year before, the school therapist had advised her father that she needed medication. How could Ruben expect her to let people know who she was, really, *really*?

'Besides,' she said, sidestepping Ruben's accusation, 'my mother's a terrible person. You would hate her. When my brother was sick, she never even visited him in the hospital.' She looked at Ruben for a reaction, but he was just staring back at her broodingly.

'Plus,' Olivia continued with her case, 'she's been gone for two years, during which she's called me all of three times! And that was only to tell me how sunny and great it was out in California. She never even *asked* me how I was doing. Plus, she's horrible to my father.' This was the crowning argument, in Olivia's opinion. If someone could be horrible to George Kidney, there had to be something desperately wrong with them.

Ruben looked at her for a moment without saying anything, his sneaker tapping lightly at the Mad

Hatter's hat. It was like he was waiting for her to admit that she was impossible to really get to know. Well, she thought, he could kick the Mad Hatter until his toes fell off – she wasn't going to give in.

Finally Ruben sighed and gave the Mat Hatter's hat a final kick. He checked his watch, which was something she'd never seen him do before when he was with her. 'Anyway, I'd better get going.'

He hopped off the mushroom, adjusted his hat, and put Jezebel on the ground. Olivia felt that she'd let him down, and it bothered her. She didn't want him to leave angry with her. Or worse, to give up on her altogether. Quickly, she searched for something safe to confide, something that he didn't already know but that wouldn't make him wonder about her sanity.

'Bye,' he said, stepping on Jezebel and preparing to push off.

'I'm afraid of elevators,' Olivia said.

'What?'

'I-have-a-fear-of-elevators,' she repeated, already beginning to regret the admission.

He shrugged. 'Then take the stairs.' He skated off, missing the point entirely.

She sat there for a while after he left, feeling by turns angry with herself then angry with Ruben. After a bit, her thoughts drifted back to the problem of her mother. Her father was right – ignoring Monica

Kidney, or even just attempting to avoid her, would only get her angry. Monica hated when people said 'No' to something that she wanted. It only made her want that thing even more.

Any which way she looked at it, Olivia came to the same conclusion: she would have to put up with Monica until Monica grew bored, which, thankfully, shouldn't take very long.

Already feeling better, she leaned back in Alice's lap, her head resting against the hard, cold tendrils of Alice's hair. Yes, once Monica got bored, she would hop on a plane back to sunny and fabulous Los Angeles and Olivia probably wouldn't hear from her again until her next birthday, when she'd get a card wishing her a *Happy 17th Birthday*.

She squashed a bug that was crawling on her shoulder, then flicked it off, past Alice's outstretched arm. There, staring back at her with its spiteful grin, was the Cheshire Cat. It seemed to be having a good laugh at her expense.

She really hated that cat.

CHAPTER THIRTEEN

The art assignment for Monday was to draw a piece of string tied in five knots. Olivia still had the entire weekend to do it, but she wanted to get a head start – maybe if she tried hard enough, she could actually draw something that Mr Pierre-Louis wouldn't rip into a hundred little pieces. She looked all over her room for string, but couldn't find any. She considered using her sneaker shoelaces, but when she started to pull one out, it was so old and frayed that it snapped in half.

She found her father down in the kitchen, where he was simmering a brownish sauce in a pan.

'Hey, Dad, I need some string. That smells good – what is it?'

'Thai garlic and basil sauce,' George said. 'Taste.' He scooped up a bit of the sauce with a spoon and held it out for Olivia.

'Spicy,' Olivia said after tasting it, then sucked in her breath twice to cool her tongue.

'Too spicy?' George fretted.

'No. But it's practically begging for a pinch more basil.'

It wasn't really, and they both knew it. It was just an excuse to run out to the garden. They had never had the luxury of a garden before, having always lived in cramped apartments. That summer George and Olivia had spent weeks clearing up Ansel's backyard, which up until then had been an untidy mess of overgrown bushes and weeds, muscling out all the sunshine from the earth. Once they'd pulled out all the weeds, trimmed back the bushes and prepared the soil, he and Olivia had purchased hollyhocks, snapdragons, asters, and even several rose bushes. They'd spent a delightful week figuring out where everything should go. Afterwards they planted a tidy herb garden, which gave off the most wonderfully tangy aroma when warmed by the midday sun. They never missed an opportunity to run out to the beautiful garden and snip a few leaves off one of the herbs for George's dishes.

But now, instead of looking pleased at the prospect, George glanced nervously out the kitchen window at the garden. He rubbed the underside of his chin with his knuckles.

'I'm not sure that it's safe to go out there, frankly,' he said.

'What do you mean?' Olivia looked out the window too, and saw that someone had placed a monstrous purple divan right smack in the middle of their garden. One of the divan's back legs was jammed in a bed of asters.

'What's that doing there!' Olivia cried, and before her father could stop her, she stormed out through the kitchen door, which led directly into the back garden.

'Careful, Olivia!' her father warned, rushing up behind her. He placed himself in front of her as if to shield her from something.

'Careful of what?'

Towards the far end of the garden, near the brick wall that separated their backyard from Ms Bender's, Ansel was on his hands and knees, poking around a thicket of bushes.

'Chester? Chester,' Ansel cooed. 'Come now, Chester, why so shy? Oh, never mind.' He stood up and brushed the dirt off his trousers. He smiled when he saw Olivia and George. 'He'll come out when he's hungry.'

'Yes, that's exactly what I'm afraid of,' George said, scurrying over to the herb garden.

'Who's Chester?' asked Olivia as Ansel collapsed on to the divan.

'He's a genuine . . . Oh, what do you call them?' Ansel said. 'Spots, claws, eats smallish animals? In any case, he's exactly like the one in the painting. You see, I was sitting in that awful board meeting with Cornwickle –' lowering his voice so that George didn't hear 'nearly expiring of boredom, when I noticed the loveliest framed print on the wall. It was of a lady sitting on a purple divan in the midst of the most beautiful jungle, with all sorts of wild beasts all around her. Well, our garden is just as pretty as that painted jungle, I thought to myself, and wouldn't it be exactly perfect if we had a purple divan and beasts and everything. The divan was easy enough to find, but it took me a bit of time to track down the beasts.'

'Beasts?' Olivia looked around the garden nervously. 'Are there more than one of them?'

'Oh, just a few parrots and several macaque monkeys.'

'Monkeys!' Olivia cried. 'Where are they?'

'Up there somewhere.' Ansel waved his slender fingers at the tall oak tree in the corner of the garden. Olivia looked up. She didn't see anything except leaves, but she supposed the foliage was thick enough that the monkeys might be hiding.

Her father returned with a handful of basil and hustled Olivia back into the kitchen and quickly shut the door.

'Did you actually see any animals out there?' George asked Olivia as he opened a drawer and pulled out the roll of string that he used to tie up pot roasts.

'No.'

'Neither did I,' he said. He snipped off some string and handed it to Olivia with a concerned looked on his face. 'You know, sometimes I think Ansel might be just a little bit mad.'

After dinner, upstairs in her room, Olivia put the length of string on her dressing table and tried to arrange it in some interesting fashion. There was only so much you could do with string, however, and the drawing came out looking like an earthworm with five tumours on it.

Before she went to bed, she opened her curtains and checked to see if the old man was sitting at his window. If so, she might try and complete her drawing. No such luck. His window was dark.

She got under the covers and was nearly asleep when she felt the edge of her bed sink down. A ghost. She was sure of it.

'Don't you people ever sleep?' Olivia groaned, her eyes still closed. There was no answer, which was odd for a ghost. Olivia opened her eyes, then gasped when she saw who it was. Throwing off her covers, she scrambled to her feet and frantically looked around for something with which she might defend herself. She caught sight of her thick world history textbook lying on the floor and edged towards it.

'Go ahead, you moron. Bash me over the head

with your book. That'll *really* hurt me.' The girl took a drag on her cigarette. The inhaled smoke clouded up the light that was pulsing out of her skin.

She was a young ghost, right around Olivia's age, but she had a hard look about her, as if she'd seen and done things that most girls her age would never have dreamed of. Her name was Abby, and Olivia had met her once, a couple of months ago, when she had entered the Exit Academy on the brownstone's first floor. It was the one and only time she'd been allowed in there. As Madame Brenda had explained, an Exit Academy was an extremely dangerous place for a Straddler. Inside the academy, Olivia's spirit was lighter than usual and could be swallowed by some of the nastier ghosts.

Abby was about as nasty as they come.

On their first meeting, she had nearly managed to toss Olivia out a window. After that, Ansel had completely banned Olivia from the first floor. But the ghosts knew she was in the house, which was why they came to visit her fairly regularly. Much to her relief, Abby had never visited her. Up till now.

'Here, you want some help?' Abby said. In a flash she had snatched up the textbook. She swatted it at her own head so hard that even Olivia winced, but it passed right through her. Of course, Olivia thought. Of course it would.

Then Abby hurled the textbook at the wall. It

crashed against it so hard that her father called out 'Olivia?' from the next room. In a moment she heard his approaching footsteps in the hallway, then a knock.

'It's OK, Dad,' Olivia called out, attempting to keep her voice casual. 'I just dropped something.'

To Olivia's consternation, he opened the door and turned on the light. Olivia glanced over at Abby. She was standing on Olivia's bed with one hip cocked to the side, smoking and staring at Olivia's father with an amused look on her pretty face.

Could her dad see Abby? Olivia wondered in alarm.

'Dropped something, huh? What was it, a hippo?' George said, smiling and looking around the room. His eyes passed right over Abby and he spotted the textbook, splayed out on the floor next to the wall, its brand-new cover torn from the binding and hanging off at an angle. Olivia had forgotten how strong Abby was. Now she winced as she recalled Abby's iron grip when she'd tried to yank Olivia out the window.

George's smile disappeared. He walked over and picked up the book, pivoting the cover so that it lay right again.

'Did you throw this, Olivia?' he asked. His usual lighthearted tone had turned serious. No, more than serious, Olivia thought. He sounded afraid.

'Not really,' Olivia said feebly.

'Either you did or you didn't.'

'I did, but I . . . I didn't mean to.'

George looked at his daughter in silence, which made Olivia fidget. Then he sighed, handed her back the textbook, and sat down on the bed. To Olivia's horror, Abby sat on his lap and hooked her arm around his neck. George didn't notice at all, but it infuriated Olivia.

'Be honest with me, Sweetpea. Is something bothering you?'

Abby took a long drag on her cigarette and blew the smoke in George's face.

'No, I'm fine, Dad. I'm just really, really tired,' Olivia said, wishing that ghosts could be throttled. 'I think I'll just go to sleep.'

She crawled into bed and pulled the covers over her head.

'Goodnight,' she mumbled. She heard her father sigh, then felt him rise from the bed.

'All right. But next time you feel like throwing things, why don't you come to me first and we can talk it over. Goodnight, Sweetpea.' As he walked towards the door, Abby hurled Olivia's wooden pencil box at George. It missed his head by an inch and crashed against the door, opening the lid and spilling the pencils all over the floor.

'Olivia!' George whipped around, and the shock on his face nearly snapped her heart in two.

'Oh, Dad! I didn't . . . I'm sorry!' What else could she say? If she told her father that a ghost had thrown the pencil box at his head, he'd *really* worry.

George stared at her for a moment. He seemed at a loss for words, but the pained look on his face said plenty. It was worse than being yelled at. In fact, she wished he would yell at her. Then she could at least feel sorry for herself, since she was only trying to spare her father some worry. Instead, he lowered his eyes and said, 'Goodnight, Olivia,' in a horrible, depressed tone and turned off the light.

The moment he shut the door, she turned to Abby, her blood rising to her face so that she felt almost feverish.

'Get out of my room!' she whispered furiously.

Abby threw her cigarette at Olivia, and as soon as it left her fingers it separated into minuscule specks of multicoloured light then faded and vanished. A moment later, so did Abby.

Olivia lay back down in bed, but something snagged at her thoughts, the way the strap of your backpack sometimes snags on a door handle and yanks you back into the room. She got out of bed and through her open curtains she could see that the old man was once again sitting by his window, staring out. Quickly, she fetched her sketchbook and the binoculars and started to sketch by the nimbus of moonlight. Her pencil scratched furiously at the paper, and she focused so hard on getting everything right – the lines of his lips, the length of his nose – that she wasn't sure how much time had passed before the old man abruptly rose from the chair and walked away. It was only then that she looked down at her sketch pad with a critical eye. To her surprise, the old man appeared quite different than before. There was great animation in his expression, a hint of excitement. A trace of anger.

He's seen what he was looking for! Olivia thought.

She gazed across the street. He'd returned to his seat and was sipping from a glass of water. Now she could see what she hadn't noticed through the binoculars' close-up view.

He was staring directly at *her*.

CHAPTER FOURTEEN

At breakfast the following morning, George broke the
bad news to Olivia.

'Your mother called a few minutes ago. She'll be
here at noon to take you out to lunch.'

'Forget it,' Olivia said.

'Now look, honey. She came all the way from
California to see you.'

'If she's feeling guilty about leaving us, that's her
problem,' Olivia answered.

'But it's not for her sake that I want you to see her,'
George said, looking a little ill at ease. 'You're
becoming a young lady –' somehow, when George
said those words, they sounded exactly like 'young
lady' and nothing else – 'and there are things that . . .
you might feel easier talking about with a
woman . . . And I've noticed that you've been sort
of angry with me lately, which is a perfectly normal
part of adolescence . . .' Olivia knew he was referring

to the pencil box that Abby had thrown at his head, and rather than revisit that ugly event, she simply gave in.

Olivia sat outside the brownstone on the front stoop, looking up and down the block for her mother, and hoping against hope that she wouldn't see her. It was already 12.15 and Monica Kidney still hadn't shown up for their 'Mother-Daughter Date'.

See! She forgot, Olivia told herself. It's OK. Whatever. I'll just grab my skateboard and head out to the park.

But just as she stood up, she felt a sudden and familiar warmth in her stomach. Out of the corner of her eye she saw something flitting around her head, like a hyperactive piece of dust.

'Christopher?' she said, in her head.

'Now come off it, kiddo,' he replied. 'You know Mom is always late.'

'My time is worth something too, you know,' Olivia replied.

'Grumble, grumble. Now plant your rump back down on the steps and give her another ten minutes.'

'Why should I?' Olivia asked without sitting back down.

'Because . . .' There was a hesitation from Christopher. 'Because Saturday is the day we usually have our field trip.'

'Oh, I forgot!' Olivia said. 'See, Mom's messing up my life already!'

Every Saturday, Olivia took Christopher on their so-called field trips. Because he could feel and taste and see all the things that Olivia could, she would think up fun outings for them.

'Well, that settles it then,' said Olivia. 'I'm not waiting around for her. Let's go down to Chinatown – we can eat that weird noodle cake you like. And then we can head on up to Little Italy—'

'No. Olivia, I don't . . . it's just . . .' He sounded embarrassed, which was very uncharacteristic of him. 'I'd like to tag along with you and Mom, if you don't mind. I haven't seen her for a really long time.'

'You actually *want* to see her?!' Olivia cried.

There was no answer, but Olivia could feel a strange squirming feeling in her chest and she realized with amazement, that she had made her brother feel uncomfortable. 'Well, I mean . . . don't you just peep in on her sometimes?' Olivia said, trying to smooth things over a bit.

'She won't let me,' Christopher admitted, which threw Olivia into a new paroxysm of indignation.

'*Won't let you?!*' Olivia was so furious that she actually said this out loud, then looked furtively up and down the street to see if anyone might have heard her. 'Does she think her life is *so* spectacular that she can't let her own son peep in on her—'

'It's not deliberate, Olivia,' Christopher said. 'Not consciously, anyway.'

'Do you look in on Dad?' she asked, suddenly curious.

'Oh, sure. The other day, when he was making a cake, I wrote "Hi, Dad" in the cake batter. He looked at it for a moment and smiled, but I think he just figured it was a coincidence.'

'All right, fine. Come along if you really want to. But you'll probably get so annoyed with her after five minutes that you'll run away screaming. Lucky you. Hey,' Olivia said, changing the subject, 'I don't suppose you've run into Branwell lately?'

She had met Branwell that past winter, in the last apartment building she'd lived in. He was the nicest boy she'd ever known – not sickeningly nice, but nice in the way that you could trust him with your most embarrassing thoughts and he'd never laugh or tell a single soul. Unfortunately, he had also been a ghost who didn't realize he was dead. It was Olivia who had helped him to see that he was dead, and in the end he left to go to the Spirit World. She was happy for him – the Spirit World was where he belonged after all – but still she missed him. She had tried to contact him many times, but there was never any answer. Sometimes she wondered if he'd simply forgotten her.

'Nope, I haven't seen the guy at all since that first

time,' said Christopher, his voice a touch bewildered. 'I've even asked around but no one else has seen him either. It's like he's just vanished.'

'Could something bad have happened to him?' Olivia asked.

'Nah. At least, I don't think so. It's a little mysterious though—' Christopher went silent for a second, then muttered, 'Wow. What the heck is she wearing?'

From up the street, a slender column of purple was making its way towards Olivia, waving. Monica was decked out in a skin-tight purple top and matching purple leggings made of some shiny, wrinkly material. The top had an attached purple hood that gripped her skull so snugly it looked like she was wearing a swimming cap. On her feet was a pair of purple and white Keds high-top sneakers.

'Ta-da! Here I am!' Monica Kidney spread her arms wide, as though she expected a round of applause.

'You're late,' Olivia said flatly.

Monica checked her watch. 'No, I'm not. I'm here exactly at twelve twenty-five, just like I said I would be.'

Olivia opened her mouth to refute this, but she felt a gentle nudge from Christopher – kind of like someone poking her in the ribs from the inside of her body.

Olivia looked up and down at her mother's outfit. 'Are you supposed to be a worm?'

Monica's arms fell and her red lips drooped a little. 'A caterpillar,' she said. Then, with unexpected good sense, Monica took off her hood. She fluffed up her hair, which had been smooshed flat, and in the end she looked like a semi-normal human being.

'I was thinking we might go to this really interesting cheese restaurant for lunch,' Monica said, as she started down the street with Olivia. 'And after that, we might go shopping for bras. Wouldn't that be fun?' she squealed and clapped her hands.

Olivia looked at her, horrified. '*I don't need a bra.*'

'Just a nice little training bra, Olivia.'

'*Training* bra? No thanks. They're not circus animals.'

Christopher laughed and Olivia turned red. She'd forgotten he was listening.

They headed down the block towards Columbus Avenue. Although he was being perfectly silent, Olivia could feel that Christopher was overjoyed to be with their mother, which Olivia found very annoying. His joy was so great, in fact, that Olivia felt a powerful urge to bounce happily as she walked, and she had to contract her calf muscles to keep this from happening.

'Be honest, Olivia. Are you happy here in New York?' Monica said suddenly.

'Sure.'

'I thought about taking you to California when I first left,' Monica said, putting her hood back on, much to Olivia's dismay, and tucking the stray hairs around her face beneath it. 'Maybe I should have. Your life would have been far more interesting. But back then you were still a fairly dull little girl . . . not *dull* in a bad way. Dull in the way that your father is dull. In a good way, I mean.' She smiled at Olivia. Olivia looked straight ahead and walked faster.

'Do you see why I can't stand her?' Olivia said to Christopher, silently, of course.

'It's just that she doesn't think before she talks,' Christopher said.

The way that Christopher was defending Monica only made Olivia angrier. And when Olivia was angry, she sometimes played dirty. Now she looked over at Monica and asked coolly, 'And what about Christopher? Did you think he was dull in a good way too?'

Monica stroked her left eyebrow several times. She didn't answer for such a long time, Olivia thought that she was simply ignoring the question. But finally Monica said, 'Christopher is . . .' She corrected herself. 'Christopher *was* immensely interesting.'

A small, ugly bubble of jealousy rose up in Olivia's throat.

So what? Olivia thought ruefully. The woman thinks cheese is interesting!

Then she remembered that Christopher could hear her thoughts.

'Sorry,' she told him.

'No problem,' Christopher said.

'You're smiling!' Olivia accused him. 'I can hear it in your voice.'

'Watch your step,' he warned, the smile still in his voice, and Olivia hopped over a pile of dog poo.

Monica prattled away about her new insect clothing line, and how she was showing it to all the most exclusive stores in New York. Olivia began to suspect that Monica had actually come to New York on business, and visiting her daughter had simply been an afterthought.

'Ah!' Monica stopped short. 'Here we are, are we not?'

The restaurant was called CHEESE, IF YOU PLEASE! The restaurant's window was plastered with a four-star review from the *New York Times*. It was blown up to ten times its original size, so that you could practically read it from New Jersey. The words 'the trendiest eatery' and 'celebrity hot spot' were highlighted in yellow. No wonder her mother was so anxious to go there.

New York is a city percolating with bad smells – car fumes, rotting garbage and, occasionally, urine. But the smell inside the cheese restaurant outstripped anything Olivia had ever smelt before.

'Man, that's revolting!' Christopher cried out, and Olivia remembered that he could smell it too.

'You're the one who wanted to tag along,' Olivia reminded him, and inhaled deeply through her nose just to drive the point home. Unfortunately, it also made her gag, prompting the hostess, a pretty dark-haired woman dressed all in black, to smile at her knowingly.

'It's a matter of surrendering to the aroma,' she told Olivia in a tinkly voice.

Good advice, Olivia thought, since the aroma (or 'the stink' to be more exact) had practically tackled her to the ground and put her in a headlock.

Monica, however, was inhaling in loud, extended sniffs and smiling exquisitely, as though she had just stepped into a flower shop.

The hostess led them to a tiny table in the midst of a cramped sea of other tiny tables, whose occupants were desperately trying to pretend that they weren't jammed tight as a box of crayons. She gave them each a menu that was shaped like a wedge of cheese and left.

Olivia wouldn't have thought it was possible, but the smell in the dining room was even worse. All around them people dined on little round wooden cutting boards full of oozy yellow and white cheese.

Olivia jammed her fist under her nose to block the smell and stared down at the menu. There was nothing but cheese. Surprise, surprise. She checked the desserts: Sheep's Milk Cheese Drizzled with Honey or Blue Cheese Pie.

'I'll order for both of us,' Monica said, shutting the menu. 'So, tell me.' She put her elbows on the table and cupped her face in her hands. 'How many boyfriends do you have, Olivia?'

Oh no, Olivia thought. This is it. This is the dreaded girl-to-girl chat.

'I don't know. How many *should* I have?'

'I always juggled two or three when I was a girl,' Monica said.

'You must be very coordinated,' Olivia said. 'Look, Mom. We don't have to do this mother–daughter stuff. I'm doing fine. We'll have a nice lunch and we'll call it even, and then you can go back to California.'

She regretted her words immediately. Monica's baby doll mouth turned all soggy and she stared into Olivia's eyes. It was worse than being stared at by Stella.

'You don't like me very much, do you?' Monica asked.

Olivia's spine curved in like a sickle, and she slumped down in her chair and pretended to study the menu.

'I asked you a question, Olivia Anne Kidney.'

Olivia found herself momentarily caught off guard. Monica could do that sometimes. Just when Olivia thought she was a complete dope, Monica would behave almost like an actual mother. Olivia hated that.

'I like you fine,' Olivia growled.

'No you don't. I know you think I'm a silly, shallow person. Well, maybe it's the truth.' Monica reached up and yanked the purple hood off her head. 'But sadly for you, I'm the only mother you have, so let's just try and have a nice time together.'

If Monica had stopped there, Olivia would have tried to be more pleasant. But after the waitress took their order ('The Scandinavian Cheese Platter for two,' Monica told her), Monica resumed the conversation.

'I know I'll never be as close to you as your father is. You two have always been like peas in a pod,' Monica continued pensively. 'I was closer to Christopher.'

Olivia felt her resentment rising again.

'Some nights, we'd stay up to the early morning hours, just talking and talking,' Monica said. 'There wasn't anyone who knew Christopher better than I did.'

Within her, Olivia could feel a mighty clash of emotions – hers and Christopher's. She was infuriated at Monica's words. How dare she claim that she knew Christopher better than Olivia herself did! She and Christopher had been practically inseparable, even though he was so much older than her. But beneath her fury, she felt Christopher's happiness start to billow up within her chest, a swell of delight that did not belong to her. It grew rapidly, expanding like a balloon, squeezing aside her resentment.

'No!' she thought. 'This is *my* body!' Her anger rushed forward to shove back Christopher's joy. Christopher pushed back. It was the first time in their lives that he and Olivia had had a serious squabble. Even when they were younger, they'd never fought like most siblings. Sure, they had disagreements, but one or the other of them would always give in. Now they were both standing their ground.

'How can you say you were close to Christopher?' Olivia said to Monica angrily. 'You were never even around long enough to get to know him. You were always skipping off to drama classes or concerts with your friends or meditation retreats.'

'It wasn't always like that,' Monica said calmly.

Christopher's happiness had skittered into her legs – it felt like a trickle of liquid electricity – and her left foot was beginning to tap happily.

'Oh yes, it was!' Olivia cried, and she stomped hard on her left foot with her right one, to stop the tapping. 'You may not remember, but I was there too!' The people at the adjacent tables were staring at them, but Olivia didn't care. Christopher said something while she was talking, and she was so upset that she absently responded out loud.

'What? I didn't hear you,' Olivia asked him.

'I said it wasn't always like that—' Monica Kidney started, but Olivia shook her head.

'No, I wasn't talking to you,' Olivia said, which made it even worse, since Monica was now looking at her as if she were a subway lunatic.

'I said,' Christopher repeated, his voice jubilant, 'ask her if she remembers the time we went to the Cloisters.'

'Forget it,' Olivia replied, in her head this time.

The waitress returned, carrying a tremendous wooden board of cheese. She set it on the table and walked away so quickly that Olivia wondered if she were trying to escape from the smell, which was truly alarming. Even the people at the other tables turned to see what was fouling up the already-violated air.

Six wedges of sickly yellow cheese were oozing all over the centre of the board, while a line of fanned-out crackers was skirting the edges, as if to get as far away from the stench as possible. Olivia drew back in her chair and opened her mouth so she wouldn't have to breathe through her nose. Monica, however, leaned forward and inhaled the stink. Then she scooped up a wad of the ooziest cheese, smeared it on a cracker, and popped it in her mouth. The other diners watched with a mix of horror and admiration.

'Yummy,' she said. Her eyes quickly darted around

at her neighbours to see if she had impressed them. Satisfied, she smeared some more on a cracker and held it out to Olivia. 'Try some.'

'I'd rather drink my own bathwater,' Olivia said.

Monica shrugged and popped the cracker in her mouth. 'More for me.'

'Go on, ask her about the Cloisters,' Christopher urged.

'I already told you, no,' Olivia said silently, folding her arms across her chest. Her mood was now officially as foul as the cheese.

Suddenly, deep in her stomach, Olivia felt as though a can of soda had been vigorously shaken and then opened. A bubbling and tickling sensation shot up through her oesophagus and into her throat. Olivia squirmed with dread as she realized that a tremendous belch was about to explode out of her mouth. She squeezed her lips shut, but the force of the thing was so powerful, she knew she was helpless to prevent it. It prised her lips apart and roared out of her mouth, loud enough to make every person in the restaurant turn and stare.

But it wasn't a belch. It was a voice. And it wasn't her own voice. It was much deeper and had an odd echo-y sound, as though it were coming through a megaphone. The words weren't hers either. They were Christopher's: 'Hey, Mom, do you remember when you and Christopher went to the Cloisters?'

Olivia clapped her hand over her mouth. It took her a moment to figure out what had happened. When she did, she was appalled. Christopher had used her! He had *forced* her to ask the question! She had never felt so betrayed in her entire life. She felt her eyes sting and her throat clog.

'Honestly, you don't have to scream. Oh, Olivia . . .' Monica hastily opened up her handbag, pulled out some tissues, and pressed them into Olivia's hand. 'Why are you crying?'

'I'm not,' Olivia said, just now realizing that she was, as she swabbed her eyes with a tissue.

'Of course I remember that trip to the Cloisters! How could I forget that?' Monica said, attempting to reassure her.

But Christopher's stunt had put Olivia in a rare temper, and she interrupted Monica's reveries with a snide question of her own: 'Do you also remember the time when Christopher was in the hospital? You know . . . back when he was dying.'

Monica's face drooped. She stared back at Olivia uneasily, as if trying to think of what to say. Then slowly and deliberately, she spread a thick layer of slightly green cheese on a cracker.

'Oh, that's right,' Olivia said, when it was clear her mother had no intention of answering. 'You *wouldn't* remember. *Because you never even came to visit him. Not once. Not even when Dad called you and said that Christopher was asking for you, over and over.'*

Instantly, Olivia felt as if her breath had been sucked out of her body, the way a tornado might suck the window out of a house. She gasped and opened her mouth to try and pull the air back in.

'What is it?' asked Monica, appearing both alarmed and relieved at the change of topic. 'Oh,' she added with sudden interest, 'you're not . . .?' She lowered her voice and narrowed her eyes at Olivia. 'Are you having menstrual cramps?'

Olivia shook her head – even managing to roll her eyes at her mother – while she caught her breath.

'Then what's wrong?' Monica asked.

'Nothing,' Olivia finally managed to utter.

But that was far from the truth. What was wrong was that Christopher had flown out of her body with breathtaking speed.

CHAPTER FIFTEEN

After leaving Monica, Olivia trekked down to the Museum of Natural History, and found that 'the chubby dude on the horse' was a statue right in front of the museum. Frannie was late, but Olivia didn't really mind. She was still fuming about what Christopher had done to her and she needed time to cool off. Yes, what she had said about Monica not visiting him in the hospital must have hurt his feelings. And surprised him too, from the way he suddenly flew out of her body. But what he did to her was even worse, in her opinion.

After a few minutes, she spied Frannie coming up the steps. Lumbering behind her was a squat, unkempt, pug-faced girl, appearing slightly bewildered. She looked to be about fourteen or so, and was wearing a little flowered skirt and a bright yellow blouse, which, considering that she was built like a very short quarterback, looked ridiculous on her. Her legs were alarmingly hairy, and below her thick, knotty calf muscles were a pair of the widest feet Olivia had ever seen. It didn't help matters that they were clad in pale pink sandals.

'Sorry I'm late!' Frannie said breathlessly. 'Couldn't be helped. I had to get Viola ready.' She patted the girl's back. Viola patted Frannie's back too, then began to smell herself, sniffing at her arms, which seemed longer than they should be.

'Soap, Viola,' Frannie told her. 'Clean. Nice and clean, you.' She pointed at the girl and smiled. The girl smiled back. Well, it wasn't quite a smile. It was more like stretching her lower lip downwards so that she exposed a band of red gums beneath a set of crooked teeth, one of which was missing entirely.

'She's Mister V's niece,' Frannie whispered to Olivia. 'All the way from Babatavia.'

'Oh! You mean she's a cavegirl?' Olivia said, staring at Viola with great interest now.

'Cave dweller is probably a nicer way to put it,' Frannie said, 'but yes, Viola grew up in a cave. Mister V asked me to take her under my wing while she's in town, and I thought she might enjoy the museum. She dressed herself, by the way. Not my idea.'

As they entered the building, they were immediately thrust into the murky half-light that was particular to that museum. It reminded Olivia of the time of day when the sun was just beginning to go down. Years ago her father had told her that this time of day was called 'the gloaming', and it was the time when lots of wild animals woke up – a piece of information that had practically ruined this museum for Olivia when she was a kid. During class trips, when they wandered through the dimly lit rooms, gazing at the stuffed lions and wild boars and panthers, Olivia was sure that the animals were about to wake up and smash through the glass to feast on the limbs of New York City school children.

Olivia remembered that now, and grabbing Frannie's arm, said quietly, 'Hey, don't you think Viola might get scared by all the wild animals? She might not understand that they're stuffed.'

Frannie nodded. 'Good point.' But before she could attempt to explain, or at least mime, to Viola that the animals were dead, Viola had rushed over to the lobby display of a tremendous dinosaur skeleton.

'Too late,' Frannie said, screwing up her face into a grimace.

At first, Viola just gawped at the skeleton. Then she opened her mouth and out came a hoarse barking cough, as though she had a bad case of bronchitis. The sound echoed loudly in the vast lobby, and people swivelled around to stare. Olivia and Frannie cringed in embarrassment. Then Viola made the sound again, but this time Olivia and Frannie could see that she was not coughing at all. She was laughing.

'Strange sense of humour,' Frannie mused.

'If you really want to talk with this Steenpister guy,' Olivia said, noting a nervous-looking security guard eyeballing Viola, 'we'd better find him pronto, before we're all kicked out.'

'Right,' Frannie said. She laid down the admission fee for all three of them, then hurried Viola out of the lobby. Off to the left was the Asian Mammals Room, which was lined with exhibits of stuffed animals and, in the centre, a very realistic herd of elephants. Olivia tried to guide Viola in the other direction, but Viola's peripheral vision appeared to be excellent. In a flash she was off and running. Although Viola was squat and chunky, they found, to their chagrin, that she was very fleet of foot.

'I don't see her,' Frannie said when they reached the room. They circled the room, even checking between the massive elephant legs. Viola had vanished.

'Great,' Frannie said. 'Now I've lost her. Maybe this was a stupid idea after all.'

'What was a stupid idea?' Olivia asked.

But before Frannie could answer, there was a loud, excited murmur of voices and a crowd of people began to gather around one of the recessed exhibits along the wall.

'There.' Olivia pointed.

'Oh no,' Frannie said.

The two of them dashed over to the crowd. There was Viola, crouched in the exhibit of a nomadic Siberian tribe – one of the few exhibits that wasn't behind a pane of glass. Viola was desperately trying to lift a big rock off the ground while chattering away in a panicked voice. Unfortunately, the rock was moulded to the craggy plaster ground, so Viola couldn't budge it. She then leaped up and pulled the spear from the hands of one of the plaster tribesmen. Drawing the spear back behind her head, the way an American football player would hold a ball right before he hurled it across the field, Viola took aim at the elephants. A cry rose up from the crowd, and some of them flung themselves on the floor while others fled.

'No!' Olivia cried out.

'They're not real elephants, Viola!' Frannie yelled.

But even if Viola had an inkling of what they were trying to tell her, she was too agitated to listen. Sweat was dripping from her forehead and Olivia could hear her rough, panting breath. She jerked the spear back and let it fly.

Even in the midst of impending disaster, Olivia had to admire Viola's throwing arm. The spear soared straight for the lead elephant's chest and would no doubt have hit its mark, but for a tall, thin, completely bald man in a button-down shirt and corduroy trousers. Without a fuss, he reached out and caught the spear a second before it hit the elephant. He examined the spear for a moment, then marched directly for Viola, who was watching him with amazement. Stepping over the low railing in front of the exhibit, he gingerly walked into the panorama. To Olivia's horror, he handed the spear back to Viola.

'Are you stupid or something?' Olivia cried out, and she leaped over the exhibit's barrier and started for Viola, fully intending to wrestle the spear from her. But the man's arm came down in front of her, and she smacked her nose against his forearm.

'Ow!' she said.

'Quiet,' the man replied, which Olivia found incredibly rude. She was gearing up to tell him so, when the man added in a hushed tone of voice, 'The Eastern European Cave Dweller will lay down her weapon if its progress has been stopped in mid-air.'

Olivia watched Viola through eyes that were still watering from the blow to her nose. Sure enough, Viola put the spear down at the feet of the plaster man from whom she'd borrowed it. She said a few words to him in her language, and when he didn't reply she cocked her head at him.

'*Frednuckle pansho binnibum*,' the bald man said to Viola. Her head swivelled towards him, an astonished look on her face.

'*Binnibum zitz*,' she replied, clearly amazed that someone in New York City could speak her language.

She turned back to the plaster man and poked at his stomach. Then she let out her explosive barking laugh.

'Everything all right?' Two security guards had arrived and were surveying the scene.

'Yes. Go away,' the bald man said testily.

The two guards hesitated. Olivia could see that they were somewhat afraid of the bald man. Still, the sight of Viola in the middle of the exhibit surrounded by a crowd of museum-goers was very suspicious.

'What's that kid doing in there?' one of the guards asked, his voice betraying a heady dose of nerves.

The bald man put a protective hand on Viola's back. 'Apparently, she was passing through when she noted something awry in our exhibit. I don't suppose either one of you boys noticed that the spear had dropped from the mannequin's hands?'

Both guards shook their heads.

'I didn't think so,' the bald man shook his head disgustedly. 'What else do you two fail to notice in the course of a day, I wonder? You should thank this girl for doing your job for you.' He bent down and picked up the spear.

'But that girl shouldn't be in—' the braver security guard started to say, but the bald man whirled around, gripping the spear in his hand in such a menacing way that the guards actually backed up.

'Scram!' the bald man growled at them. 'This isn't

a coffee break.' Then, to Viola, he said in a gentler tone, 'Let's just put this spear back where it belongs, shall we?'

'I know where I'd like to put that spear,' one of the security guards muttered, but when the bald man shot him a look, he said loudly, 'Good day, Doctor.'

The bald man led Viola out of the exhibit, and Frannie stepped forward, her hand extended.

'Doctor Steenpister, I presume,' Frannie said. Although she was so small, she had an air of tremendous authority. Even the bald man seemed impressed by her. He took her hand and shook it – not in the limp way adults usually shake hands with children, but a firm, respectful shake.

'You presume correctly,' he said. 'Should I know you?'

'I'm Frannie Smithers. Look, do you think we could go somewhere and talk?'

'No,' he said coldly. He turned to Viola. '*Magnus ishi*,' he said to her and started to walk off, gesturing for Viola to come along. But Frannie hooked her arm through Viola's and stood fast.

'She's with me,' Frannie said. Her elfin face had turned as icy as Dr Steenpister's. He looked at her carefully now, as though he were sizing up an opponent. He rubbed the crown of his shiny head.

'I assume *she's* with you, as well?' he asked, pointing disdainfully at Olivia.

'You assume correctly,' Frannie said.

For a split second Dr Steenpister actually looked amused. He let out a sound like *hnnn*, which Olivia guessed was his version of hysterical laughter. Then his face turned stony again. He nodded shortly. 'Come along.'

They had to travel up to the offices in an elevator, which Olivia was not too happy about, particularly since this was the sort of elevator that made a horrible grinding noise as it ascended. It stopped on the third floor and they followed Dr Steenpister through a short hallway until they arrived at a door that bore a plaque engraved 'Dr J. P. Steenpister, Curator of Indigenous Cultures'.

'Don't touch anything,' Dr Steenpister warned ominously as he opened the door. It took a few moments before Olivia could even see what it was that she was not supposed to touch. The light was so bright in the room that it virtually blinded her and she had to close her eyes and open them several times before they adjusted.

They were no longer *in* the museum, but rather on the roof of the museum, in a tremendous greenhouse. It was large enough to accommodate some good-sized trees, and it stretched back so far, and was so crowded with plants, that Olivia could not make out where it ended. Many of the plants and trees were awfully strange-looking. There were huge lumpy,

mossy things that were shaped like melting snow-
men. There were trees that sprouted only two or three
leaves, but each leaf was as big as beach umbrella.
There were tall, skinny trees with naked bluish
branches that quivered constantly, as if they were
freezing. Which was surely impossible, Olivia
thought, since the temperature inside the greenhouse
was stiflingly hot.

'Follow me,' Dr Steenpister said, and walked
towards a copse of trees, with thick foliage that
dripped so low off the branches the leaves scraped
the ground. Parting the leaves, Dr Steenpister walked
through and disappeared into the depths of greenery.

For a moment Frannie and Olivia looked at each
other in confusion. Then Frannie darted through the
leaves and disappeared from sight. There was nothing
to do but follow, so Olivia stepped forward and with
hands that were pressed together as though she was
praying (which wasn't too far from the truth), she
parted the leaves and stepped in. More leaves tickled
her face and she had to keep parting them, since they
appeared to hang several feet deep. As she pro-
gressed the air grew cooler and quite pleasant.
Finally, the leaves opened up to a clearing, surrounded on all sides by trees. There, in the centre of
the clearing, were Dr Steenpister and Frannie,
perched on what looked to be huge lumpy, cream-
coloured stools.

'Amazing, huh?' said Frannie, beaming.

'I guess,' Olivia said unconvincingly. 'At least it's nice and cool in here.'

'No, don't you see?' Frannie said, patting the stool she was sitting on. 'These are mushrooms. *Mushrooms!* Isn't that the most original thing you've ever seen?' Frannie said.

On closer examination, Olivia saw that all the furniture in Dr Steenpister's 'office' was made of giant mushrooms sitting in tremendous pots. Some of them grew in tight clusters while others grew singly. Dr Steenpister's stool was one of the clustered mushrooms, with several smaller mushrooms sprouting around the main stool. On one of these smaller mushrooms – the one that was a bit taller than the stool – he had placed his laptop and a phone whose cord trailed off and disappeared beneath the foliage. The tiniest mushroom, which was near his left knee, held a collection of pens and pencils, their points stuck into the white flesh. All across the top of that mushroom were tiny dots of blue, black and red ink, where other pens had once been stuck.

Olivia thought that it really was one of the most original things she'd ever seen. Until she remembered that it wasn't.

'It's just a copy of *Alice in Wonderland*,' she said.

'You think so?' Dr Steenpister said arrogantly. 'And who, may I ask, wrote *Alice in Wonderland*?'

'Lewis Carroll!' Frannie piped up, which was a good thing since for the life of her, Olivia could not remember who wrote it. 'And,' Frannie continued, 'he was an amateur botanist, so I bet he knew about these giant mushrooms.'

'Exactly!' Dr Steenpister cried. 'These are *boletus maximus* from Java, and Lewis Carroll studied them at Oxford. As did my own father, who built this greenhouse.'

Now he gazed at Frannie with frank admiration, which annoyed Olivia, especially since she herself had not even known the name of *Alice in Wonderland's* author, much less that he was an amateur botanist.

'She's older than she looks, you know,' Olivia said crossly. When that failed to wipe the admiration from Dr Steenpister's face, Olivia added. 'She's fourteen, if you want to know the truth.'

This produced the desired effect. Dr Steenpister furrowed his brow and gazed down at Frannie.

'Impossible,' he declared. 'This girl can't be any more than eight.' The snarly arrogance was gone from his voice, however. In fact, he now looked uneasy, as though someone were playing a trick on him.

'Actually, it's the truth,' Frannie said, and right away Olivia felt very petty for having blurted out her age. 'I stopped growing when I was seven. It's why I wanted to see you.'

Dr Steenpister tapped his finger on the mushroom that held his laptop and shook his head. 'I don't see what that has to do with me . . .'

'I read your father's book, *A Botanical History of the Dreaded Pitta-Pitta Tribe of New Guinea*,' Frannie explained. 'As you may imagine,' she spread her hands downward to indicate her body, 'I have a particular interest in finding the plant that Blup ate.'

'Well, if you read the book *carefully* –' the arrogance had returned to his voice – 'you would know that my father never found the plant.'

'I did read the book carefully, Doctor Steenpister,' Frannie said. 'That's why I believe the plant is somewhere in this greenhouse.'

Dr Steenpister glowered and began to polish his head with the palm of his hand uneasily.

'Most people believe that there are no more Eastern European Cave Dwellers left in the world,' Frannie continued, looking Dr Steenpister right in the eye. 'I'm guessing that someone like Viola would be of great interest to someone like you.'

Olivia glanced over at Frannie. So that was why she'd brought Viola with her!

Dr Steenpister cleared his throat uncomfortably. After a moment he said, 'Certainly, she is of some interest . . .'

I bet you're not so happy that Frannie's clever now, Olivia thought.

'Well, Viola will be in town for a week. I'd be happy to bring her over to chat,' Frannie said amiably. 'And in return, you could show me which plant Blup ate.'

Dr Steenpister's glower deepened. He hopped off the mushroom and began to pace. Every so often he shot out a question, like 'How do you know Viola?' and 'Who else has met her?' until finally he stopped pacing and exhaled noisily.

'Agreed,' he said grudgingly. 'Bring her back on Monday. I'll have to conduct some cognitive tests, record her voice, et cetera, and I'll need some time to prepare.'

It all sounded dead boring. Olivia was already beginning to feel very sorry for Viola.

'Where is Viola anyway?' Olivia asked.

They called for her several times, and when there was no response, they all pushed back out through the leaves. Once again, Viola was nowhere to be seen. Dr Steenpister called out something in her own language, but the only sound they heard was the off-and-on hiss of a sprinkler and the muffled noise of traffic on the street below.

Suddenly there was a rustling from behind a thicket of tall bushes and out came one of the smallest adult women that Olivia had ever seen. She barely reached Olivia's hip. The woman had skin the colour of peanut butter and short, tightly curled black hair that formed a thick helmet above her head. Her eyes were black and bright, and seemed extremely amused.

'Where's the girl?' Dr Steenpister demanded of the woman. His tone was sharp and rude, but the woman didn't appear to mind.

With her bright, amused eyes she looked around at all of them. Olivia found the woman vaguely disconcerting – as though she considered them all slightly ridiculous. She pointed at a shelf full of very pretty potted flowers. They had silky violet and white speckled petals and their plump centres looked eerily like tiny sad faces. Olivia leaned forward and noticed that each flower had tiny tears dripping from its 'eyes'.

'Cool,' Olivia said. She stuck out a finger to dab the tear from one of the unhappy flowers when Dr Steenpister reached out quickly and yanked her hand back.

'What?' Olivia turned on him angrily. But then she noticed Frannie staring at the flower with a shocked look on her face. The 'mouth' of the flower that Olivia had almost touched was now yawning open, baring two rows of needle-sharp teeth.

'*Monstrum Bellus,*' said Dr Steenpister ominously. 'That's the flower's Latin name. It means Beautiful Monster.'

'Would it really have bitten me?' Olivia asked. Dr Steenpister didn't have to answer since at that moment Viola emerged from the thicket with bandages on three of her right-hand fingers and eyes that were still red from crying. The tiny woman pointed at Viola and laughed.

'That's not funny,' Olivia said.

'No, it's OK, Olivia,' Frannie said. She turned to Dr Steenpister and asked, 'She's a Pitta-Pitta, isn't she?'

'Yes, as a matter of fact, Lippa *is* a Pitta-Pitta.'

'In the book,' Frannie told Olivia, 'it says that the Pitta-Pittas laugh at tragedy. It's a cultural thing.'

Olivia eyed the tiny woman, Lippa, who was laughing so hard that all the brilliant white teeth in her mouth showed, even the back molars. 'It's a *rude* thing,' Olivia said.

Lippa turned her bright, laughing eyes on Olivia. Her lips snapped shut over her teeth and her face turned very serious, which Olivia found a bit alarming.

'She didn't mean anything by that,' Frannie hurriedly explained. 'My friend just says what's on her mind without thinking.'

'Well, I don't see how that's possible,' Olivia grumbled. 'If it was on my mind, I was obviously thinking about it.'

Dr Steenpister spoke a few words to Lippa in her own language and she let out a noise that sounded something like a raspberry. Then she disappeared again behind the thicket.

'Monday, then.' Dr Steenpister opened the door for them to leave. He nodded curtly to Frannie. 'I think we'll both be pleased with the results of our bargain, young lady.'

Dr Steenpister's 'young lady' sounded like 'I will treat you exactly the way I would treat an adult', which, in Olivia's opinion, was the scariest way to say 'young lady'.

'I don't like him,' said Olivia when all three of them were back in the elevator. She was trying to ignore the elevator's grinding noise as they descended.

'You like the Princepessa, don't you?' Frannie asked.

'Yeah. So?'

'So she and Doctor Steenpister are cut from the same cloth. Both of them are way too proud and suspicious, but basically OK. Although, I have to say it, the Princepessa is driving us all mad these days. The other day she accused my mother's dog of jumping on the coffee table and peeing in her tea, which is totally ridiculous since Mister Snuggles has arthritis and only pees in the Princepessa's shoes.'

CHAPTER SIXTEEN

'Master Plover and your father are dining in the garden tonight,' Cornwickle informed Olivia when she came home that evening.

'What about that . . . that animal in the garden? Chester?'

'I suspect it has gone the way of the parrots and the macaque monkeys – over the garden wall, never to be seen again.' Cornwickle sniffed. 'One hopes.'

A table had been set out in the centre of the garden, with a large silver candelabrum in the middle and bunches of cut flowers strewn across the tablecloth, between the platters of food. Ansel and George had already started eating, and now looked up happily when Olivia entered the garden.

'Excellent, the family is all here,' Ansel said as Cornwickle pulled out Olivia's chair for her. 'Really, Cornwickle, I wish you would sit with us. We're not contagious.'

'It wouldn't be proper, sir,' Cornwickle said, sitting down at a small table a few feet away. He spread a napkin across his lap, picked up his fork, and began to spear a shrimp on his plate. Ansel watched him for a moment, his expression turning sulky.

'Cornwickle,' Ansel said with sudden vigour, as though an idea had just occurred to him, 'what are you thinking, man? The monkeys must be fed!'

'Sir,' Cornwickle said, a forkful of shrimp poised in the air, 'I believe the monkeys have all run away.'

'Nonsense. They're just bashful.' He reached across the table, piled a heaping mound of food on his salad plate, and held it out petulantly. 'Here. You can give them this.'

Cornwickle sighed, put down his fork, and rose. He looked down at the plate that Ansel had prepared.

'Shrimp Carbonara, sir?' Cornwickle said questioningly.

'Do you have a problem with George's cooking, Cornwickle?' Ansel raised his finely moulded chin combatively.

'Of course not, Master Plover. It's just that the monkeys—'

'Exactly. Now off with you.' He shooed him away with his fingers. 'And did you have a good time with your mother, my dear Olivia?'

'No, it was awful—' Olivia started, but Ansel interrupted her with, 'No, no, Cornwickle! Not there!'

Cornwickle had laid the plate of pasta by the base of the tall oak tree.

'Sir?' he said.

'Where do monkeys live, Cornwickle?' Ansel said as though he were talking to a small child.

'In trees, sir,' Cornwickle said wearily.

'Exactly. *In* trees, not *under* trees. No, you must place the plate up in the tree, Cornwickle. Way up there, at the tippy-top, there's a good fellow.'

Cornwickle gazed up at the oak. His moustache twitched.

'You know, Ansel,' George said quietly, 'that's quite a climb, and Cornwickle is a largish man . . .'

'My mother wants me to have a *proper* butler, and a *proper* butler would climb that tree,' Ansel said loudly.

'Certainly, sir,' Cornwickle sighed. He pulled his chair up to the tree and used it to boost his hefty body to the lowest limb.

'Now, what were we saying?' Ansel turned back to Olivia, smiling. 'Oh yes. I was telling you how much I enjoyed talking to your mother this afternoon. She was dressed like a cockroach.'

'An earwig,' George corrected him, a note of embarrassment in his voice.

'She was here *again*?' Olivia cried.

'She stopped by after your lunch with her,' George said.

There was a loud scuffle coming from the oak tree, and they all turned. Cornwickle had managed to climb a good way up the tree, but was now clinging precariously with one arm as his right foot struggled to find the branch beneath it.

'A little to the left, Cornwickle. There you go!' Ansel called to him. 'You'll be at the top in no time!'

'Ansel, really. Don't you think you should let the poor man come down?' George watched nervously as Cornwickle proceeded to inch his way up the tree again.

'Don't you dare feel sorry for him.' Ansel waggled a finger at George. 'He doesn't deserve it. He's been plaguing me for days.'

'What did she want?' Olivia tried to turn the conversation back to her mother.

'She wants to see you again, Sweetpea. On Thursday. She seems determined to buy you a bra.'

'You told her no, didn't you?' Olivia's voice was rising.

'As a matter of fact, I told her yes,' George said.

'Well, you can call her up and tell her no. I'm not going bra shopping with a woman who dresses like a cockroach!'

'An earwig,' George corrected.

'Bravo! Nearly there, Cornwickle!' Ansel put down his fork and applauded. All that could be seen was

Cornwickle's large backside parting the branches close to the top of the oak. 'The monkeys will be so glad.'

There was a rustling from the top of the tree as Cornwickle placed the plate of pasta in the crook of the top branches. Then, slowly and with great care, he began to climb down.

'He's rather agile for a fat man,' Ansel mused with some annoyance. 'Oh, and speaking of which, no one ought to go for a swim in the lagoon just yet. It seems we missed one of the snapping turtles. It nearly removed a chunk of flesh from Cornwickle's hide this morning.'

It was a few moments later that they heard an ear-splitting cry for help from the other side of the garden wall.

'Not to worry, Ms Bender!' Ansel hastily called over the wall. 'That's just my butler in the tree! Not a peeper or anything naughty!'

There was a hesitation before her shaky voice called back, 'No, not *him*! I just saw something . . . an animal . . . lurking in my boxwood shrub! It nearly bit me!'

'Ah.' Ansel clapped his hands delightedly and exclaimed to Olivia and George, 'That must be Chester!'

'Sir.' Cornwickle had successfully descended and was now approaching Ansel. 'I think it is best if you don't mention to your neighbour that the beast belongs to you.'

'You do, do you?' Ansel eyed Cornwickle with hostility. Then Ansel cupped his mouth with his hands and called loudly over the wall, 'Thank you, dear Ms Bender, for finding *my pet,* Chester! I will send Cornwickle right over to fetch him!' And with a defiant snort he turned back to his meal.

Cornwickle sighed and brushed some stray leaves off the front of his waistcoat. 'Just as you wish, sir,' he said, and headed off to Ms Bender's.

'Ms Bender is going to kill you, you know,' Olivia said to Ansel.

'Not at all. Ms Bender finds me charming.' He smiled at her – and indeed it was a very charming smile. 'Although I doubt poor Cornwickle would say the same. Excellent meal, George. As usual.'

CHAPTER SEVENTEEN

Just after the lunch bell on Monday, Olivia loitered on the first floor, waiting for the crowds of cafeteria-bound students to clear the hallway. While she waited, she passed the time pretending to be fascinated by the legion of autographed photos hanging on the wall. These were the people who had attended the school and had gone on to be successful artists or musicians or dancers. Olivia could pretty much guarantee that her own photo would never grace that wall.

As the crowds started to thin, Olivia casually began to stroll closer and closer to Room 114. She stopped every few steps, pretending to be riveted by a particular photo, until one of them really did catch her eye. It was of a very young ballerina dancing on stage. The photo caught her in mid-leap, her legs stretched impossibly high off the ground. On the bottom right-hand corner was the ballerina's autograph: Mona Monsoon.

Just then the door to Room 114 opened and a young woman poked her head out.

'Olivia?' the woman said.

'Yes.'

'Oh good! Come on in!'

The woman disappeared behind the door, and after a quick glance around the hall to check that no one was looking, Olivia entered Room 114. At first, she just stood there, confused. The woman sitting behind the desk was not her idea of how a school counsellor should look. If anything, she looked like she'd popped right out of one of those autographed photos in the hall – all glossy and white-toothed, and with skin so flawless that you knew the photographer had done something tricky with the photo. Only in her case, there were no tricks, except possibly for a little Maybelline. Her shoulder-length hair was a screamingly bright, almost Technicolor red, and except for the fact that she was wearing a frumpy navy blue jacket over a matching skirt, she looked just like a bonafide old-time movie starlet, right down to the beauty mark just above the left side of her mouth.

'Are you really *Gwen*?' Olivia asked astonished. 'Gwen, the school counsellor?'

By way of answer, the woman put her foot up on the desk so that Olivia could see the pinchy-toed shoes.

'Have a seat.' Gwen nodded towards the chair on

the other side of her desk and put her foot back down. She fished out a crumpled paper bag from her desk drawer and removed two containers of yogurt and two plastic spoons. 'Did you bring lunch? Because I brought extra, just in case.'

'No, thanks. My dad always packs something for me.' She opened her knapsack and pulled out the nylon lunch box. Inside was a small wild-mushroom focaccia, a container full of marinated artichoke hearts, four fat little dumplings along with their own container of dipping sauce, a small thermos of iced tea and a large slice of a chocolate raspberry torte. Olivia pulled out the items and placed them on the desk.

'My dad's a cook,' Olivia explained, suddenly embarrassed by the feast spread out in front of her. She ripped the focaccia and handed half of it to Gwen, who hesitated a moment then took it, and bit into it in a nice, dainty way.

'What's the matter?' Gwen asked when she saw Olivia watching her.

'Nothing. You eat nicely. The person I usually have lunch with eats like an animal.'

'Oh. Thanks, I guess. So,' Gwen said after she popped the last bit of focaccia in her mouth, 'how was your weekend?'

Olivia pressed her back against the chair. 'Is this the part where you start nosing around?' she asked.

'No, this is the part where I find out how your weekend was,' Gwen replied evenly.

Olivia peeled back the plastic tops on the container of dumplings and the sauce. She pushed the containers towards Gwen, who plucked one of the little round dumplings out, dipped it in the red sauce, and took a bite.

'Not too fabulous, if you want to know the truth,' Olivia said.

'Did your father make these things from scratch?' Gwen asked, taking another bite of the dumpling.

'Yes. Are you listening?' Olivia asked, which struck her as a funny thing to say to a counsellor.

'"Not too fabulous." I'm listening. Why not too fabulous?' She helped herself to another dumpling.

'I had this huge fight with my brother,' Olivia said. It was funny to hear those words coming out of her mouth – as though she had a completely ordinary life.

'What about? If you don't mind me asking.'

'He . . .' This part was harder to explain. 'He put words in my mouth.'

'Really?' Gwen said. 'You don't seem like you need any help in that department.'

'Do you mean that in a snotty way?' Olivia asked.

'A little bit,' Gwen said. 'What words did he put in your mouth?'

'Well, it wasn't the words so much as the fact that he thinks our mother is actually a good person.'

'She's not?'

'No. She's awful.' Olivia folded her arms across her chest, not feeling inclined to elaborate. There was a short pause, after which Gwen reached across the desk and opened the container of artichoke hearts.

'Do you mind?' she asked.

'Help yourself.' Olivia shrugged.

'So,' Gwen said, holding a heart and gently shaking off the dripping marinade into the container, 'what's he like anyway?'

'Who, Christopher? He's tallish, blondish—'

'No, not what he *looks* like. What's he *like*?'

'Oh, he's great. Smart, funny. Everyone likes him. If you met him, you'd like him too.' And, Olivia realized suddenly, Christopher would have probably liked Gwen right back. She had eyes the colour of Dr Pepper.

'How old is he?' Gwen asked, as though she might be thinking the same thing.

'He would have been—' She caught herself. 'He's going to be twenty-one in October.'

'Wow! So he's a lot older than you.'

'Doesn't matter. We're really close. We know each other better than anyone else in the world. Which is why it's so strange to find out that he actually *likes* our mother.'

183

'Mmm.' Gwen seemed to consider the last bite of artichoke heart pinched between her fingers. 'But if you think about it, you weren't even around for the first eight years of Christopher's life. And then you probably don't remember much of the first five years of *your* life. So all in all –' she quickly licked a drip of brine off the heart – 'you've only known your brother for *less than half of his life*. Weird when you think about it that way, huh?'

More than weird. The realization stunned Olivia. It was so stupidly obvious, but she had never thought of that before.

'So who's this person who eats like an animal?' Gwen asked. Her mind seemed to flit about like a hummingbird.

Olivia told Gwen about Stella and the fact that she could sleep with her eyes open, to which Gwen responded, 'But why would you want to?'

'My point exactly,' Olivia agreed. But Gwen seemed to ponder this question.

'Is she afraid of something?' Gwen picked up her yogurt spoon and scooped up a hunk of the chocolate raspberry torte, her brow furrowed slightly. 'Or someone?'

'Really, she's just a freak,' Olivia assured her, digging into the cake with her own spoon. All of a sudden, she noticed Gwen's name placard, which had been shoved to the edge of her desk: *G. Pinkus, Counsellor.*

'I thought you said your last name was Riley?' Olivia said.

'I never did.'

'But that's the name you signed on my excuse note,' Olivia said. She pulled out the note from the front pocket of her knapsack. 'See?'

'Ms Riley is the school nurse,' Gwen said. 'I figured you'd prefer to have your teacher think you had a headache rather than a psycho attack.'

'You *forged* her signature?' Olivia asked incredulously.

'I've been doing it since I was thirteen,' Gwen said, smiling. Her teeth were so white it looked like she'd never drunk anything but milk. 'Ms Riley was the school nurse when I went to this school too. I used to get lots of headaches back then.' She winked when she said 'headaches'. It was a good sort of wink too, not the kind that made Olivia embarrassed for the winker. It was a wink that Christopher would have appreciated.

'How come you didn't come to art class on Friday?' Stella whispered as Olivia took her seat beside her easel. 'Mister Pierre-Louis was not happy about it. You should have see his face—' Her mouth clamped shut as Mr Pierre-Louis walked in the room. To Olivia's dismay, he walked straight up to her, his cheeks sucked in. Clearly, he'd been looking forward to this moment. Olivia doubted that she'd disappoint him.

'Where were you on Friday?' he asked.

Olivia had the note ready in the palm of her hand. She gave it to him and he read it, then crumpled it up, looking distinctly unimpressed.

'The portrait, please.' He folded his arms across his chest and gazed up at the ceiling.

Olivia fumbled with her knapsack, pulling at the sketch pad, which was so large its edges caught beneath the knapsack's zipper.

'Today, please,' Mr Pierre-Louis said.

She gave a good solid yank and the sketchbook came out.

Olivia flipped to the page, took a deep breath and held it back behind her teeth as she handed the pad to Mr Pierre-Louis. Plunking the pad on the easel's ledge, he looked at the drawing. He sucked on his cheeks so hard that you could have tucked golf balls in the divots below his cheekbones. The rest of the class watched in perfect silence with the same morbid interest people take in seeing a boa constrictor strangle and devour a rabbit. Well, she wouldn't give them the satisfaction of seeing her squirm, Olivia decided. She examined her fingernails nonchalantly, then pretended to brush something off her shirt, then crossed and uncrossed and recrossed her feet.

Finally, Mr Pierre-Louis spanked the side of her easel and handed her back her sketch pad.

'Nice work,' he said.

She was so shocked that she didn't even reach for her sketch pad. She just stood there, frowning at him in confusion.

'Are you ill, Miss Kidney? Shall we call for a stretcher?' Mr Pierre-Louis asked. The class sniggered.

'No, I'm fine,' she said, avoiding the eyes of her classmates.

'Your drawing skills are abominable, of course,' Mr Pierre-Louis declared. 'Despite that, you've done something quite remarkable. You've managed to show us what this man has hidden behind his rusty can of corn niblets.' He nodded to her approvingly. 'Bravo, Olivia.'

After he left her, Olivia looked at her drawing, perplexed. What did he mean? She held up the sketchbook for Stella to see.

'What do you think?' Olivia asked her. 'What's hidden behind his can of corn niblets?'

When there was no answer, Olivia put her sketchbook back on the easel and sighed. She opened her knapsack, fished around for a tissue, and wiped the drool off Stella's chin.

CHAPTER EIGHTEEN

At the dismissal buzzer, Olivia hurried down the stairs with everyone else. Maybe it was because Mr Pierre-Louis had approved of her drawing. Or maybe it was because she had passed right by Renee on the steps and impulsively smiled at her, which startled Renee and made her stumble against the girl in front of her, who called her a clod. In any case, Olivia found herself in a really good mood. She was beginning to get the hang of the school, beginning to feel a part of its rhythm. More importantly, she was beginning to feel like a regular, normal kid. In this happy state of mind, she trotted down the street towards the subway, nearly passing right by the old woman who was waiting on the corner, standing beside a gleaming silver car.

'Oh! Christina Lilli!' Olivia exclaimed, careful to leave off the 'Princepessa' part. 'What are you doing here?'

'I've come to fetch you. Your dress is ready and it needs to be fitted.' She'd obviously made a recent visit to the beauty parlour. Her hair was poufed up and dyed a strange lavender-white. She gazed around, her face pinched with disapproval. 'I don't like the looks of some of these children.'

'They're just artistic, that's all,' Olivia said.

'Artistic? Pah! They're hoodlums. They look like they don't bathe. Speaking of which . . .' She rapped sharply on the tinted window of the silver car, and in a moment the window lowered and a woman stuck her head out. Beneath a mop of black hair, she had a square, pugnacious face and a pair of glinting dark eyes. She was wearing a dress made of some dun-coloured hide.

'Keep – window – OPEN,' the Princepessa said, pointing to the window and then motioning downward with the palm of her hand. And then to Olivia, she said, 'The woman smells like the inside of an old army boot.'

'One of Arthur's family?' Olivia guessed.

'His baby sister. Mertha. She likes to ride around in the car. Much like a Labrador retriever.'

The Princepessa's attention was momentarily diverted by a boy whose green hair was gelled and spiked so that he resembled a startled parrot.

The Princepessa turned to Olivia and in a very

accusatory way said, 'I won't tolerate strangely coloured hair at my wedding, Olivia.'

'Right,' Olivia said, eyeing the Princepessa's own hair. The Princepessa squinted at Olivia, as though she were trying to decide if she was being impertinent. But Mertha was beginning to scroll up the window again, so the Princepessa hurried Olivia into the car. She scolded Mertha as she climbed in, and then told the driver to take them directly home.

Olivia sat between the two women, which seemed to suit both of them just fine. As they drove through the streets, the Princepessa occasionally shot irritated looks at Mertha, who was staring out the window, ignoring her. The Princepessa suddenly leaned across Olivia and said to Mertha in a loud voice, 'Do you have any idea how ridiculous you look in those clothes?'

'Shush!' Olivia whispered to the Princepessa.

'You're lucky the driver hasn't mistaken you for a rag and used you to wipe the windscreen,' the Princepessa continued.

'Stop it,' Olivia said, but the Princepessa just flipped her hand in the air and sat back in the seat.

'Oh, the woman doesn't understand a word I'm saying.' She shook her head. 'Cave people at a royal wedding! It's appalling.'

'You're marrying a caveman,' Olivia reminded her.

'Yes, and one of them at a wedding is bad enough. But we're to have a whole herd of them!'

'How many are there?' Olivia asked.

'Two.'

'That's hardly a herd, you know,' Olivia said.

'They smell like there's a herd of them.' Here, the Princepessa leaned across Olivia again and made several loud sniffing noises to make her point.

Olivia peeked over at Mertha. The woman was still staring fixedly out the window, but Olivia detected a grim set to her lips. Olivia got the feeling that, like Viola, she had some pretty good peripheral vision. Olivia noted the stitching on Mertha's dress was done with slender leather strips that were sewn with careful, dainty little stitches. Tiny bones that might have come from fish were sewn along the edge of the collar in a zigzag decoration. It was actually a very nice dress, Olivia thought. She took a small, silent whiff. Yes, there was an odour. But it wasn't awful. Certainly not as bad as the CHEESE, IF YOU PLEASE! restaurant. Mertha smelt sort of like a recently extinguished campfire. With maybe a touch of elephant.

'At least her daughter has begun to dress like a human being,' the Princepessa said.

'Oh! Of course. She's Viola's mother,' Olivia said.

At the mention of her daughter's name, Mertha turned to Olivia with a frown and said something sternly in her own language, which sounded like a series of whoops and howls, much like the noises that come from angry fans at the Yankee Stadium stands. Then she turned back to the window and resumed staring at the passing view.

'What was that about?' Olivia asked.

'Arthur says that Viola has been getting very rebellious lately.' She leaned across Olivia and said loudly to Mertha, 'Teenagers are despicable creatures, Mertha. The sooner you accept that, the happier you will be.'

Without taking her eyes off the streets, Mertha squared her broad shoulders and grunted in a way that sounded very much like she agreed.

In the Vondychomps' mansion they passed through the grim antechamber and entered the throne room, which was all aflutter with people in white chef outfits. They were anxiously brandishing silver trays of elaborate appetizers, slabs of roasted meats and tiny, prettily decorated cakes. Arthur Vondychomps sat at a small table set up in the room, sampling the items on the trays. By his feet, Mimi's dog, Mr Snuggles, was gazing up him, waiting for falling scraps.

'Yes, yes, it's all delicious,' he was saying to one of the chefs, who was looking very put out. 'But we want *authentic* Babatavian cuisine.'

'But this is Babatavian cuisine!' the chef insisted.

The Princepessa swept over to the tray nearest her

and snatched up one of the thick slices of meat. After a moment of chewing she spat it out on the floor. Mr Snuggles rushed forward and gobbled it up instantly.

'I'm surprised the dog didn't spit it out as well,' the Princepessa said to the chef, whose face had turned crimson red.

The chef clapped his hands sharply and announced to his staff, 'We will leave now! This very moment!'

'Yes, it's probably for the best,' Arthur said resignedly, as all the people in white began to collect up the trays and file out of the room. 'Still,' he said to the Princepessa, 'don't you think you should lower your standards just a smidgen, my dear?'

'If I was able to do that, I would have married someone else long ago.'

It took Arthur a moment to extract the compliment from those words, but when he did, he beamed beautifully, and lowered his eyes.

The Princepessa sniffed and said, 'Come along' to Olivia, who suppressed a smile herself, so as not to embarrass the Princepessa.

They travelled up the dark stairs, the narrow space trapping the reptilian scent of the greenish snake oil in the sconces. The fat seamstress was waiting for them on the second floor. When she saw Olivia, her eyes squinched in a smile, and all her pretty white teeth showed.

'Hallo to the little girlie,' she said. The cuff of her sleeve was gleaming menacingly with pins. 'We maken she a beee-aa-uuutiful gown!' Then she went to the closet and flung it open, pulling out a long silver dress on a silk hanger. It was indeed a beautiful gown. The bodice was stitched with tiny little pearls and the shimmery silver material fanned out like an upside-down tulip. She held it up against Olivia.

'It looks too big,' the Princepessa said.

The seamstress cocked her head. 'Ooops! Maybe I make it a little too biggin in the waist,' she said happily. Her fat fingers tickled the pins stuck in her cuff, like a swordsman trying to select his weapon.

'She did that deliberately,' Olivia said.

'Oh, no problem, no problem. You put it on, girlie.' The seamstress indicated a screen that Olivia should go behind, pushing the gown at Olivia eagerly. 'I will take in a little bitten here, a little bitten there . . .'

The door flew open then and Frannie burst in, breathless. Her eyes darted around the room quickly before she flashed a strained smile at them. 'Hey. Hi. Nice dress. So, has anyone happened to see Viola?'

'If you want my opinion,' said the Princepessa, walking past her to leave the room, 'you're getting far too chummy with that girl. She's a bad influence.'

'Yep, you're probably right,' Frannie said, then made a quick motion to Olivia, pointing down the hall and mouthing, 'My room. Later.'

Olivia nodded before the seamstress put one of her butcher's hands on the back of Olivia's neck and pushed her behind the screen.

'So?' the seamstress asked cheerfully as Olivia put on the dress. 'Has any body tried to killing you dead yet?'

'To kill me?' Olivia said. 'No! Why would anyone be trying to kill me?'

'Oh, nothing nothing, little girlie.' There was an awful sound coming from the other side of the screen. Olivia peeked around it and saw that the seamstress was laughing.

'Does this have something to do with the assassin?' Olivia asked.

'You might be a littling bittling careful these days, girlie, that's all I say.' The seamstress pretended to zip up her lip.

'I thought that the assassin only tries to kill the Princepessa at the actual wedding,' Olivia said.

'If the assassin finding out who Royal Imposter is before wedding, well . . .' The seamstress made a swift motion with her fat finger across her thick neck, like a knife cutting a throat. Then she shook her head with a look of mock tragedy. 'Bad luck for the Princepessa if her imposter getsing killed before wedding.' She laughed again. 'Bad luck for imposter too!'

CHAPTER NINETEEN

Twenty-five minutes and seven pinpricks later, three of which drew blood, the seamstress dismissed Olivia. She hurried down the hall and crept into Frannie's cave. A low fire was burning in the pit. Frannie was sitting on the pile of skins, gnawing at her cuticles. For a moment Olivia thought the Princepessa might be right. Except for her school uniform, Frannie looked quite wild.

Taped to the wall above her bed was a piece of paper that said, 'Everybody should do two things each day that he hates to do, just for practice – William James.'

'Well,' Olivia said, touching her ribs, which still smarted from the seamstress's needles, 'that's one down, one to go.'

'What?' Frannie looked up, just then realizing that she had company. 'Oh, it's you. Oh, Olivia, I am in *such* trouble!' Frannie moaned.

'What did you do?' Olivia asked, finding it hard to believe that Frannie was capable of doing anything worse than harbouring an overdue library book.

'I lost Viola,' Frannie said. She looked up at Olivia with wide eyes. 'She's somewhere in the city. Probably frightened to death. Anything could happen to her.'

'I don't know. She seemed pretty good at taking care of herself.'

'Yes, maybe if she has a spear and she's facing an angry hippo!' Frannie cried indignantly.

'How did you lose her anyway?' Olivia asked.

'I was taking her to see Doctor Steenpister after school today,' Frannie said. 'We were heading for the subway and I peeked in the bookstore window for just one minute – well, maybe a little longer – and when I turned back, Viola was gone. She must not have realized that I stopped and just kept walking and got swept up in the crowds, and oh, she must have been so scared when she found I wasn't there any more!' Frannie buried her head miserably in her tiny hands.

Olivia remembered how Viola had spotted the Asian Mammal Room out of the corner of her eye. She doubted that Viola hadn't seen Frannie stop.

'How was she acting before you lost her?' Olivia asked. Frannie was so bereft that Olivia had to repeat the question before Frannie lifted her head to answer.

'I don't know. Like she usually does, I guess.' Frannie took a moment to consider, then said, 'Well, to be honest, she didn't seem really keen on going back to Doctor Steenpister's. When I said his name, she made this funny face – it's the same expression people get when they first smell the snake-oil lamps.'

'I don't think she's lost, Frannie,' Olivia said. 'I think she just gave you the slip.'

'Really?' Frannie said, already looking relieved.

There was an angry whooping sound coming from the hallway outside. In a moment Mertha entered the cave and whooped again.

'Viola's not here,' Frannie said.

Mertha frowned and looked around. When she didn't see her daughter, she let out a low, guttural sound. Frannie quickly stood, grabbed a piece of paper from beneath her stack of books, and began to draw. It was a picture of Viola, and not a very flattering one at that. Viola's body was shaped like a breeze block and her neck was almost non-existent. Next, Frannie drew several cages filled with animal-ish creatures (truth be told, Olivia thought, Frannie was a pretty awful artist). When she was finished, she held the drawing up for Mertha to see.

'Understand? Viola is at the zoo,' Frannie said, smiling in a very unnatural way. (She's a pretty awful liar too, Olivia thought.)

Mertha's grunts sounded a little less angry now. Encouraged, Frannie put a long spear in Viola's hands, and Mertha grinned and nodded, completely satisfied that her daughter was finally coming to her senses.

'I hate lying!' Frannie said after Mertha left. 'I just didn't want Viola to get into even more hot water than she already is. Ever since Viola started wearing normal clothes, she and her mom have been fighting like mad. Well, anyway,' Frannie sighed miserably, 'I guess that's that. I'll never find out what Blup's plant was.'

'Don't worry, Viola will show up,' Olivia said. 'You can take her over there tomorrow.'

Frannie shook her head. 'It really is kind of a lousy thing to do to her, when you think about it . . . using Viola like that. It's just that I'm sort of desperate. But that's no excuse. She obviously doesn't want to go.' She attempted a smile. 'Anyway, there are worse things than looking like a seven-year-old for the rest of your life.' But the very next moment, Frannie began to cry, turning away from Olivia and clamping her hand over her mouth to muffle the sobs.

Olivia hated to see people cry, but it was especially awful to see such a dignified person crying. She laid her hand on Frannie's narrow back, touching the slender spine that refused to grow.

'We're going to the museum, Frannie,' Olivia said

with sudden decisiveness. 'Right now.' She stood up, cracking her head against the ceiling. 'Ow!'

'What's the point?' Frannie said miserably, still huddled on her pelts. 'Without Viola, Doctor Steenpister won't help me.'

'We'll convince him to,' Olivia said, rubbing her sore skull.

'How?'

'We'll beg him,' Olivia said.

'I hate begging,' Frannie said.

'Then William James will be very proud of you,' Olivia replied, grabbing Frannie's arm and pulling her to her feet. 'You hate lying and you hate begging. You already told a lie. If we go to the museum and beg, you'll have done your two things for the day.'

Unable to argue with the wisdom of William James, Frannie allowed Olivia to lead her out of the cave and uptown to the American Museum of Natural History.

CHAPTER TWENTY

They found Dr Steenpister in his office, sitting on the *boletus maximus* mushroom, tapping at the keys of his laptop. He had looked up eagerly when he saw them push through the heavy foliage, but his pleasant expression quickly faded.

'Aren't we missing someone?' he asked.

'I'm sorry, Doctor Steenpister,' Frannie began, rubbing her hands together nervously, 'but Viola isn't coming.'

Dr Steenpister looked from Frannie to Olivia, as though he suspected they were making a joke at his expense. Without a word, he stood up and walked past them, disappearing between the trees. In a minute they heard him angrily calling for Lippa. Frannie bit her lip and eyed Olivia anxiously before they both followed him out, passing back into the sweltering greenhouse air.

'Is the girl in here somewhere?' he was demanding

of Lippa. She was holding a potted plant that looked like a half-dozen flesh-coloured straws, standing upright and weaving around. 'The cave-dwelling girl?'

Lippa smiled widely and shook her head in such a way that she seemed like she was blatantly lying. No wonder Dr Steenpister always looked like he suspected people were playing tricks on him, Olivia thought.

Dr Steenpister turned to Frannie, his expression stony. 'I thought we had an arrangement, young lady.' His voice was tight with anger. His 'young lady' sounded distinctly like 'fingernail filth'.

'I know, Doctor Steenpister,' Frannie said, her words tumbling out quickly, 'but Viola didn't want to come, and it wouldn't be right for me to make her, I'm sure you would agree, but I was hoping that you'd show me Blup's plant anyway.'

Dr Steenpister gazed down at Frannie with a look of profound disbelief. 'It appears that not only is your body stunted, but your brain is too.'

'Excuse me?' Frannie said weakly.

'Or maybe you thought I would have pity for you because you're deformed?'

'Apologize for that!' Olivia cried.

'You two have wasted enough of my time.' Dr Steenpister turned away from them and headed back to his office. Olivia started to follow him, ready to pursue her demand for an apology, but Frannie held her back.

'It doesn't matter, Olivia,' she said. 'Let's just go.'

'You want talk to his father?' This came from Lippa.

Both girls turned, startled. Lippa was tickling one of the potted straws.

'You speak English?' Frannie said.

'You want talk to Franklin Steenpister?' Lippa asked again.

'I'd love to,' Frannie said, 'but unfortunately he's dead.'

'Ssst-ssst-ssst.' Lippa shook her head. 'Not dead.' The straw that she tickled now bent towards her. The tip of the straw widened like a funnel. Lippa picked up a beaker of some green-coloured liquid and poured it in the straw, which waved around appreciatively as it swallowed it.

'Franklin Steenpister is alive?' Olivia asked.

Lippa nodded her head, grinning in a way that made her look like she was lying.

'But the book said he died,' Frannie objected.

'*He* tell everyone that.' She jerked her head towards Dr Steenpister's office. 'But it is not true.'

Bewildered, both girls watched in silence as Lippa put down the beaker and closely examined one of the other straws. She frowned at a thin brown line that ran diagonally across it like a scar, then swiftly snapped the straw in half, just below the line. The plant let out a disturbing asthmatic wheeze.

'If he's alive, where is he?' Frannie asked.

One of Lippa's peanut-butter-coloured fingers pointed down.

'He's down in the museum?' Frannie asked.

Lippa shook her head. 'More down.'

Olivia and Frannie exchanged confused looks, so Lippa placed the plant on a shelf and gestured for them to follow her. They did, weaving their way through the tight rows of plants and flowers till they came to a door at the far end of the greenhouse. Lippa opened it and they found themselves outside, on the museum's roof. Lippa walked straight to the edge of the roof, and once again pointed down. Frannie and Olivia followed and peered over the roofline to see what she was pointing to.

It was the 81st Street subway station.

'Franklin Steenpister lives in the subway?' Olivia asked Lippa incredulously.

Lippa nodded and smiled broadly. 'He not well. His mind is . . .' She tapped the side of her head, then made a fluttery motion with her hand, like a bird flying away. 'Phhht! Bye-bye.' Her eyes were bright with a rush of fresh amusement.

'He's crazy?' Olivia said.

'Yes, crazy,' Lippa nodded happily. 'Him in there, the *son* –' she indicated the greenhouse with a hint of disdain – 'he ashamed. He say his papa is dead.'

'Lippa, are you sure that Franklin Steenpister is still alive?' Frannie asked, a measure of hope returning the dignity to her demeanour.

'Of course I sure,' Lippa said. 'I am his wife.'

This stunned both girls into silence. Then, as though Lippa anticipated their objections, she added, 'Second wife. Not the mother of that one.' Again, she indicated Dr Steenpister by a nod towards the greenhouse and a look of contempt.

'Where in the subway does he live?' Olivia asked.

Lippa shrugged.

Olivia saw Frannie's hopeful expression fade slightly. The New York City subway system was a huge maze. It was rumoured that homeless people lived in nooks and crannies in the tunnels, of which there were probably thousands.

'Wait a second, maybe we don't even need to find him,' Olivia said to Frannie. 'Maybe Lippa knows what Blup ate to make him grow.'

'Me?' The brightness in Lippa's eyes suddenly dimmed as she shook her head solemnly. 'So many plants in there. Who knows? My husband know. And that one.' She nodded again towards the greenhouse. '*He* know. Not me.'

A muffled call for Lippa came from inside the greenhouse, and Lippa hustled Frannie and Olivia through a door opposite the greenhouse, which led back into the second-floor hallway.

'When you find my husband, you tell him I miss my little bishi-snoot – that is what I used to call him,' Lippa said before she left. There were tears in her eyes. 'You remember! *Bishi-snoot.*'

'We'll tell him,' Olivia said. Then, when the door closed behind them, she said to Frannie, 'What do you suppose a bishi-snoot is?'

To Olivia's surprise, Frannie knew the answer. 'It's a little rodent that lives underground in New Guinea. Kind of looks like a giant hairless rat.'

'Wow! That's a lousy thing to call someone.'

'Yeah, maybe,' Frannie said vaguely. She seemed distracted. Olivia left her to her thoughts while she herself began to work out how in the world they were going to find a man who obviously did not want to be found.

CHAPTER TWENTY-ONE

Mister Pierre-Louis was in an unusually good mood the next afternoon. A scarily good mood, in Olivia's opinion.

'Good afternoon, my precious geniuses!' he cried as he strode in, holding a small wooden crate and flashing a brilliant smile at the class of puzzled faces. 'I have been looking forward to our session today so much that I have brought you each a gift.'

'I don't like the sound of this,' Olivia muttered to Stella.

'Me neither,' Stella said, tugging the collar of her turtleneck up over her lip.

The other kids in the class were looking equally nervous, and one girl even went so far as to blurt out, 'What if I don't want your gift?'

'Then you would hurt my feelings,' Mr Pierre-Louis said ominously.

Olivia guessed that would be a far more unpleasant option.

Mr Pierre-Louis cheerfully put his hand into the crate and pulled out a small white egg. He held it between his fingers and said, 'Can anyone tell me what this object is?'

No one was brave enough to answer.

'What?' Mr Pierre-Louis opened his eyes wide. 'Not a single one of you stunningly brilliant children knows what this object is? Perhaps I have overestimated you.'

'It's an egg,' said Carl, unable to resist the goading.

Mr Pierre-Louis smiled at him in a way that made Carl play nervously with his nose ring. Mr Pierre-Louis walked up to him and held out the egg.

'I want you to put your ear against this egg. Now, now, nothing to be frightened of,' Mr Pierre-Louis said when Carl shook his head.

After a hesitation, Carl leaned forward and put his ear against the egg.

'I hear something inside it,' he said, frowning.

'That's because there *is* something inside the egg. In fact, there is that same something inside each and every egg in this crate – twelve to be exact, one for each of you.' And Mr Pierre-Louis proceeded to hand each student an egg, the last ones going to Stella and Olivia.

Olivia examined it. It was larger than a chicken

egg, with a slightly greenish hue, and was so weight-less it felt as though it had no yolk. Still, it definitely contained *something*. She could feel the thing ping-ing around inside, making the egg jump a little now and then. On one end of the egg there was a round piece of shell that had been removed and then glued back to cover the hole, just like an Easter Egg.

'As you may have noticed,' Mr Pierre-Louis said, putting the wooden carton down on the floor and clasping his hands behind his back, 'these are no ordinary chicken eggs, mmm. In my country, these are called "Good Luck Eggs". I give you each this extraordinary gift because I find you to be a most extraordinary class.'

A few of the students smiled.

'You are all extraordinarily *bad* artists,' Mr Pierre-Louis continued. 'You strangle your pencils with your clumsy pork-sausage fingers and you attack the paper as though it were your mortal enemy. Today, my cherubs, your "paper" will indeed be your mortal enemy, and you will learn – the hard way, unfortu-nately – to draw with a hand that is as light as a puff of air.' He puckered his lips and blew a delicate *fhooo* of air. 'Inside each egg is a very small tick.'

'That's disgusting!' one of the girls cried out, hold-ing the egg as far away from her as possible.

'Careful! Don't drop it,' Mr Pierre-Louis warned gravely. 'The second that egg breaks, the tick will bite the first patch of skin it sees. The bite won't look like much at first. Just a round red circle with a white dot in the centre.'

'I don't believe you,' one boy said. 'And anyway, why would they be called Good Luck Eggs if all they've got inside them is a tick that will bite you?'

'Because if you are very lucky, the bite will simply itch for several days.'

He paused and waited for the question, which Stella finally asked: 'And if we're not lucky?'

'Ahhh.' Mr Pierre-Louis's eyes glinted. 'If you are not lucky, your skin will develop tiny purple pustules all over. They're permanent, my friends. And they ooze – very unattractive, I assure you. Which is why it is so important for you to use a very light hand as you draw on your egg with these . . .' He walked to the supply cabinet and pulled out a can full of capped pens. Removing one of their caps, he held the pen up for everyone to see. Its nib was a fine-pointed needle.

'Are you kidding?' Carl cried. 'We'll break the shell if we draw on it with that.'

'Mmm . . . you're right,' Mr Pierre-Louis said, nodding as though deep in thought. After a moment he said, 'You probably should be very, very careful then.' And he proceeded to hand out the pens.

'My parents will have you fired!' one girl said furiously.

210

'Which reminds me of the most interesting thing about these ticks,' Mr Pierre-Louis said cheerfully. 'If you're bitten – and you are one of the unlucky ones – the symptoms won't appear for seven years. You'll be perfectly fine until one day . . . well, you won't. But by that time, I will be happily retired, swinging in a hammock beneath a cloudless Hawaiian sky, having mercifully forgotten about every last one of you.'

'What do you want us to draw?' Olivia asked, once they all had their pens.

'Draw something that makes you happy, mmm,' Mr Pierre-Louis said merrily. Then he hopped up on the windowsill and gazed blissfully out at the view.

Olivia looked at the egg in the palm of her hand, careful not to hold it too tight. Something that made her happy? She ran down a list of things in her mind: her father's chocolate lava cake, the garden in the back of the brownstone. Christopher? No, she was still mad at him. And he was probably still mad at her too. Ruben? No, their last encounter had been too unpleasant.

Then she thought of Branwell.

She imagined his face, remembering the dark eyes, the nose that was neatly squared off at the bottom, the wide mouth with its sharp peaks – a mouth that was both serious and then, suddenly, full of good humour.

Taking the cap off her pen with her teeth, she

lightly touched the pointed nib to her egg. It scratched a fine black line across the rough surface. She made another line, then another, cautiously attempting to draw Branwell's eyes. She held the pen so lightly that she could barely control its movements. The tip began to make it own graceful little twists and turns, creating feathery lines that looked nothing like an eye. Still, she didn't dare grip the pen any tighter and try to force it to do what she wanted. Instead, she kept picturing Branwell in her mind while the pen danced crazily across the surface of the egg. The studio was so quiet that you could hear the scritch, scritch, scritch of the pens on the shells and the slow, careful breathing of twelve very tense people.

After several minutes, Olivia stopped and examined her drawing. Amazingly, Branwell's eyes were beginning to emerge from the tangle of ink. They weren't the eyes that Olivia had pictured – they were more alive somehow. They looked both worried and watchful, and as though they were trying to let her know something important.

Right then she began to feel a melting warmth in her gut. It was the same sensation she always felt whenever she contacted Christopher. He must be coming through. Maybe he wanted to apologize.

She listened for his voice, but instead she only heard static. That happened sometimes when the connection wasn't good. Madame Brenda had once told Olivia that tuning into the dead was like tuning a radio – first you would hear static, and then, if you listened long enough, a voice would come through. Now she heard a steady *zzzzz*, with short blasts of voices all tangled together, then the *zzzzz* again. Finally, a single voice emerged. It was faint, like hearing a distant shout during the thickest snowstorm. It said, 'Olivia! Finally!'

'Branwell!' she said, in her head, with barely contained excitement. This was it! Branwell was finally coming through from the Spirit World. She must have been focusing so hard on him that she'd broken through the many months of silence.

'Olivia!' The cry did not come from Branwell this time, but from Stella, who was staring at Olivia's egg with horror. A crack had formed across the shell. In her excitement, Olivia must have absently pressed down too hard with her pen.

Stella's hand shot out and she covered the crack in Olivia's egg with her own hand.

For a moment the two girls stared at each other, too afraid to move. A slick of perspiration appeared on Stella's forehead.

'Oh, Stella, oh, Stella, why did you . . .?' Olivia said, feeling her own hand begin to shake.

'It's OK,' Stella said. The fear was beginning to leave her eyes. 'I don't think the crack went all the way through the egg. Wait, I'll tell you for sure . . .'

Slowly, Stella lifted her hand off the top of the egg and peeked.

'Careful,' Olivia said.

'See, it's only a hairline crack. The egg is still sealed.' Stella put her ear to the shell, then said, 'Yup, I still hear him in there. Listen.'

'I believe you.' Olivia took a few deep breaths to steady herself, and then looked at Stella in wonder. 'Thank you.'

'You would have done the same for me.'

Olivia wasn't so sure about that, but Mr Pierre-Louis was scowling at them now, so Olivia ducked her head and went back to work.

Miraculously, not a single student broke their egg. When the period bell rang, there was a collective sigh of relief. One girl actually passed out, but luckily had put her egg down before she toppled over.

'Congratulations!' Mr Pierre-Louis said as he hopped off the windowsill. 'You can all look forward to a future without pustules!'

He went around the room, collecting all the eggs and putting them carefully back in the wooden crate.

'I thought you were giving them to us as gifts,' one boy objected, holding his egg to his chest.

'You want to keep yours?' Mr Pierre-Louis asked.

'Yes.'

'Then you are either an idiot or a psychopath. Hand it over.'

As Olivia left the class, stepping around the girl who had fainted, she couldn't stop herself from smiling. *She had contacted Branwell!* He was OK. And he hadn't forgotten her.

CHAPTER TWENTY-TWO

'I've been thinking about something Lippa said.' Frannie sounded excited when she called Olivia at home that afternoon. 'About how she nicknamed Franklin Steenpister a "bishi-snoot".'

'A what? Oh yeah, the rat thing.'

'See, I think she meant it as a clue to find him,' Frannie said.

'Balderbash,' Olivia said, because it was a word she'd always wanted to say, and she was in the right sort of mood to try it out.

'What?'

'I said, balderbash.' She said it a little weakly now. It wasn't the kind of word you could say twice in a row.

'That's balder-*dash*,' Frannie corrected. 'Anyway, it's not *balderdash* that she would give us a hint about Franklin Steenpister. It's exactly the sort of thing a Pitta-Pitta would do. They love riddles. And besides, I noticed something about Lippa. Whenever she was telling the truth, she looked like she was teasing. So I'm guessing that when she's teasing, she looks dead serious. And when she told us that his nickname was "bishi-snoot", she had tears in her eyes.'

'So she called her husband a giant hairless rat. Big deal. That's no clue.'

'A giant hairless rat that lives in a maze of under-ground tunnels. Something like the subway system. And from the photos in the book, Steenpister is as hairless as his son. Plus, he mentions in the book that he is six foot five – that's hairless and giant, I'd say. But the most important thing is that the bishi-snoot has one peculiar habit. Whenever it rains, he pops out of the tunnels and goes hunting. That's the only time you ever see a bishi-snoot.'

'What does it eat?'

'Earthworms mostly.'

'Maybe my mother should take a trip to New Guinea,' Olivia mused out loud.

'You're really weird today, you know that?' Frannie sounded exasperated. 'I would call you back later if it weren't for the sky.'

'What guy?' Olivia asked.

'The "sky", not the "guy". Jeez, Olivia, have Cornwickle bring you a cup of coffee or something.'

'Oh, sorry. What's wrong with the sky?' Olivia said, craning her neck around to look out the window. It looked dim and hazy.

'Rain clouds. Big nasty purple ones, heading over from New Jersey. It's going to rain like mad pretty soon. So get dressed and meet me down at the Natural History Museum ASAP. In front of Roosevelt . . . I mean the chubby dude on the horse. If I'm right about bishi-snoot being a clue, Steenpister should pop out of his hole today.'

'I think there's more of a chance we'll see an *actual* bishi-snoot than Steenpister, but fine. I'll be right down there.'

Fifteen minutes later, Olivia strolled up to the statue in front of the museum, her umbrella opened to shield her from the fine sprinkling of rain. Frannie was already waiting, standing beneath a child-sized red umbrella and talking to a police officer. She kept shaking her head vehemently, her expression decidedly livid.

'I already told you a half-dozen times,' Olivia heard Frannie saying to the officer as she approached, 'I am *waiting* for someone. Oh, here she is! Thank goodness.'

The police officer looked at Olivia sternly. 'Are you her babysitter?' he asked Olivia.

'Her what?' Olivia said.

'Yes, yes, for heaven's sake, she's my *babysitter*!' Frannie said disgustedly.

'Well, you should know better than to let a little

kid stand on the street all by herself,' the officer scolded Olivia. 'It isn't safe.'

'OK,' Olivia said, throwing a confused glance at Frannie.

The officer gave Olivia a final hard look of warning before leaving.

'How mortifying!' Frannie said, her face flushed. 'He thought I was running away from home. He actually offered to buy me a Happy Meal if I told him my "mommy's phone number"! I'm fourteen years old, for pity's sake! I could babysit *you*!'

'Hey, speaking of running away, whatever happened to Viola?' Olivia asked.

'Oh, she came back last night, looking all sheepish and proud of herself. She got an earful from her mother. I couldn't understand a word of it, but Mister V was turning all kinds of colours so it must have been bad. And Mertha doesn't know the half of it. You know what that crazy Viola did? She got herself a tattoo!'

'No kidding?' Olivia said. 'Where?'

'On her upper arm. It's a big nasty one of a skull with a knife going right through the top of it. I lent her all my long-sleeve shirts for the time being, but oh ho! Just wait until Mertha sees it!'

The rain started to come down harder and Frannie said, 'We'd better go and keep an eye on the subway entrance.'

'Which one? There's loads of stations.'

'The one right in front of us,' Frannie said, nodding towards the 81st station. 'The station Lippa pointed to.'

Olivia followed Frannie down the block, and they stopped a few feet from the station.

'What now?' Olivia asked.

Beneath her red umbrella, Frannie's little peaked face was resolute. 'We just wait.'

'All right,' Olivia sighed. 'But I'll bet Lippa is up on the roof right now, watching us and laughing her head off.'

'If she's laughing, that just means we're on the right track,' Frannie said firmly.

The rain began to come down harder. It pecked at their umbrellas so loudly that when they tried to talk, neither one could hear unless the other was shouting. Finally, they resigned themselves to not speaking while they waited side by side, staring intently at the subway entrance. Loads of people came out of the station, but not a single one of them was a tall, bald man.

A rumble of thunder sounded, slow and stuttering at first and then exploding so loudly that Olivia jumped. She reached out and grabbed Frannie's elbow.

'This is crazy! Let's just go!' she yelled through the rain.

Frannie shook her head and tipped her umbrella down to block Olivia from her view.

'You are so stubborn!' Olivia yelled, but if Frannie heard her she couldn't tell. Briefly, she considered leaving, but she didn't like the thought of Frannie waiting alone. Yes, she was two years older than Olivia, but there was something too pitiful about such a tiny person standing alone in the rain, under a child's red umbrella.

It was then that the bishi-snoot popped his head up from his hole. It took a moment for the girls to realize that they had sighted him. At first all they saw was a very tall man emerging from the station, holding a long black trench coat over his head to shield it from the rain. It was when he turned to head east that they caught a brief glimpse of his face – close-set, pale eyes with deep pouches beneath them, scooped-out grizzled cheeks, a long chin, and the edges of what appeared to be a completely bald head. Olivia looked over at Frannie. Frannie tipped her umbrella up and looked at Olivia. Then, without a word, they began to follow him.

The thunder simmered again, then roared, but Olivia barely paid attention to it now. Steenpister was walking at a fast clip, his thin, sockless ankles poking out from his too-short pants. He crossed the street and seemed to be heading straight for the park. Frannie and Olivia hurried after him. Luckily the rain had driven most people from the streets, so it was easy enough to keep a safe distance yet not lose sight of him. He entered the park, keeping to the paved path as he continued east, while the storm raged all around them. It whipped the trees, flinging the branches hither and thither and hurling leaves to the ground. Yet Steenpister showed no sign of stopping, his trench coat already soaked through and dripping at the hem. Even Olivia's umbrella couldn't keep the wind from spraying rain on her, drenching the left side of her shirt.

They passed the Delacorte Theatre, where the rain slipped off the bronze statue of Romeo and Juliet in slick sheets. Suddenly Steenpister slowed. Frannie and Olivia did too. He veered to the right, heading directly for the pretty little pond adjacent to the theatre. Usually the pond banks were packed with chattering people and romping dogs, but now there wasn't a soul around.

The emptiness gave Olivia an eerie feeling – the same sort of feeling she had during a huge snowstorm three years before, when the streets, mounded with snow higher than her head, were hushed and deserted. Without the crowds, New York City seemed very old and melancholy, like someone who had seen many sad things and tried to fill their life with hullabaloo in order to keep from thinking too much.

Olivia and Frannie ducked behind a tree as they

watched Franklin Steenpister walk purposefully across the bank and towards the water. The wind had picked up and the rain pummelled the pond, forming thousands of pinpricks on its surface. Was Steenpister going to take a swim in this weather? Olivia wondered. She moved close to Frannie, who folded up her own umbrella and stood beneath Olivia's.

'Let's just ask him about Blup now,' Olivia said.

'No. Don't you see? He's on a mission of some sort,' Frannie said. Her damp fringe was plastered against her forehead. 'I don't think he'll appreciate being disturbed, and I don't want to risk making him mad.'

Steenpister had hesitated for a moment on the edge of the pond, near the part of the bank where the tree branches hung low, their storm-torn leaves forming a shifting green mosaic on the pond's surface. Then he walked right into the water, shoes and all. His trench coat floated out behind him as he walked in deeper and deeper, until the water was up to the middle of his thighs.

'He's going to drown himself!' Olivia cried, and she started for the pond, but Frannie held her back.

'No. The bishi-snoot *hunts* in the rain,' she said.

'He's not a bishi-snoot, Frannie! He's a crazy old man!' But just as Olivia broke free of Frannie's grasp, Steenpister crouched down in the water and began feeling around. Olivia stopped and the two girls watched. The trench coat still covered his head as he pawed beneath the water, impervious to the crash of thunder and the silver ribbon of lightning that scratched at the sky.

'He'll get fried in there,' Olivia said. She was more than a little concerned for their own safety as well, and she pulled Frannie away from the tree and herded her into a portaloo on the field opposite the pond. She folded up her umbrella and squeezed in beside Frannie, keeping the door open so they could see what Steenpister was up to.

'He'll see us in here. We'll scare him off,' Frannie objected, raising her voice to be heard above the next crash of thunder.

'Good! Then maybe he'll get out of the water, the idiot!'

Frannie covered her nose and started to protest about the smell, which Olivia had to admit wasn't too fabulous, when Steenpister suddenly stood up straight, his right hand pulling out something large and rectangular from the pond. It was hard to tell what the thing was – the rain blurred their view and in a flash Steenpister had removed his trench coat from his head and wrapped it around the object.

He waded out of the pond, holding the concealed object in front of him. His brisk purposeful walk had changed. Now he strolled leisurely across the bank, just as if the day was sunny and clear, his long arms wrapped tenderly around the lump beneath his trench coat. Olivia and Frannie stepped back into the portaloo as he came near, but closing the door would have simply attracted his attention.

Steenpister's pale eyes abruptly darted in their direction, as though some animal instinct had alerted him their presence. He looked right at them. Olivia held her breath. His face was clearly visible now. There was something familiar about him, Olivia thought. Maybe it was simply that he and his son looked so much alike. But no, there was something else . . . Suddenly she knew. It was his expression. He had the same look on his face as the Pitta-Pittas in Frannie's book – the look of someone who knew a secret. And wasn't telling.

'Good afternoon, Mister Steenpister.' Frannie walked out of the toilet, snapped open her red umbrella, and extended her hand. Steenpister's eyes narrowed with suspicion. He backed up, tightly clutching the thing wrapped in his trench coat. Then, without a word, he turned and ran.

'Follow him!' Frannie said to Olivia. And they did. He didn't take the path this time, but ran in zigzags across the sodden grass, as if he were being hunted and didn't want to provide them with an easy target.

For an old man, he was pretty nimble. While the mud sucked hard at Olivia's sneakers, slowing her down, Steenpister's feet seemed to barely touch the ground, his arms carefully cradling the thing beneath his coat.

'Mister Steenpister!' Frannie called after him. 'We just want to ask you something . . . please, Mister Steenpister!'

But Steenpister didn't even break his stride. From the corner of her eye, Olivia could see that Frannie was beginning to fall behind, which made Olivia run even faster. If Franklin Steenpister wasn't going to stop, at least she could find out where he was heading.

He had gained a lot of distance while he moved through the mud, but when he hit the paved bike path Olivia began to catch up. The rain was starting to let up bit by bit until it stopped completely. There were more people in the park now, jogging and biking along the path, and Steenpister had to dodge between them as he sprinted. He presented a strange sight, even by New York standards. Several joggers paused, running in place, to give him a second look, then paused again when they saw the lanky, soaking-wet girl who appeared to be chasing him.

'Pick your knees up, kid!' one of the joggers yelled at her. 'You'll never catch him running like that!'

Olivia tried it, lifting her knees higher, and she did begin to gain some speed. Soon Steenpister was just a few yards ahead of her. Funny thing was, Steenpister never once glanced back to see how close Olivia was, or even if she was still following him. It was as though he wasn't at all worried about her seeing where he went. He only cared that she wouldn't catch him.

Without warning, he darted off the path and headed up a grassy incline. The ground was muddy here too, but this time Olivia could manage it better, lifting her knees even higher. She followed him as he took a sharp turn to the right, past a thick stand of trees, and halfway up a double set of stone stairs, where he stopped. Olivia was just a few yards from the steps now. She watched him kneel down and fidget with something on the ground. A split second later, Steenpister disappeared beneath the pavement. Just like that.

Olivia stood still for a moment, panting and gazing around, thinking that it had been a trick somehow, that he was hiding behind one of the trees. Slowly she approached the steps and walked up the first flight. There, on the landing, she saw a metal grate set into the ground, large enough for a man to climb through. She knelt beside it, laced her fingers through, and gave it a tug. It was locked. The bishi-snoot had escaped.

CHAPTER TWENTY-THREE

Frannie caught up to her a few minutes later, soaked to the skin and breathing hard.

'Well?' she gasped, her hands on her hips and her chest heaving. 'Did you see where he went?'

Olivia pointed down to the grate.

'Don't bother,' she said when Frannie started to kneel down. 'It's locked.'

Frannie sighed. She sat down on the steps to catch her breath, and Olivia sat down beside her.

'What do you suppose he pulled out of the pond?' Frannie asked.

'I don't know, but I think he was afraid we wanted to take it from him,' Olivia said. 'Well,' she shrugged. 'We gave it a good try, didn't we?'

'What do you mean? That's it? You're giving up so easily?' Frannie asked.

'Are you kidding? I just practically ran a marathon! I wouldn't exactly call that giving up easily.'

'"Most people never run far enough on their first wind to find out they've got a second."' Frannie tapped her red umbrella on the step for emphasis. 'William James.'

'Yeah, well, William James never ran after a bishisnoot.'

Before she headed home, Olivia decided to take a quick peek at the park's band shell pavilion to see if Ruben was around. She still felt sort of bad about their last conversation and she wanted to make sure that he wasn't angry with her.

The sun had come out, and there was a smattering of skateboarders around. Olivia checked all Ruben's favourite stretches of pavement in the pavilion, but he was nowhere to be seen. Two of the three Groupies were there, however, parked on a bench and eating salad out of plastic containers.

'Looking for your boyfriend?' one of the girls asked.

'Maybe,' Olivia answered cautiously.

'We know where he is,' the other one said. She made a funny pucker-twist with her lips, which were oily with dressing, then exchanged a significant look with her friend.

'Well?' Olivia asked after waiting a few moments. 'Are you going to tell me or what?'

'He's with *her*,' the first girl said, jabbing her

plastic fork at the empty spot beside her, where the third Groupie usually sat. Olivia now saw that there was an unopened plastic container of salad sitting on her spot.

Olivia felt a hard yank in her gut. So Ruben had taken off with one of The Groupies! She struggled to compose herself, inhaling a deep breath and even managing a tight smile – there was no way she was going to let these two nitwits see that they'd upset her.

'No problem.' Olivia shrugged and began to walk away. She stopped short and added, 'Oh, and if they come back any time soon, don't bother telling him that I was here.'

'They've been gone for, like, for*ever* already! I'd bet anything they won't be coming back at all,' one of The Groupies said with a smirk.

Olivia always walked fast when she was angry. Now her feet pounded the pavement so hard that her ankle bones vibrated as she walked back to the brownstone, reaching it in record time.

CHAPTER TWENTY-FOUR

Parked right in front of the brownstone was a large black van with its hatch open. Two men were stacking boxes into the back. They weren't dressed like people who were accustomed to stacking boxes. They wore very stodgy tweed jackets, one grey and one brown, over white dress shirts.

Marching down the brownstone's front steps, carrying a clipboard, was a man in a very grim-looking dark suit and a matching expression on his pouchy face. George Kidney was trotting down the stairs right behind him, looking more than a little unhinged.

'But don't you think you're being a little unfair?' Olivia heard her father saying to the man with the clipboard. 'You didn't even give him any notice. I'm sure he would have gotten rid of the animal if you'd told him he had to.'

The man completely ignored George. He went up

to the two other men and jotted something on the cartons with a magic marker.

'I mean, I don't even think this is legal,' George said, his voice rising. He spotted Olivia and tried to iron out his distressed expression.

'Hi, Sweetpea.'

'What's going on?' she asked him. George stepped away from the man in the black suit and in a quiet voice told her, 'They're evicting Ansel.'

'They're throwing him out of the brownstone? Why?'

'Chester. It seems that there was a complaint from guess who.' He jerked his thumb towards Ms Bender's school.

'But I thought he owned the brownstone,' Olivia said.

'So did I. But apparently these guys do. They've been moving things out all afternoon.'

Olivia looked at the men by the van. They were standing around now, conferring with each other, their brows furrowed. All together they looked like a group of irate college professors. Olivia pinched at her lower lip, wondering.

'Where's Ansel?' Olivia asked.

'In the garden, pouting. He won't even try to help himself out of this mess,' George said in a rare display of exasperation at his boss.

'Maybe he can't,' Olivia replied. She headed up

the brownstone steps, leaving George to continue pleading with the men.

She found Ansel draped across the purple divan in the garden, wrapped in a light cotton blanket, his face concealed behind a travel book on Italy.

'Ansel?' Olivia said tentatively.

'Hmm?' he said without putting down the book.

'Are those men out there from the Board of Exit Academies?'

'So it seems.' There was an air of indifference in his voice, but it was a little *too* indifferent.

'Are we being kicked out?'

'So it seems.'

Olivia tried to control a surge of sickness at the thought of having to move again. She sat down on the divan, forcing Ansel to curl his legs back to make room for her.

'Did you tell them you'd get rid of Chester?' Olivia asked, trying to peer at his face behind the book.

'They've already captured him. He's been taken to the zoo.' Ansel sighed and put his book down on his lap. His face was a wreck of misery. 'Poor fellow. How will he stand it? He has such a lively nature.'

'But if Chester's gone, why are they still evicting us?' Olivia asked, her voice rising uncontrollably. She was conscious of a thickening in her throat, and quickly told herself that she was not to cry under any circumstances.

Ansel tipped his chin up and the wings of his nostrils flared indignantly. 'Because they're a bunch of tweedy snobs, that's why.' He picked up his book again. 'It doesn't matter. I've decided to go to Italy. I hear they have lovely old things there. And there is a carnival in Venice with masks and parades and hoopla. There's nothing I like better than hoopla.'

But what will Dad and I do? Olivia almost asked before the more stoical part of herself thought: We'll manage. We always have.

Instead, she asked, 'What about all the people who come for their lessons at the Exit Academy?'

'The board has transferred their scripts to another Exit Academy in the city, so they'll automatically be re-routed in their dreams. They won't have nearly as much fun at the other place. It's all very ho-hum and by the book.'

The kitchen door opened and Cornwickle entered the garden, carrying a silver tray that held a doll-size porcelain cup and saucer.

'Your espresso, sir.' Cornwickle handed the little cup to Ansel.

'Thank you, Cornwickle, you're very kind,' Ansel said, smiling up at Cornwickle weakly, just like a sick little boy who had been handed a bowl of soup. 'Have they gone yet?'

'Not quite, sir. But I think they've nearly cleared out the Academy.'

Ansel made a small, wretched noise in his throat.

'Is there anything else I can do for you, sir?' Cornwickle asked.

'No, thank you, Cornwickle. Yes, wait. Do you . . . do you think you might go with me to the zoo tomorrow? To visit Chester? The more, the merrier, you know. For poor Chester, I mean.'

'It would be my pleasure, sir,' Cornwickle answered with sincerity, and retreated back to the house. Olivia got up and followed him to the kitchen, closing the door behind her.

'Will we really have to leave the brownstone?' Olivia asked Cornwickle. He put the tray on the kitchen table and wearily dropped his bulk down on one of the chairs.

'I'm afraid so, Miss Kidney. They've given Master Plover two weeks to clear out.'

'But they can't! I mean, he's already gotten rid of Chester!' She hadn't meant to get upset, but the sound of hopelessness in Cornwickle's voice made the whole thing seem more real.

'It's not just Chester, Miss Kidney. The Board of Exit Academies has disapproved of Master Plover for some time. He doesn't attend meetings or return their phone calls. And his teaching style is . . . more experimental than most.'

'He's a *great* teacher,' Olivia objected. 'I know he is. I was in the Academy once and I saw it for myself.'

'Yes, I know you were.' Cornwickle looked at Olivia oddly. 'They disapproved of that as well. To bring a Straddler into an Exit Academy was a very risky thing to do. "Criminally reckless", according to them. They said he might have thought of another tactic under the circumstances.'

Olivia fell silent. The thought that she might have played a part in this eviction made her queasy.

'Please don't worry yourself, Miss Kidney. Your father is a wonderful cook. I'm sure he'll find a suitable job elsewhere.'

'We've been elsewhere,' Olivia said, the tears finally spilling uncontrollably. 'We've been elsewhere twenty-three times. I hate elsewhere.'

After dinner, Olivia went upstairs and ploughed through her history homework distractedly until she came to the last question, which was about medicine in the Middle Ages. She looked it up in her textbook and found that they believed people were made up of four elements – yellow bile, black bile, phlegm and blood.

How repulsive, Olivia thought. According to the book, if a person had too much yellow bile, they were supposed to be choleric, which meant they were 'bad-tempered' and 'easily angered'.

I suppose Ruben would say I was loaded with yellow bile, she thought bitterly. She looked up bile in the dictionary. 'A yellow or greenish fluid secreted by the liver.' Oh, fabulous.

She looked at herself in the dressing-table mirror. Her skin always had a yellowish tinge. Her father said she had an olive complexion, but really it was yellow. Bile yellow. She wondered what sort of fluid The Groupies were made up of. Probably that slimy, greasy stuff they put in lava lamps.

The house was soggy with silence that night. Olivia tossed and turned in bed, unable to sleep without the nightly cacophony of visitors' voices, and the Exit Academy's random eruptions of thumps and birds cawing and hands clapping. Not to mention her worries about where on earth she and her dad would live.

After a while, she went downstairs and out into the garden. It was a beautiful, cool evening, with a breeze that lightly nudged at her face and her bare ankles. The long-stemmed hollyhocks and snapdragons swayed slightly. Their brilliant purples and pinks and corals were muted by the night, yet they seemed more awake now than in the daytime. Awake and watching.

She considered contacting Christopher. He would know what to say to ease her mind. But her thoughts automatically leaped back to the lunch with her mother, and the way Christopher had made her speak for him. 'Just as if I were a puppet or something!' she said out loud.

The very next moment she heard an unmistakable *thup*. It came from behind a thick privet hedge, close to the back of the garden. Olivia held her breath. Her first thought was that Chester had escaped and found his way back to the garden, but that seemed unlikely. Then she heard a man's voice, deep and resonant.

'Are you there, littling bittling girlie?'

Olivia's eyes widened, but she said nothing, not daring to move and make a noise.

'I know you been seeing me across the street, girlie.'

Olivia clapped her hand to her mouth. It was the old man from across the street! It had to be!

'I am Ivan Simko,' the voice said. Olivia thought she could see a shadowy form by the tall oak tree. 'I know you is here, girlie.'

Olivia ran. She dashed across the garden, through the kitchen door, locking it behind her, her heart punching at her ribs. Peering through the kitchen curtains, she caught a glimpse of a man slipping out through the garden gate. Olivia yanked the phone book off of the shelf and with shaky hands flipped through the pages until she found Vondychomps, Arthur. She dialled the number and in a moment she heard the Princepessa's voice snap, 'Who's calling this late?'

'Olivia,' she said, keeping her voice low. 'Listen, I think there really might be a Royal Assassin.'

There was a pause. Then, 'Really? Well! I didn't think anyone would care enough to make an attempt.' She actually seemed pleased.

'He has an accent exactly like the seamstress.' She peered nervously out the window again. 'He said his name was Ivan Simko.'

'Well, then there's nothing to worry about. That's a Yurkistani name,' the Princiepessa said disdainfully. 'No Yurkistani has ever tried to assassinate one of the Royals. Yurkistanis are far too stupid.'

'They can't *all* be stupid,' Olivia protested.

'Oh, but they are. Look at the seamstress.' The Princepessa sniffed. 'Dumb oafs, every last one of them. When I was a girl, we hired a Yurkistani boy to feed our Royal tigers. I told him that I didn't like the way the tigers' breath smelt after they ate, and I ordered him to brush their teeth. He did, and the male tiger bit off his finger. Now is that clever, I ask you?'

'But you ordered him to do it,' Olivia said.

'Pah!' was the Princepessa's only response.

Olivia made a mental note to check that Mr Simko had all his fingers.

CHAPTER TWENTY-FIVE

Stella waited for Olivia by the water fountain at lunchtime, as usual, but today she invited Olivia to have lunch at her house. Considering that Stella had saved her from a lifetime of pustules, Olivia couldn't very well refuse.

Stella lived only one block from the school in a grimy white-brick apartment building. To Olivia's horror, they had to travel up in an ancient, trembling elevator to the sixth floor. Olivia plastered herself against the back wall and stared up at the numbers that lit up over the elevator door, counting backwards. Six more floors, five more floors, oh no, what was that creaking?! Four more floors, three more floors, the cables on this thing must be a hundred years old, two more floors, can cables rust away and snap? One more floor . . . The elevator stopped on the seventh floor, bouncing up and down several times before the door opened and Olivia darted out.

Stella turned right down the short hall, which smelt of cat litter and ketchup, and opened the door marked 7F with her key. From inside came a blast of TV voices.

'It's me!' Stella bellowed cheerfully over the TV noise as she walked in the apartment.

They walked down a short wallpapered foyer, which was cluttered with framed school photos of Stella from the time that she was a small, weird-looking child with clumps of knots bunching up her stringy hair, to more recent photos where she was a larger, even weirder-looking kid.

They entered a living room dominated by a huge ugly couch on which sat a sloppy-looking woman with a mean, squinty-eyed face. Her socked feet were up on the coffee table and she was sipping at a bottle of Gatorade from a straw, watching TV glumly.

'Anything good on?' Stella asked her conversationally.

The woman didn't answer. She just cackled loudly along with the TV audience laughter.

No wonder Stella's so weird, Olivia thought.

'This is my friend, Olivia,' Stella said.

The woman looked up briefly and nodded, then stared back at the TV. Her mouth looked like it had been sawed into her face with a dull knife. She certainly didn't seem like the kind of mother who would cover her foyer with her daughter's school photos.

Just then an old woman shuffled into the living room, smiling brightly at Stella. She was neat and cheerful-looking, with huge blue eyes and a short, wide nose with a little upturn at the tip. Her hair was carefully coiffed and it curled like white silk ribbons all over head.

'Ooof!' the old woman said as she squeezed Stella's face between her little hands. 'Such a beauty, isn't she?' The old lady addressed the question to Olivia, who gave a non-committal smile, and decided that it must have been Stella's grandmother who hung up all those school photos.

'Grandma, this is my new friend, Olivia,' Stella said, presenting her with an awkward flourish of her hand, like an amateur magician.

'You're hungry, Olivia? I made some noodle soup, and a nice chicken salad with the crunchy things, what do you call it . . .? Would you like some nice chicken salad, Marva?' Stella's grandmother suddenly called out to the woman on the couch.

'Later,' Marva answered, her eyes never leaving the TV screen.

Stella's grandmother ushered them into the kitchen, sat them down at a lopsided Formica table, and placed a steaming bowl of soup and a sandwich in front of each of them. Then she sat down at the table with them and watched them eat with a contented look on her face, as if it were the most fascinating thing in the world.

By the end of the meal, Stella had a noodle plastered to the side of her face and a chunk of chicken salad wedged in the corner of her mouth, but miraculously there was nothing in her hair.

'OK, Grandma,' Stella said, standing up and eyeing her grandmother carefully. 'We'd better get going now.' Instantly her grandmother's soft pale skin flushed an angry pink. She slammed her fist against the table so hard the plates rattled.

'NO!' she screamed.

'Now, Grandma, you know I have to get back to school.' Stella's voice suddenly sounded very high and loud, as though she were talking to a toddler.

'You always leave me!' her grandmother screeched, her eyes pooling with tears. 'It's not fair. I HATE YOU!'

'Don't say that, Grandma,' Stella pleaded.

Marva rose from the couch and lazily ambled over. 'Now that's enough,' she said to the old woman. 'Stella is your granddaughter. She is not your mother.'

'She's my granddaughter? She can't be. I'm only this many years old.' The old woman held up her hand to show five fingers. The anger had left her face, and now she simply looked confused.

'It's OK, Grandma,' Stella said gently. 'Why don't you lie down and rest. You look tired.'

The old woman blinked her large blue eyes several

times, then nodded. She took Marva's arm and trudged off to the bedroom.

Stella gave Olivia a small, embarrassed smile. 'She forgets things.'

'Oh sure,' Olivia said, shrugging and trying not to show how shocked she was by the whole scene. After an awkward moment of silence, she added, 'She seems really nice.'

'She is!' Stella said. 'She brought me up all by herself, without any help.'

'But isn't that other woman your mother?' Olivia asked.

'Who, *Marva*?' Stella seemed to think this was an absolute scream, and she laughed in a wheezy, head-bobbing way, until she was finally able to squeak out, 'Olivia, you are so weird sometimes.'

It took all of Olivia's self-control not to point out that at least, in her case, it was only 'sometimes' and not every minute of every day.

'Marva's the *day nurse*,' Stella said. 'She makes sure Grandma doesn't do anything awful. You know, like wander out of the apartment and get lost. Or set the curtains on fire, like that one time. Marva watches Grandma during the day, and I watch her at night.'

'Shouldn't you be sleeping at night?' Olivia asked.

'I am sleeping.' Stella smiled proudly. 'Remember how I told you I trained myself to sleep with my eyes open? Well, that's why. I sit out here on the couch all night long, fast asleep but with my eyes open. If Grandma wanders out of her room in the middle of the night and sees me, she thinks I'm wide awake and goes back to bed.'

'Are you sure you're *not* wide awake?' asked Olivia, thinking of all the times Stella had nodded off in class.

'Don't be ridiculous,' Stella snorted. 'Of course I'm asleep! I know because I can hear myself snoring.'

CHAPTER TWENTY-SIX

Olivia returned home to find a trail of blood on the front steps of the brownstone. Since the trail was rather thin and splattery on the bottom steps and grew thicker and blobbier as Olivia walked up the steps, it seemed to be coming *from* the brownstone rather than going *into* the brownstone. Olivia remembered the man across the street and felt a sickening feeling bloom in her belly.

The front door was ajar, and inside the hallway entrance the beautiful rug was a mess of bloody footprints. She listened for any sounds, but it was eerily silent. Suddenly, she heard something within the house. Footsteps. They sounded hollow, as if the sound was pinging off all the walls. Olivia held her breath, caught between the urge to run and the desire to know what was going on.

All of a sudden the white double doors flew open and Olivia jumped back, one hand on the front door knob, ready to flee. But it was Cornwickle who emerged, looking very annoyed. He was carrying a bucket sloshing with soapy water, a rag slung over the side of the bucket and a scrubbing brush floating inside.

'What happened?' Olivia asked when she caught her breath.

'I have worked in many, many households, Miss Kidney.' Cornwickle's voice was tight with anger. 'But never, *ever* have I been called upon to mop up the blood from a man's severed nose!'

'Dad!?' Olivia cried in panic, imagining the man across the street wielding a knife and attacking her father.

'No, no, Miss Kidney,' Cornwickle hastened to reassure her. 'It was a gentleman from the Board of Exit Academies.'

'Did Ansel do it?' Olivia asked in a horrified whisper.

'Certainly not, Miss Kidney. I don't pretend to know what Master Plover is capable of, but I shouldn't think that he would go so far as removing someone's nose from their face.'

There was a loud peal of laughter from behind the doors, in the lagoon.

'However,' Cornwickle added, putting down his bucket, pulling out the scrubbing brush, then kneeling down to work on the carpet, 'he is not beyond finding it all very funny.'

Olivia entered the living room intending to question Ansel as to what had happened, but she got no further than two steps before she stopped cold and gawped. The water in the lagoon was gone. What was left was an empty basin with a few sad little puddles. Scattered haphazardly on the still-damp ground were pieces of furniture on their rafts. The pedalos, still tied to the moorings on the marble walkway, were heaped together in the basin like colourful beached fish.

In the middle of all this, reclining in his lawn chair sheltered by an umbrella, was Ansel. His eyes looked a little wild, and he had a deliriously happy smile on his face, which Olivia found to be alarming under the circumstances.

'Hello, Olivia, love!' His voice echoed off the walls. 'What do you think of our new arrangements?' He spread his arms wide. 'It was the idea of the tweedy things at the Board of Exit Academies. They disapprove of travelling by boat in one's home, it appears, so they have drained our lovely lagoon.' His voice faltered a little here, and Olivia was afraid he might actually cry.

'Oh, Ansel,' was all Olivia could say. Then she remembered. 'But what happened to that man's nose?'

Ansel smiled in a very wicked way, pressing his lips together as if to stifle a laugh. 'I've always thought noses were silly, irresponsible things. They stick out of one's face when all the other bits and pieces are set flush against one's head, nice and tidy and minding their own business. But noses are always poking about where they shouldn't be. Until along comes an enormous snapping turtle . . .'

'Oh no!' Olivia cried.

'Yes. They'd just finished draining the lagoon when one of the tweedy things discovered our turtle, hiding under a sofa cushion. He went to retrieve it and, *voila*! Off comes the nose. Luckily for the tweedy thing, the turtle spat the nose out and Cornwickle wrapped it in ice. The nice ambulance folks said there was a seventy per cent chance that the doctors could reattach it. Now I call that excellent odds!'

Olivia doubted the tweedy thing would agree.

'Where is the turtle now?' Olivia asked, looking around nervously.

'In the downstairs bathtub. Don't worry, the bathroom door is shut. Your father is cooking up some chicken and sweet potatoes for the creature as we speak.'

The brownstone was a sad place that evening. Ansel moped around or sat in an armchair, staring off aimlessly, the book about Italy lying on his lap, face down. Even George's cooking seemed half-hearted.

His quiche was wet in the centre and his flounder was rubbery. At the rate he was going, even 'elsewhere' was not going to hire him.

Before she went to bed, Olivia checked out her window to see if the old man was there, but his light was off. He might be watching in the dark, a thought that made Olivia's skin feel prickly.

She needed to talk to Christopher. Never mind their fight. Her life was being turned upside down and she wanted him to spin it right side up again. To give her perspective. To hear him say that everything was going to be all right. Lying in bed, she closed her eyes and pictured him. But every time she did, the memory of what happened at the cheese restaurant flooded her thoughts and made her mad all over again. How dare he use her like that! She was still so angry – he'd never be able to come through like that, and she knew it.

'What a bore!' came a voice right beside her. Olivia's eyes flew open. Abby was stretched out next to her, her head sharing Olivia's pillow, smoking a cigarette. The smoke she blew out was much thinner than regular cigarette smoke, and the spot where it touched Olivia's cheek felt damp and cold. 'This place is like a tomb.'

'I guess you'll be leaving too?' Olivia asked, moving her head to the far edge of the pillow.

'No. Why should I?' Abby asked belligerently.

'Well, since it's not going to be an Exit Academy any more . . .'

'You don't know much, do you?' Abby sneered. 'Once an Exit Academy, always an Exit Academy. They'll just replace Ansel, that's all, and good riddance to him! He and his mother have done their best to make my life wretched.'

Olivia hesitated, then asked the question she had wondered about for some time. 'How did you die, Abby? I mean, you're really young.'

'Not that it's any of your business,' Abby said, 'but I was murdered.'

This took Olivia by surprise and she was silent for a moment. 'Who did it?' Olivia asked. She was going to ask 'How?', but that seemed like a gruesome sort of question.

'My sister,' Abby said. She took a puff from her cigarette and blew the smoke up towards the ceiling, where it hung like a patch of gossamer fog before it melted into the darkness. 'She pushed me out a seventh-storey window.'

'Why?' Olivia asked. She couldn't help but think about the time Abby tried to do the exact same thing to her, up in the Exit Academy.

'What do you mean, why?' Abby sat up and stared with an appalled look on her face. 'Because my sister was crazy, that's why! I didn't do anything to deserve such a horrible death!'

Olivia wondered now if dying like that had made Abby into such a nasty ghost. She'd once read in one of Christopher's books that murder victims whose killers were never punished often turned into ghosts.

'Did your sister go to jail?' Olivia asked.

'*Her?* Go to *jail?* Oh no, she was too *delicate* for jail,' Abby scoffed. 'They just put her in a home for crazy people. After six months, they let her out. End of story. She went on to live a nice little life and I went on being dead.'

'I'm sorry,' Olivia said. And she actually meant it too, right up until Abby told her to take her 'sorry' and stuff it, stubbed out her cigarette on Olivia's pillow, and vanished into the night.

CHAPTER TWENTY-SEVEN

New York City is so huge that you'd think you would never bump into the same person twice. But that morning on the IRT, Olivia recognized a woman with a blonde ponytail and wire-rimmed glasses. They'd been in the same train carriage every day the week before. When she happened to catch the woman's eye, Olivia nodded and smiled a little. The woman returned the smile with an irritated frown, as if to say, 'How rude! We're not bus people, for heaven's sake.'

Olivia occupied herself by staring out the subway car window, checking for black-tongued ghosts and thinking that she might try riding the bus to school every now and then. Yes, it was swarming with noisy little kids who wiped their mucusy hands all over the backs of the seats, but at least people would admit to recognizing each other now and then.

When the train stopped at the 72nd Street station,

however, a passenger entered who not only recognized Olivia, but called her by her name.

'Ohhh-lanky Ohhh-livia!' the bubble-wrap lady cried, then hustled over, rustling loudly as she pushed her way through the crowds.

'Oh no!' Olivia said out loud.

'Aren't you surprised that I remembered your name?' The bubble-wrap lady smiled a broad, lip-sticky smile at Olivia and grabbed the same pole. Her fingernails were crusted black around the edges.

'Hnnn.' Olivia couldn't completely ignore her but she didn't want to encourage conversation either.

'I'm good with names. Had to be. I have seven older brothers: *SamTobyTommyRobertKipPeterAndyJunior*.' She whipped off the names lightning fast. 'Backwards: *AndyJuniorPeterKipRobertTommyTobySam*.' Truth be told, it was sort of impressive, in a crazy-person kind of way.

'So where's that handsome fella you were with the other day?' the bubble-wrap lady asked.

Olivia shrugged, trying to avoid looking at her hat, which seemed to have a few more items hanging from it, like a miniature tube of antifungal cream and a few packets of Sweet & Low.

'Nice fella,' she said, smooshing her pasty flaming-red lips together in approval. 'You just don't meet too many nice fellas these days. He noticed my hat. That's something in this day and age. I mean, look around!' She swept her arm around and the bubbles in her bubble wrap squeaked loudly. 'Look at them all . . . pretending not to notice me. Bunch of sneaky Peeping Toms.'

All the people who had been watching her out of the corners of their eyes quickly looked out the window or down at their books or up at the advertisements. It made Olivia laugh, which made the bubble-wrap lady laugh, and for a split second Olivia felt very much on the side of subway lunatics. It was right then she thought of something.

'By any chance, do you know someone named Franklin Steenpister?' Olivia asked.

'I'm good with names. Had to be, with eight older brothers.'

'Seven. I know, you told me already.'

'*SamTobyTommySteenpisterRobertKipPeterAndy-Junior.*' The bubble-wrap lady popped a bubble around her belly button for emphasis.

Olivia frowned at her for a moment. 'Did you say Steenpister?'

'Backwards:*AndyJuniorPeterKipRobertTommyToby Sam.*'

Now Olivia remembered the thing that she hated about crazy people. Just when you're convinced that they're actually fairly normal and rational, they slip in their nutty stuff, which makes you all discombobulated – just like them.

'Yeah, that's great.' Olivia turned her back on the bubble lady. She should have known better than to try and have a real conversation with a woman dressed in packing material.

'Skinny old man. Tall. Bald as a peeled grape,' the bubble-wrap lady said. Olivia turned.

'What?'

'Franklin Steenpister. I know him. He lives in the tunnels. But I have to warn you. He's got a few screws loose in the old topper.' She flicked a miniature bottle of mouthwash hanging from her hat.

'Where in the tunnels?' Olivia said. Her stop was coming up any minute.

'The worst part.' The bubble-wrap lady's lips turned grim, and she shook her head. 'It's way downtown. Under Warren Street. No one ever goes there, not even the craziest, meanest tunnel people. They're too afraid. Except for Steenpister.'

'Warren Street, you said?' Olivia asked.

'You won't find him,' the bubble-wrap lady warned. 'The tunnels are very twisty-turvy down there. Lots of places to get lost. Lots of bad things down that end.'

'Why? What's down there?' Olivia asked. She already could imagine a whole host of things to be terrified of: rats, subway lunatics, murderers . . .

'The tunnel that he lives in, it's not like any of the others. It's much older. It's got a piano that really plays and couches and a crystal chandelier. Real fancy, real cosy, real hobnobby. Every so often a tunnel person will try to live there. But they never stay long.'

Olivia felt the train slowing down for her stop.

'Why?' she asked.

'It's haunted.'

Olivia snorted. 'I doubt that,' she said. She glanced around the car quickly, and finding that no one was interested in them any more, added, 'Ghosts hate to be alone in the dark, even the nasty ones.' It was sort of pleasant to talk openly about ghosts, even if it was with a subway lunatic.

'But they're not alone. The place is infested with ghosts. Worse than rats,' the bubble-wrap lady said. 'They're children, the ghosts. Little ghost kids.'

'Really?' Olivia said, her interest peaked. She couldn't help but ask it: 'Do they have black tongues?'

'Black tongues? Black tongues!' The bubble-wrap lady started laughing so hard that her bottles clacked together. 'You're a strange one, Ooh-livia!' The woman with the blonde ponytail and wire-rimmed glasses glanced at her now, smiling a little, as though she completely agreed.

Miss Monsoon swept into the homeroom classroom again, her hair pulled back into a single braid that reached her bony tail bone. She faced the class, raised her drawn-on eyebrows, and looked at all their faces seriously.

'This period, we will talk about . . . the Muse,' she said.

'The moose! What moose?' one of the boys asked, looking around with feigned surprise.

'You . . . Johnny-boy,' Miss Monsoon said to the boy.

'Me?' the boy pointed to himself. 'My name is Scott.'

'You're a ballet dancer, Johnny, aren't you?' Miss Monsoon asked. This made all the other boys titter.

'I play the trumpet,' Scott said angrily.

'And have you any friends, Johnny-boy?' Miss Monsoon continued.

'A couple, yeah,' he said, although it didn't seem like any of them were currently in the room, since nearly everyone was laughing at him.

'Get rid of them instantly!' Miss Monsoon cried, tossing her slender arms in the air dramatically. 'A dancer needs only one friend! She is called the Muse, Johnny-boy, and she will teach you how to leap like a gazelle!'

This sent most of class into peals of hysteria.

Then Miss Monsoon did something that made the laughter cease on the spot. She leaped high into the air, twice in a row, between the aisles. On the third leap she sailed across the room, astonishingly high off the ground. She landed squarely and executed a dizzying series of twirls that made her long braid look like yellow ribbon whipping around a pole. The laughter had ceased and a murmur of awe sounded through the classroom.

'Mark my words, you are wasting your time in this school, children,' said Miss Monsoon. She wasn't even out of breath. 'They will only teach you silly tricks to impress silly people. Find the Muse . . . find the Muse . . .' Miss Monsoon waved her arms around the room, as though the Muse might be lurking beneath one of their desks. 'Just when the world tells you something is impossible to do, the Muse will whisper to you. She'll show you how to make the impossible possible.'

All day at school, Olivia debated whether or not to tell Frannie about what the bubble-wrap lady had said. Certainly she wanted Frannie to find Steenpister, but walking through subway tunnels – even ghostless ones – was not a particularly smart thing to do. And Frannie was just desperate enough to attempt it, which meant that Olivia would feel duty-bound to go with her, since sitting at home and thinking about Frannie wandering through dark, dangerous subway tunnels alone was far worse than actually wandering them with her.

I won't tell her, Olivia decided finally. Yet when she got home, she changed her mind again, picked up the phone, and dialled her number.

Stacy, Frannie's sister, picked up and shouted 'Yeah?' In the background, there was a frightening commotion of yelping and wailing.

'Holy cow, what are they doing to Mister Snuggles?' Olivia asked.

'Mister Snuggles?' Stacy shouted. 'Oh, *that*. Nah, that's the wedding singer. Babatavian guy. He's giving them a preview.'

'Well, he's really going to be howling when the Princepessa tosses him out on his ear.'

'What? Nah, she loves it. So does Mister V. The guy is singing Babatavian ballads, and the two of them are holding hands and melting all over each other right now. It's pretty freakin' disgusting.'

'Is Frannie around?' Olivia asked. In the background, she could hear what sounded like a very good imitation of a cat fighting with a dentist's drill.

'Yeah, hang on.'

Suddenly Olivia could hear the howling and yelping sounds begin to grow fainter, so she guessed that Stacy was bringing the phone to Frannie's cave. In a few minutes she heard an echoey 'Hello?'

'Hi, Frannie. Listen, there's something I thought I should tell you.' Olivia recounted everything the woman had told her that morning. She took care to add that the woman was dressed in bubble wrap and wore a coat hanger on her head in the hopes that Frannie wouldn't take the story too seriously.

Frannie listened in silence. When Olivia was finished Frannie said, 'Well, the woman is obviously a crackpot. A piano in a subway station? Not to mention the ghosts. Oh, *please.*'

Olivia winced a little at this last comment.

'But she did seem to know who Steenpister is,' Olivia said, feeling rather defensive all of a sudden. 'And really, she seemed sort of normal.'

'What did you say she was wearing on her head? Miniature bottles of mouthwash and tubes of anti-bacterial cream?'

'Foot-fungus cream,' Olivia corrected, feeling that her argument was badly faltering.

Still, after Olivia hung up she felt a rush of relief that Frannie hadn't believed the bubble-wrap lady's story.

Olivia found her father in the kitchen, surrounded by open cookbooks. The counters were littered with shopping bags full of food, some of it very peculiar-looking.

'What's all this?' Olivia asked.

'The Princepessa asked me to cater for her wedding,' George said, looking worried. 'She wants me to make authentic Babatavian cuisine. Pickled yams.

Liver tarts. Something called yarba-yarba, which as far as I can tell is mashed cabbage in pork fat. Frankly, I don't know if I'm up for the challenge. Oh, and by the way, Olivia, your mom is coming over in an hour.'

'What? No!' Olivia wailed.

'Come on, Sweetpea. She's going back to LA in a few days. She just wants to spend a little time with you.'

'Tell her she can mail me a bra from California. For my *tenth* birthday.' Olivia flipped through one of the cookbooks absently, frowning. 'Hey, Dad? Was Christopher very close with Mom?'

'When he was younger, he was. Oh, he adored her. And Lord knows Monica loves being adored.'

'Didn't he get that she was a nitwit?'

'She's not a nitwit, Olivia,' George warned, continuing to unload his groceries. 'Not really. And anyway, Christopher was always very different from you.'

'You mean he was a lot nicer, don't you?'

'Christopher was one of the nicest people I've ever known,' George said. He smiled. 'But you've always been wiser. He saw people the way he wanted to see them. You see them the way they are. I think that's why Monica has always been nervous around you.'

'Well, that's just stupid,' Olivia snapped.

'Hmm,' George said to her response, as though it only proved his point.

'And anyway, what's all the fuss about me getting a bra?' Olivia said, quickly changing the subject. 'You don't see *me* going around telling people they need a bra.'

'That's probably a good policy, Sweetpea. Hey, look at this thing.' He handed her something shaped like a potato with little brown hairs growing all over it. 'Do you think I should peel it before boiling it?'

'I think you should shampoo it before boiling it,' Olivia said, handing it back to her father. She sat down at the kitchen table and watched as her father began to scrape at the thing with a peeler.

'What's going to happen to us after Ansel is evicted?' she asked, broaching the topic that they'd both been avoiding.

'We'll find someplace else to live, Olivia. We always do.' He forced a smile. 'Just think about it this way. Most people live in the same old place with the same old neighbours, year after year. But look at us! Every few months we get to choose a brand-new life.' He examined the peeled vegetable, then pitched it into a pot. 'So . . . any requests for your brand-new life, Sweetpea?'

'A normal one, please,' said Olivia. 'That would be nice for a change.'

CHAPTER TWENTY-EIGHT

Olivia slipped out of the house before her mother arrived and headed for Central Park. She could hang out there for a couple of hours, and with any luck her mother would give up waiting at the brownstone and go away.

If Olivia were to admit it to herself, she was also hoping to see Ruben there. But she was in no mood to admit anything to herself today.

Once in the park, she stopped to get herself a hot dog and a bag of chips at the first vendor she saw. She strangled the bag of chips right there at the cart, not caring that the vendor was giving her a funny look, and then dumped the crumbled chips on top of her hot dog.

'That's a first,' the vendor said, shaking his head.

Olivia ignored him. She'd eaten her hot dogs that way since she was a little girl, and no one could convince her that there was a better way to eat them. She nibbled as she walked, ambling aimlessly (at least she told herself that she was ambling aimlessly. In fact she was taking a rather direct route to the band-shell pavilion), and after a bit she found herself right near the band-shell pavilion. She started to walk towards it, shoving the rest of the hot dog in her mouth and swallowing it without bothering to taste it. Then she stopped short. Yes, Ruben might be there, but so would The Groupies.

She hastily changed direction and continued her amble, with somewhat less enthusiasm. The afternoon stretched out before her dully. She wished she hadn't eaten her hot dog so quickly.

Before long, she found herself at the boat pond. She amused herself for a while, watching the model boats tottering in the water, then headed for the Alice in Wonderland statue. She liked to go to the statue when she was feeling out of sorts. There was something about the place – like nothing bad could ever happen to you there. She could kill some time in Alice's lap, and then start back home. But her plans were spoiled when she saw that Alice's tremendous legs were already occupied by two little girls who were kicking at each other. She almost turned to leave when she noticed a brown suede hat hooked on one of the White Rabbit's ears.

Ruben's hat.

She gazed around for him, then circled the statue.

No Ruben, yet it certainly looked like his hat hanging limply off the rabbit's ear. She climbed up on the edge of the giant mushroom to get a better look.

'Hey!' One of the little girls on Alice's lap stopped fighting with her friend and pointed a finger at Olivia. 'This is private property!'

'Oh shut up,' Olivia told her. Sometimes she really hated little kids.

Unhooking the hat from the White Rabbit's ear, she turned it over in her hands. It looked like Ruben's hat all right. She brought it to her nose and smelt it, which was sort of silly since she couldn't have said what Ruben's head smelt like. To her surprise, it had a sickly sweet strawberry smell. An unmistakably girlish sort of smell. The Groupies. That girl had probably put it on her head. Olivia felt her yellow bile begin to simmer.

'Hey, lady. Why are you smelling my hat?'

Olivia looked down and there was Ruben, holding a soda and smiling up at her, his wild black curls much wilder without the hat pressing them down. Olivia checked her urge to smile back by clenching her brow into a scowl.

'I was hoping you'd be here,' Ruben said, and again Olivia had to carefully control the little muscles around her mouth, which seemed more numerous and wilful than she remembered. 'I just got thirsty waiting, so I left my hat, in case you came.'

'Why were you hoping I'd come here?' Olivia asked confrontationally.

'To see you, you idiot – why do you think? So you're OK then, huh?'

'Why wouldn't I be?' Her eyes narrowed. Was he feeling guilty about going off with one of The Groupies?

'Because one of my friends saw you running across the park the other day, chasing The Turtle.'

It took a moment for Olivia to decipher this. 'The Turtle? Oh, you mean Steenpister!' A more amiable tone accidentally slipped into her voice.

'You know The Turtle by name?' Ruben asked in surprise. It occurred to her then that Steenpister actually did look like a turtle with his close-set little eyes and his bald head poking up out of his trench coat.

Olivia remembered that she was angry, and spat back, 'That's pretty superficial, don't you think – making fun of the way a person looks? Maybe the people *you* hang out with these days think that's really hilarious, but personally—'

'We don't call him The Turtle because of how he looks,' Ruben said, his upper lip lifting a little bit, as though he were beginning to suspect that she was crazy. 'We call him The Turtle because of what he does. He *catches turtles*. Sheesh, Olivia!' He shook his head.

So that was what Steenpister was doing in the pond, Olivia thought.

'What does he do with them?' she asked, her anger beginning to wilt under the weight of her curiosity. Ruben started to say something, but the two little girls in Alice's lap began screaming at each other at the top of their lungs, and Olivia couldn't hear a word.

'Hey!' Olivia clapped her hands at them, and jerked her thumb at the ground. 'Down! *Now!*'

The little girls looked at her in astonishment for a moment. Olivia stared back at them.

'My butt's getting cold anyway,' the girl closest to Olivia said before hurriedly getting up off of Alice's lap, followed by her friend, and running to the pond.

Olivia moved to Alice's right knee, and Ruben climbed up and sat on her left one.

'So what does he do with the turtles?' Olivia asked.

'Who knows? Eats them maybe.' Ruben shrugged. 'From what I hear, he only catches snapping turtles. People dump them in that pond and they get really big and nasty. He puts cages in the pond and traps them. He's a weird guy.'

Olivia nodded as she took in this information.

'I looked all over for you the other day,' Ruben said.

'Oh?' Olivia said, turning a cool gaze on Ruben. 'Funny, I was looking for you too.' He appeared genuinely confused for a moment, but then his face registered some understanding and he actually blushed. It was a funny blush that produced a thick red stripe on either cheek.

'Did you by any chance speak to The Groupies?' he asked.

'I spoke to *two* of them,' Olivia replied, with a significant look on her face.

Ruben appeared ready to defend himself, drawing his chin up and cinching his brows. Then he stopped. He smiled at her, and asked, 'Why were you smelling my hat?'

Now it was Olivia's turn to feel her face grow hot.

'Were you checking to see if I let her wear my hat?' he asked.

'It's *your* hat. You can put it on a chimp, for all I care,' Olivia said, flicking her fingers at the bronze kitten that was sharing Alice's right leg with her.

'She smells nice, doesn't she?' Ruben said, waggling his eyebrows and grinning. Olivia was seriously close to punching him.

'She smells like jelly,' Olivia snapped back. She slid off the statue and started to walk away quickly.

'Olivia!' Ruben called after her. She heard him running behind her, then he grabbed her by her elbow to stop her. 'Oh, come on. Do you honestly think I'd be interested in one of those goons? I never would have gone off with her at all except she overheard my friend telling me about The Turtle. And when I got all worried, The Groupie rushed up and said that she knew where you were and she'd show me, so I went with her. We walked all over the park before she admitted she had no idea where you were. I was so mad I could have clocked her with my skateboard, only her big fat head would probably have snapped poor Jezebel in two.'

This made Olivia feel much better, until she remembered: 'What about the smell in your hat, though?'

Ruben shoved his head right under Olivia's nose. She drew back in surprise, then bent down and took a sniff. Strawberry jelly.

'My mother buys whatever shampoo is on sale,' he explained with a little embarrassment. He put his hat on Olivia's head.

'There. Now it's yours,' he said. 'You won't ever have to worry about someone else wearing it.'

'I wasn't worried,' Olivia said and started to walk off in the direction of home. Then, on impulse, she stopped and turned back around. 'Hey! What are you doing this Sunday?'

'Nothing.'

'Want to go to a wedding with me?' Olivia asked.

Ruben looked surprised, then tremendously pleased, before he tried to hide it with an easy shrug. 'Sure. Why not.'

'Great,' Olivia said, and told him the address of the

Vondychomps' mansion. 'Be there at three o'clock. And dress snappy.'

Then she turned and started to walk off again, tugging Ruben's hat down over her head so that it fit more snugly.

After dinner, during which Olivia received some hard words from her father for successfully avoiding her mother and hurting her feelings, Cornwickle knocked on her bedroom door. 'Miss Smithers on the line for you, Miss Kidney.'

'Guess what!' Frannie said. 'Your bubble-wrap lady actually knew what she was talking about! I did a little research, and it turns out that there is an old abandoned subway station under Warren Street. It was an experimental subway built way back in eighteen-seventy. The train was just a giant tube that was sucked back and forth between two stations by a pair of huge fans, something like those little whooshy tubes at drive-through banks. Amazing, huh? '

'Yeah, but what about the piano and the fountain and ghosts and all that stuff?'

'Turns out she was right about that too! They built this fancy waiting room at the station. There was a piano and a crystal chandelier and a fountain where goldfish swam. As for the ghosts . . . well, isn't it obvious? It's just a story that someone made up to keep people away from there. Steenpister himself, I'll bet you. Which also makes it much safer.'

'Frannie, we can't go down there. Even the bubble-wrap lady said that it's really easy to get lost in that part of the tunnel.'

'You said "we". Are you thinking of going too?'

'I was speaking hypothetically,' Olivia said.

'*Hypothetically!* Why, Olivia Kidney! You haven't been reading books or anything crazy like that?'

'As a matter of fact I have been reading books,' Olivia said. 'In particular, my history textbook, which tells all about the black plague in the Middle Ages and how it all got started because of rats, which (PS) the subway tunnels happen to be crawling with.'

'It was the *black* rat that carried the plague. The rats in New York are just the plain old brown variety,' Frannie informed her.

'Really? Well, I'll remind you of that when one of them is crawling up your pants leg,' Olivia replied tartly. 'Why don't you just wait for the next rainy day when Steenpister will come up again?'

'We called him by his name. He knows he's being hunted. The bishi-snoot is very slippery. He won't come up the same way again. Anyway, I spent the afternoon at the public library and found a bunch of old subway maps. According to them, there's an entrance that leads directly into the tunnels down on Warren Street, and we'd only have to go a short way to get to Steenpister. As far as I can tell there's only one or two really tricky parts on the map, and I've found a solution for that too. We could go tomorrow, except that I haven't figured out how to get Steenpister to talk to me.'

There was a long pause, then Olivia asked, 'Does your mother have a pet carrier?'

'I think she has one for Mr Snuggles. Why?'

'Then we can go tomorrow. Just bring the pet carrier here after school.'

'No kidding? You're really going to do this with me?' Frannie asked.

'Why not?' Olivia answered easily.

A funny thing happens when your world is crumbling to pieces, Olivia thought after she hung up the phone. Things suddenly seem less frightening. Or maybe it's that *everything* seems so frightening, and one more frightening thing hardly matters at all.

CHAPTER TWENTY-NINE

After school on Friday, Olivia waited for Frannie on the brownstone's porch, not wanting to explain the sight of the waterless lagoon to her. It was too sad, and anyway she didn't feel like talking about the eviction.

On her head was Ruben's hat and by her side was a pillowcase, tied at the top and wriggling about frantically. It hadn't been hard to catch the turtle. Some leftover chicken had been enough to occupy him while Olivia slipped the pillowcase over him. But now that she had him, the pillowcase's fabric seemed dangerously thin. If Frannie didn't hurry, there might be a very angry snapping turtle crawling down 84th Street.

Across the street the front door of the pretty little brownstone opened, and to Olivia's horror Ivan Simko appeared at the top of the building's porch. Olivia yanked down the brim of Ruben's hat to cover her face as best as she could.

Ivan Simko walked down the stairs slowly, his posture very upright. At the bottom of the stairs, he patted down his gleaming white hair before looking up the street. For a moment it seemed like he was staring directly at her. She felt a prickling coldness spread across the nape of her neck and she pulled the brim of the hat down even further. Just in case, she gripped the top of the pillowcase, ready to run. But the hat, it seemed, had done the trick. Ivan Simko turned his attention to a taxi rolling up the street. He hailed the taxi with a quick, almost elegant flourish. That was when Olivia spotted the noticeable gap on his right hand, where his index finger should have been.

'Are you OK, Olivia?' Frannie asked. Olivia hadn't even seen her approach, her eyes had been so fixed on the old man. 'You look all flustered.'

'I'm fine,' Olivia said, checking up the street to watch the taxi turn the corner and drive out of sight. She shifted her gaze to Frannie. She was holding a pet carrier and Viola was trailing behind her, wearing a pair of headphones and bobbing her head to the tinny crash of rock music coming from them.

'What's with the hat?' Frannie asked.

'It's for good luck.' Olivia said, tightening her grip on the wiggling pillowcase. She looked askance at Frannie. 'Why are you bringing *Viola*?'

'We're going to need her,' Frannie said. 'Think

about it. We're going into a dark tunnel, which is pretty much like a cave. So who better to bring with us than an actual cave-dweller?'

Olivia wasn't entirely convinced, but at that moment the tip of the turtle's claws punctured the pillowcase. She hustled the creature into the carrying case and quickly latched it. Frannie looked at him through the clear plastic lid.

'A *turtle*?' she said in the same doubtful tone that Olivia had uttered 'Viola?'

'We're going to need him,' Olivia said.

They took the downtown subway. Today Olivia was glad to be surrounded by subway people who were dutifully pretending not to notice the huge turtle in the carrying case or the thuggish-looking girl with excessively hairy legs.

They got off at a stop way downtown, a part of New York City that Olivia rarely visited. Once they were on the street, Frannie took out a small square of paper from her back pocket, which she unfolded carefully. On it, there was a mess of diagrams and sloppy writing that Olivia, peering over Frannie's shoulder, could make no sense of.

'This way,' Frannie said decisively, turning left up the street.

This was the very snout of New York City, where the island was squeezed to a narrow point. Consequently, the streets twisted in unreasonable ways. Holding the pet carrier, Olivia followed Frannie through the confusing maze of narrow avenues, while Viola trailed several steps behind, absorbed by the music blasting from her headphones.

Finally Frannie stopped, glanced at her paper again, then looked up at a number carved into the wood above the door of one of the buildings.

'This is it,' Frannie said.

The sign above the store said, 'Ooo Lala Hosiery & Intimate Apparel'. Olivia was not sure what hosiery & intimate apparel was, but she presumed from the window display that it was a fancy name for knickers and bras.

'The tunnel is in here?' Olivia asked incredulously.

'According to the map there's an entrance right in this building,' Frannie said.

'How old was that map?' Olivia asked.

'Eighteen eighty-one,' Frannie said. 'But if we're lucky, the original passages should still be there.'

The door tinkled when they opened it, and they found themselves in a gauzy maze of underthings. The tiny store, with its creaky old-fashioned wooden floor, was crammed tight with racks and racks of girdles and slips and nightgowny-looking things. Pantyhose hung from the ceiling and circular racks were dripping with bras. It was an impressive sight. Even Viola had pushed the headphones off her ears and was now examining a silky white top with spaghetti straps.

'Frannie?' she said, holding the top up for Frannie to see. 'Good, Frannie?'

'No, not good, Viola,' Frannie said sternly, taking the top out of her hands. 'She's been picking up a little English,' Frannie explained to Olivia.

'Very pretty, isn't it?' A saleswoman had appeared from within the depths of the store. She had a helmet of streaked blonde hair, coarse as a lion's mane, and she had a round, tan lion-ish face, but her voice was very purry and pleasant. Viola looked at her with her mouth gaping open slightly. Olivia wondered if she was wishing she had her spear.

'Yes, it's quite pretty,' Frannie said, drawing herself up, 'but unfortunately, my friend has gotten herself a tattoo – a big ugly one on her upper arm – and a sleeveless top is out of the question.'

'But it's meant to be worn *beneath* her clothing.' The saleslady took the top out of Frannie's hands and placed it up against Viola. 'That way, she could cover her tattoo, and she would still feel dainty and feminine underneath.'

Olivia laughed out loud at this, and the saleslady turned her huntress eyes on Olivia, looking her up and down.

'And you, my dear, are in need of a bra.'

Olivia turned bright red. She wished Viola really did have a spear.

'A nice little training bra,' the saleslady assured her. 'I have just the one for you, with a sweet little pink bow in the middle. We can try on a few and see what we like.' And the saleslady slinked off towards the back of the store.

'I am not trying on bras,' Olivia whispered to Frannie.

'Please, Olivia. It's perfect. While she's fussing over you, Viola and I can look around for the entrance.' She took the pet carrier out of Olivia's hands. 'Go on.' She gave Olivia a little shove towards the back of the store.

Olivia groaned, but went, wading through the racks of underthings, the top of her head tickled occasionally by pantyhose.

This is like going through an underwear carwash, she thought.

In the back of the store there were lots of circular double-tiered racks of bras in every colour and shape imaginable. Too bad Mom isn't here, she thought wryly. She'd be in heaven.

'Hmm.' The saleswoman stared at Olivia's chest. 'I'm guessing you're an A cup.'

Olivia cringed at the word 'cup.'

The saleslady gave one of the racks a hearty spin and the bras all flew around in a circle until her hand clamped down on the rack and stopped it. She pulled out a ruffled white bra with a pink bow sewn in the middle.

'Try this one on, dear. The clasp fastens in the back, like so . . .' She gave Olivia a demonstration, and then showed her how to adjust the arm straps, but Olivia was too mortified to pay attention.

'Yeah OK, thanks,' Olivia muttered, taking the bra from the saleslady. She slunk over to one of the fitting rooms and yanked the heavy blue curtain shut.

At first she just sat on the little upholstered stool, the bra hanging limply from her fingers. She figured she'd just wait a respectable time before coming out and telling the saleslady it didn't fit. But then she grew a little curious and decided to try the bra on after all. It took a little while to figure it all out, and when she finally did get it on, the whole stupid thing was all twisted so she had to start all over again.

'Everything all right in there?' the saleslady asked. 'Do you need any help?'

'NO!' Olivia shouted, holding the curtain closed.

When she finally did get it on the right way, she scrutinized herself in the mirror. It looked like she had slapped two doilies on her chest. She decided then and there that when she finally did get a bra it would be a plain white one, the plainest white one imaginable.

'Hey, Olivia?' Frannie was outside the curtain, whispering.

'Don't come in,' she said quickly, then whispered, 'Did you find it?'

'No. Can you keep the saleslady busy a little longer?'

Olivia sighed loudly. 'I'll try,' she said.

She got dressed again and pulled the curtain back. The saleslady was there in a flash. 'So? What did you think?'

'I didn't like the pink bow,' Olivia replied.

The saleslady looked genuinely surprised, as if she hadn't yet met a girl who wasn't just loopy over a bra that had a pink bow.

'Maybe something more sporty?' the woman said. 'For a girl-on-the-go.'

Olivia liked the sound of that. She sincerely hoped she'd be going, the sooner the better.

'Yeah, something more sporty,' Olivia agreed.

While the saleswoman spun another rack, Olivia cut a glance towards Frannie and Viola. Frannie was walking along the left wall, her eyes scanning the wall, while Viola was meandering in the middle of the store, looking on the ground, and, inexplicably, up at the ceiling.

The whole plan was pretty goofy, Olivia thought. Even if there had been some kind of entrance to the tunnel once, what were the chances it would still be here more than a hundred years later?

'This one!' The saleslady held up a hanger with a powder-blue bra. 'And there's another sporty one on this rack . . .' While she spun the next rack, Olivia went over to a rack in the corner with some unusual-looking bras. Some had fur on them and others were covered with sequins. A few of them even had feathers tufting up along the edges.

'Those are our novelty bras,' the saleslady called to Olivia as her rack squealed in a circle. 'Nothing you'd be interested in.'

But there *was* something Olivia was interested in. She spied it through the bare spot on the rack between the D cups and the Double-D cups. There was a door in the floor. It was right smack in the centre of the novelty bra rack.

'Here we go!' The saleslady jiggled a hanger with another bra that had all sorts of criss-crossy stitching on it. 'This one has great support for smaller bosoms.'

Olivia cringed again.

'Shall we try these on?'

'Sure, but let me get my friend's opinion this time,' Olivia said, and she rushed off to fetch Frannie.

'This turtle is going to give himself concussion,' Frannie said when they were inside the dressing room. There were loud thumps coming from inside the carrier, and when Frannie put it down it rocked wildly.

'Listen, Frannie,' Olivia whispered. 'There's a door

in the floor, right under the rack of bras with all the fur and junk on them. As far as I can tell, there's just a little latch on the door, no keyhole or anything.'

'Really? Great! OK. Listen, Olivia. The best thing you can do is to keep the saleslady busy with the bras, while Viola and I go down there,' Frannie said. 'All three of us don't need to go. And there *are* rats, even if they're brown ones.'

It should have been a tempting offer. But now that the passageway was found, Olivia felt a strange urge to go through it.

'No,' Olivia said. 'I'm going too. We'll just have to slip by the saleslady somehow.'

Their problem was solved the very next minute. The store's front door tinkled, and the saleslady called to them, 'I'll be up front if you need me, girls!'

Olivia grabbed Frannie's arm and pulled her out of the dressing room. While the saleswoman was making her way through the store to greet the new customer, Olivia and Frannie frantically looked for Viola. She was nowhere to be found. Frannie's expression was teetering between panic and fury, but suddenly it turned suspicious. She marched to the dressing rooms and drew back one of the curtains. There was Viola, in the silky white camisole, grinning at herself in the mirror.

There was nothing to do but for Frannie to grab Viola just as she was and drag her to the novelty bra rack. Frannie dropped to the floor, pet carrier in hand, and crawled beneath the bras to the centre of the rack. Olivia watched as she flicked the latch and raised the trapdoor. Cold, damp air wafted up through the blackness.

Frannie whipped out a small flashlight from the side pocket of her pants. She shone it down into the hole, then grabbed the carrier and lowered herself into the darkness. Viola went next – eagerly, in fact. She probably missed being underground.

When it came to Olivia's turn, she hesitated. A flutter of fear squeezed her chest. There was no sound at all coming from the trapdoor. To her left, she could hear the saleslady purring to the new customer, a purr that was slowly approaching.

Olivia dropped down and crawled under the bras. The ones on the lowest tier tickled her neck with their feathers and fur. Now she could see that there was a metal ladder attached to the stone wall just below the door. How far down it went was impossible to tell, since only six or seven rungs were visible before they were lost in the thick blackness below.

Olivia lowered herself on to the ladder and began to climb down. The climb seemed to go on forever. There was a musty, basement-ish odour, mingled with the scent of burning electrical wires and something else. Something vast and friendless.

After a few minutes she put her foot down to feel for

the rung below and instead of metal she felt gravel. She had reached the bottom. Looking around, she tried to pick out shapes, but there was only blackness.

A sudden beam of light bored into her eyes and she quickly shaded them.

'Frannie?' Her voice sounded hollow.

The light left her face and now illuminated Frannie, who was holding the flashlight under her chin, smiling.

'This is it. We're in the tunnel.' She shone the flashlight around, and Olivia could see stone walls arching above them and bare gravel on the ground.

'Where are the tracks?' Olivia asked.

'They never put them in. This was part of a subway line that was started but never completed. There's a bunch of them down here, according to the map. Steenpister's station is further downtown, but these old tunnels hook right into it.'

'Ga!' Viola cried, shaking her head, her eyes glinting. She was sniffing the air in long, loud inhalations.

'Yes, this must feel very much like your *ga*,' Frannie said. 'I was afraid it might make her a bit homesick,' Frannie said to Olivia.

Viola grabbed the flashlight out of Frannie's hand and turned it off. They were once again immersed in the blinding darkness.

'Hey, Viola,' Olivia said a little nervously, 'let's just keep that thing on.'

'Actually, we need to keep it off,' Frannie explained. 'The tunnels are a little confusing at this stretch – even the maps were a little vague – which is why we need Viola to guide us. But she says she needs to do it in the dark. She says the lights confuse her. She can find things more easily in the dark. At least I think that's what she was saying. My translations are still a little rough.'

'Maybe what she really said was "No flashlights, so I can lead you into the middle of nowhere and leave you there for the giant rats to eat,"' Olivia said.

'*Bah Nitna!*' Viola snapped.

'What's that mean?' Olivia asked.

'Nothing nice,' Frannie said. 'For heaven's sake, she does understand a little English, Olivia.'

'Sorry, Viola,' Olivia said.

Their eyes gradually grew accustomed to the dark, and now Olivia could make out the shadowy shapes of her companions. The white camisole gleamed in the blackness, and Olivia wondered if Viola was cleverer than she seemed. Or maybe she just wanted to feel dainty and feminine underneath.

Viola made a gruff sound and started to walk, so Frannie and Olivia followed, Olivia taking the pet carrier out of Frannie's hands. They travelled slowly over the chunky gravel, their feet stumbling at first before they got the hang of it. Off in the distance they could hear the occasional rumble of trains, but other than that there was silence. An awful, thick silence. Olivia's gaze was fixed to the ground for any signs of scurrying rodents, but she imagined that if a rat was at all stealthy it could clamber over her shoes and up her pants leg without her seeing a thing in this darkness. A person could hide from them too, Olivia supposed, curled into one of the crevices in the tunnel walls. It gave her a goosepimply feeling all over.

The tunnel twisted and turned, and Olivia had the sensation of descending deeper and deeper into the bowels of the city, miles below the sidewalk. Every so often she became gripped with the fear that they would never find their way out again, that they would be trapped down here, and no one would hear their cries for help. That was when she put her hand on Ruben's hat and rubbed it.

Up ahead, Olivia could see that Viola had stopped and was pacing back and forth, the faint beacon of her camisole illuminating her movements.

'What's wrong?' Olivia called ahead. There was no answer, but a second later she saw what the problem was. The tunnel had ended without warning, sealed by a solid brick wall.

'Well, that's that,' Olivia said. She wasn't sorry. She's had enough of the adventure. It wasn't even so much the rats any more. It was the silence. It felt suffocating.

But Viola had not given up so easily. She was back-tracking now, her crouched body creeping along the edge of the tunnel wall. She backtracked so far that Frannie and Olivia lost sight of her altogether. Olivia felt a moment of panic. Down here, Viola's presence was actually reassuring.

'Frannie!' They heard Viola shout suddenly. 'Frannie!'

Frannie and Olivia rushed across the gravel towards Viola's voice. Frannie switched on the flash-light and they found Viola crouched down and searching the ground for something. Set into the wall beside her was a short, wooden door, its edges black and rotted. Viola picked up a piece of gravel with a narrow, shard-like rim. Jamming the narrow end into the edge of the door she deftly manoeuvred the stone, jemmying it back and forth until there was a squeak of wood. Then a crack. The door flew open and without a moment's hesitation Viola crawled through, followed, a little more tentatively, by Olivia and Frannie.

On the other side of the door, they stood up and looked around. The tunnel was quite different here. It was a long cylinder made of brick rather than stone, with wooden ribs curving across it for bracing. There was no gravel on the ground, just smooth brick and two rails running along the bottom. The tunnel wall bricks were painted white, which should have made it easier for them to see. But instead the visibility here was even worse than in the other tunnel due to a thick cold mist that clouded the air. Even though they were all standing close together, they passed in and out of each other's sight as the mist swirled and shifted.

'*Keeegh,*' Viola said in a quiet voice.

'What does that mean?' Olivia asked Frannie.

'I don't know. But she doesn't sound happy.'

In fact, Viola seemed positively disorientated. When the mist occasionally parted to allow her glimpses of her surroundings, Viola turned this way and that, smelling the air, her eyes shut. Then she stretched out her thick hand and took hold of Frannie's. Frannie took hold of Olivia's, and in this way they started to move, dragged along by Viola.

'Do you think she really knows where she's going?' Olivia asked. The mist now completely cloaked the air in front of her, so she felt as though she were talking to herself. But she was answered by an angry, '*Bah Nitna!*'

'Sorry, Viola,' Olivia said.

They walked in silence, stopping every so often to take turns holding the pet carrier. Eventually, the mist began to thin out enough that they could let go of each other's hands. Here and there, hanging on the sooty whitewashed walls of the tunnel, were beautiful wrought-iron sconces, each with two glass globes set on their little holders.

'Gas lights,' Frannie said. 'This place is old. Really old.'

'Maybe we're close to Steenpister's station,' Olivia said hopefully.

It was right then that Olivia saw the little girl. She wore a thin yellow dress and was perched in a very ladylike way on the lower rung of a metal ladder that was attached to the tunnel wall. Olivia stopped short, staring up at her in bewilderment. The girl returned the stare, appearing equally puzzled.

'Hi,' Olivia said to her.

Frannie stopped and looked back at Olivia.

'Who are you talking to?' Frannie asked.

'Look on the ladder,' Olivia whispered, nodding towards it. 'The little girl.' It was still misty in the tunnel, but the girl was plainly visible. Olivia watched as Frannie gazed at the ladder, frowning, then turned back to Olivia.

'There's no one there,' Frannie said. 'Are you trying to spook me?'

Olivia looked back at the little girl. She noticed the girl's luminescent skin that appeared lit from within. Now Olivia understood. She should have realized it before, but the tunnel's weird lighting had confused her.

The little girl was a ghost.

'It worked, didn't it?' Olivia said to Frannie, smiling, trying to keep her voice light. Out of the corner of her eye, she watched as the little girl descended the ladder, her little black shoes touching each rung delicately, as though she was trying not to scuff them.

'Let's go,' Olivia urged.

Olivia Kidney was afraid of several things. Snakes, rats and, most definitely, elevators. The one thing she was not afraid of was ghosts. They were as normal and natural to her as living people. Sometimes even *more* normal and natural than living people. But she was afraid now. It was that squirmy, heeby-jeeby feeling – a feeling that Madame Brenda had once warned her to take seriously. She was taking it seriously now, especially since the girl was following them, her thin legs keeping pace behind them, stepping lightly between the rails.

'What do you want?' Olivia tried to 'think' to the girl, but there was no answer. Up ahead, Viola seemed unnerved. She kept stopping and looking behind her, her head cocked as though she could hear something in the distance. But Olivia watched as Viola's eyes passed right over the little girl without seeing her.

Suddenly, a few feet ahead, they could make out a blue glow that seemed to float in mid-air.

'What's that?' Frannie asked, her voice betraying the panic of someone who'd been recently spooked.

No one knew. They kept walking and Olivia could hear Frannie nervously muttering to herself, '"A hero is no braver than an ordinary man, but he is brave five minutes longer." – Emerson.'

Presently they saw a reddish glow appear just beyond the blue one.

'It's the gas lamps!' Olivia said. 'Look at the glass covers.' She pointed to the nearest sconce. 'They alternate red and blue. Someone's lit the lamps up ahead.'

'Steenpister!' Frannie said, her voice markedly relieved. 'We must be close to the station.'

Olivia glanced back and saw that the little girl had begun to run. She scurried past them, just inches away in the narrow tunnel. Frannie took no notice. Viola's head swivelled towards the little girl just as she passed, but that was all.

As they came upon the lit globes, they could see that the tunnel ended just a few feet ahead. Off to the left was a small platform with a set of stairs leading up to a second storey.

'This must be it!' Frannie exclaimed.

Olivia scanned the area for the little girl, but she had vanished.

For good, I hope, Olivia thought.

They climbed up on to the platform, but Frannie paused at the bottom of the steps.

'I feel like we should knock or something,' she said.

'I think he knows we're here,' Olivia said. She had the feeling that their approach was being watched as soon as they had reached the lit gas lamps.

'Mister Steenpister!' Frannie called up the steps. 'We don't want to bother you or anything, but we've gone to a lot of trouble to find you, and—'

'We brought you a present! A turtle!' Olivia interrupted. 'A very large snapping turtle! A few days ago he bit a man's nose clean off his face!'

There was no answer, but Olivia thought she could hear someone stirring.

'You can leave the turtle at the bottom of the stairs,' a voice finally came from upstairs.

'But we want to ask you a question, Mister Steenpister,' Frannie said, 'in exchange for the turtle.'

'Then it isn't really a present, is it?' he said quite sensibly.

'No, I guess it's not,' Frannie admitted.

'It looks like we've begun this relationship with a lie,' Mister Steenpister said, still remaining hidden. 'That's a bad beginning, in my opinion. I suggest we end it here and now, before we grow to hate each other.'

Viola had been listening to the conversation, not understanding it word for word, but certainly catching the gist of it. Patience for silly squabbling had never been her strong point. Once, when her cousins in the cave back home were bickering over who got to suck on the crispy tail of the roasted boar, Viola had simply plucked the tail from the embers and tossed it up in the air, and the person who caught it kept it fair and square.

Now she bent down and opened the latch of the pet carrier. She flipped the carrier on its side so that the turtle could crawl out.

'No, Viola!' Olivia cried, backing away from the creature, which could crawl faster than you would imagine. The turtle wasn't happy either. It raised its ugly head and looked around as if trying to choose the best piece of flesh to bite.

In an instant, Steenpister was down the stairs. He snatched up the turtle by its shell and held it in the air.

'Well, hello, you handsome devil,' Steenpister said to the turtle with a friendly smile. He was wearing a green sweater that was not at all ripped or nasty-looking and his trousers were perfectly respectable, except that they were too short. 'Took someone's nose off, did you?'

'There was blood all over,' Olivia affirmed.

'Bad boy.' Franklin Steenpister shook a finger at the turtle, careful to keep a safe distance from its snapping jaws. 'All right then. I'll take him.' Steenpister started up the stairs with the turtle.

'But our question . . .' Frannie called after him.

'You can ask it upstairs as well as downstairs, I assume,' he said.

CHAPTER THIRTY

They followed him up the stairs, and there, on the second-level landing, was the most extraordinary subway station Olivia had ever seen. The wainscoted walls were covered with beautifully framed paintings, and scattered about were cushiony armchairs and couches. Off in the corner towards the back was a gleaming black piano. The centrepiece of the room was a marble fountain carved with angels, and lolling about in its water-filled basin were dozens of tremendous turtles.

But what Olivia found most extraordinary was the children. There were three of them, including the little girl who had followed them, dressed in odd, old-fashioned clothing and watching them with great interest. They were ghosts, all of them. Olivia could see that plainly now. One little girl was nestled in an armchair, a boy sat at the piano bench biting his thumbnail, and the little girl who had followed them stood by Steenpister, her arms crossed in front of her chest suspiciously.

Steenpister put the turtle in the fountain. 'Play nice,' he told him as he let him go.

Does he know the ghosts are here? Olivia wondered.

He walked over to a little table with a hotplate on top of it and grabbed the kettle that was sitting on its burner. Climbing up on a chair, he reached for a valve set in one of the overhead pipes and turned it. A stream of water poured out from a crack in the pipe and into the kettle. He then placed the kettle on the hotplate, which had a long extension cord that snaked along the floor and disappeared into a hole that had been sliced into one of the walls.

'Make yourselves at home,' he said to them as he sat on a round antimacassar, his tall frame bending forward and his elbows resting on his knees. The girl in the yellow dress sat on the floor by his feet, still managing to look ladylike, and busied herself by straightening her stockings.

They each sat down, Frannie choosing the armchair that was occupied by one of the ghosts – a terribly thin little girl in a shabby dress the colour of an old bruise. The girl scooted over before Frannie sat down, and the two of them were so small they could sit side by side without even touching. The little ghost-girl stared at Frannie with unabashed fascination, her lower lip drooping a bit.

'I remember you two from the park,' Steenpister said, nodding towards Frannie and Olivia. 'I thought you might be after my turtles. Last month a couple of kids tried to steal one of my catches from me, but I outran them. The blessing of long legs,' he slapped at his thighs. He didn't seem particularly crazy, Olivia thought. But then she remembered how tricky crazy people could be, and decided it was best to reserve judgement. 'How did you find me?' Steenpister asked.

'Your wife told us how,' Frannie said.

'Lippa!' he said with a grin. 'I do miss my old girl. But she won't live down here. She likes the sunshine too much.'

The boy at the piano began to plink a few keys, and everyone turned towards him.

'Did that piano just play by itself?' Frannie asked, the spooked voice returning.

Steenpister sighed. 'It does that every now and again. I don't know why. It's just a regular old piano, nothing special. Sometimes it plays whole songs on its own, quite well.'

The boy began to play a song now, his fingers flying across the keys, his hands making little flourishes in the air as he played.

Show-off, Olivia thought.

Poor Frannie's eyes grew wide. The little girl sitting next to her smiled a little. One of her front teeth was missing.

'Some folks say this station is haunted. Well, maybe it is. It doesn't bother me in the slightest. Anyway, it's nice to have a little music now and then.'

The kettle screeched and Steenpister rose quickly to fetch it, followed by the girl in the yellow dress. He took out four mismatched teacups from a crate on the floor, as well as a tin of tea and a chipped sugar bowl with a spoon in it. The little girl in the yellow dress licked her finger and stuck it in the sugar bowl, then licked the sugar off her finger. The boy at the piano quit playing and rushed over to do the same. Their tongues were pink, Olivia noted with some relief.

'Oh, it stopped,' Frannie said, looking over at the piano sadly, which made the boy rush back to play some more.

The skinny, sickly little girl next to Frannie kept her seat, looking almost too weak to run like the others. Olivia wished that she would dip her finger in the bowl too. That was silly of her, she knew. The sugar wouldn't make her any plumper or healthier-looking, but it bothered Olivia anyway.

Steenpister returned and handed out the tea to them. Olivia examined her cup carefully for dried bits clinging to the outside or something nasty floating in the tea, but the cup was perfectly clean. So was Steenpister, for that matter. She had taken a whiff of him as he handed her the tea, expecting him to have that awful sour subway-lunatic smell. But instead he smelt rather pleasantly of nothing at all.

'You don't really believe in ghosts, do you?' Frannie asked incredulously.

'There are more things in heaven and earth, Horatio, than are dreamt of in your philosophy,' he said, taking his seat again.

'That's from Shakespeare,' Frannie said approvingly. '*Hamlet.*'

'Well,' Steenpister looked at Frannie in surprise. 'Aren't you a clever little girl. How old are you?'

'I'm going to be fifteen in a few months,' Frannie said. The little girl sitting beside her raised her eyebrows.

'Ahh,' Franklin Steenpister nodded, frowning. He seemed to be turning this information over in his brain. 'You've come about Blup, haven't you?'

Frannie nodded, her face pale with anticipation.

Franklin Steenpister gazed down at his tea, then looked back up at Frannie sadly. 'I'm sorry,' he said, 'but you've come a long way for nothing. I never found Blup's plant.'

'I don't believe you,' Frannie said staunchly. 'You did find that plant. That's why the Pitta-Pittas poisoned you. Besides, your son knew what Blup ate! He was even going to tell me, except . . . things just didn't work out.'

'*My son,*' Steenpister shook his head disgustedly. 'My son likes to hide the fact that his father was a very silly man. But I am silly. The Pitta-Pittas proved it. They made a great silly fool out of me.'

'How?' Frannie asked, spitting out the word like a dare.

'Oh, it was true that they sent Blup off on his rite of passage and he came back three feet taller. But it wasn't Blup who returned. It was another boy, a member of a nearby tribe called the Chumboos. The Pitta-Pittas are very good friends with the Chumboos, who are all quite tall, while the Pitta-Pittas are, as you know, very short. They simply switched. It wasn't hard to fool me. I never paid much attention to the children – always had my nose stuck in the plants. It's an old trick the two tribes have played on anthropologists for hundreds of years. Of course, they have had to change the tribal names every so often to keep their little game going but it's worth it to them. They love a good prank.'

That sounded so much like something the Pitta-Pittas would do, that Frannie went silent.

'How did you find out about the trick?' Olivia asked.

'Oh, it was weeks later. I was wandering through the jungle, trying to find what Blup had eaten, when

I ran into Blup himself, still three feet tall and trying to reach a mango on a high branch. I fetched the mango for him and he told me everything, laughing his head off as he did. I should have been insulted. I had spent weeks trying to solve the puzzle of Blup's growth. But the jungle had changed me. I started to laugh too, just like a Pitta-Pitta. I found I no longer cared about research and statistics and awards. After that, I gave up my old life and stayed with the Pitta-Pittas. I married Lippa, and would have lived in the jungle for the rest of my life if Lippa hadn't poisoned me. She wanted to go to New York City, you see, and I wanted to stay in the jungle. So she slipped me a nasty little concoction that made me just sick enough to have to leave. Cunning woman!' He smiled with admiration. 'We returned to New York and after I recovered I tried to live a so-called normal life, but I just couldn't do it. Things seemed much saner down here, below the streets, so I set up house and live a cosy little life, thank you very much.'

Olivia had been so interested in the story she had momentarily forgotten about Frannie. When she looked at her now, she saw that her friend was clearly crushed. Frannie was gazing off at nothing, her eyes damp. She was pressing one hand against her belly, as though she felt sick. The little girl who shared her seat rested her chin on Frannie's shoulder.

'Of course,' said Steenpister, 'I will understand if you want to take back your turtle.'

'No,' Olivia said quickly. 'Keep him.'

Steenpister looked very relieved to hear this, which made Olivia remember that there was always a little nugget of crazy lurking in the heart of every subway lunatic. But just as she had decided that Steenpister's crazy nugget was his love of snapping turtles, he said, 'There's nothing like a snapping turtle for keeping away the rats.' Which, after all, seemed very sensible.

Out of appreciation for the turtle, Steenpister offered to show them a short cut to the street, so they wouldn't have to face the dismal tunnels again. He led them out of the room through a padlocked back door, which he opened with a key. Then they followed him down a long, wide hallway with rough-cut stone walls – not anything like the elegant station or even the neat, brick-lined tunnel. This hallway looked like it had been hastily excavated out of solid rock. The girl in the yellow dress walked by Steenpister's side, but the other children had stayed behind in the station.

Along the way they came upon a chaos of dust-covered rubble and splintered shards of wood, as though some great digging machine had ploughed right through a home without warning. And then, a few feet further on, there was a gaping hole in the side of the passage, revealing a threadbare apartment, with a mattress on the floor in the back, a blackened stove in the corner, and in the centre of the room a kitchen table where two boys – one small and the other quite a bit older – were engrossed in a game of chequers. Their heads were bent low and cupped in their hands, their elbows resting on the table with the chequerboard between them. Olivia watched them for a moment as she walked, accidentally kicking a stray chunk of rubble against Viola's ankle.

'Oi!' Viola cried.

The boys looked up. Olivia stopped, frozen in her tracks. She stared at the older boy. Her eyes grew wide and she had to cover her mouth to keep from crying out.

It was Branwell.

CHAPTER THIRTY-ONE

Branwell looked just as surprised as Olivia. He rose from his seat, a huge grin spreading across his face as he started towards her.

'Ah, you're noticing the old apartment,' Steenpister said. 'A sad story. Watch your step.' He put a hand on her shoulder and guided her around a pile of plaster, then past the ruined apartment. Olivia looked back at Branwell. His smile had disappeared. He raised one hand to say goodbye.

'What happened to that place?' Olivia asked as they rounded a bend and Branwell vanished from her view.

'Many years ago, when they blasted through the rock to make this station,' Steenpister explained, 'there was a family living down here illegally. The parents were away at work, but the children were home at the time they tunnelled through. They died in the blast. Very tragic.'

Olivia glanced at the little girl in the yellow dress. She was skipping back and forth down the passage in a bored sort of way.

They rounded a sharp curve and came upon a patch of sunlight streaming through a grating above their heads. Steenpister stopped here and showed them how they could climb a network of pipes along the wall to reach the grating. It was locked from the outside, but from down here they could just turn the latch and push, he said, and the grating would flip open.

'Goodbye,' Franklin Steenpister said. Then he added to Frannie, 'The Pitta-Pittas have a saying: "Problems are like parrots. If you hold them upside down by their feet and flick their beaks with your fingers, they will eventually throw up."'

Frannie looked markedly unimpressed, but thanked him anyway before Olivia gave her a boost to the first pipe. Viola went next. Last came Olivia, who had pocketed a loose stone. Before closing the grate, she carefully shoved the stone beneath the grating's edge.

They found themselves in a little alley beside a Chinese restaurant, right next to a garbage dumpster. Frannie promptly reached into her pocket and took out the paper on which she had written all her notes and diagrams. She balled it up and threw it into the dumpster.

'All this trouble for a cup of tea and some advice on how to make a parrot vomit.'

Olivia walked Frannie and Viola to the subway station, her mind somersaulting with conflicting emotions. She felt awful for Frannie, yet overjoyed at seeing Branwell again. What was he doing down there? Had he been there a long time? Was that why she couldn't contact him?

When they reached the train station, Olivia said, 'You two go ahead. I think I'm going to have a look at that bra place again.'

'For what?' Frannie asked. But then she dropped her eyes to Olivia's chest and said, 'Oh, right. Probably a good idea.'

Olivia bit back a tart reply.

She headed back the way she'd come, but when she turned down the alley by the Chinese restaurant, she found it wasn't empty this time. There was an old Chinese woman sitting on a chair outside the restaurant's back door, cutting the ends off of green beans with a pair of scissors and dropping them into a metal bowl on her lap. She looked like she was in no hurry either. As she snipped, she was singing something in a very tuneless way, one foot tapping just inches away from the subway grating. Olivia had no choice but to walk around the block several times until finally she saw the woman slowly rise and disappear back inside the restaurant.

Olivia hurried down the alley and knelt by the grating, half afraid that the piece of rubble she'd wedged beneath it had fallen out. A quick check found that it was still in place and, after she looked once more up the alley and saw that no one was around, she lifted the grating and slipped down the hole. Her foot found the top pipe easily and she lowered the grating over her head, the metal making a gloomy clanking sound as it shut. The light from the street above made it easy for her to spot the rest of the pipes and she scrambled down, then made a final, long leap to the ground from the lowest pipe.

'How come you dress like a boy?' There, standing with her hands on her hips, was the girl in the yellow dress.

'How did you know I was here?' Olivia asked, finding that she was actually relived to find herself with company.

'You're a very noisy person,' the little girl said. She had a frosty, proper little voice. 'How come you dress like a boy?'

'It doesn't make much sense to wear a nice dress in a subway tunnel, does it?' Olivia asked. 'You'll just get it all sooty.'

'Not if you're very careful.' She stared at Olivia for a moment. 'Can you really see me?' she asked.

'Of course. You have blonde hair and your dress is yellow and isn't at all sooty.'

The little girl smiled. 'My name is Harriet,' she said.

'I'm Olivia.'

'I know. Branwell told us,' the little girl said, rearranging her fringe. 'He's doing Geography with Joey now. Come on.' She turned daintily on her heels and led the way down the passage, turning once to give a vague warning: 'Don't be alarmed if Joey does something.'

'What does he do?' Olivia asked.

'I don't want to say.' And Harriet continued on, leaving Olivia to wonder what it could possibly be.

After a few minutes they turned a corner, and up ahead Olivia saw Branwell. He was writing on the wall with a piece of chalk while the small black-haired boy he'd been playing chequers with was hopping from foot to foot.

'I have a bee in my sock,' the boy said.

'No you don't. Now, think,' Branwell said.

The boy stood still for a moment and stared at the wall, then pointed.

'East,' he declared and began to hop around again.

'Nope, that's west. North-East-South-West.' Branwell pointed at different spots on the wall. Olivia guessed by the sound of his voice that they'd been at this for some time. 'Remember it this way, Joey: Never-Eat-Soggy-Worms.'

'I like them soggy,' Joey said. 'They slip down nice and quick that way.'

Branwell spotted Olivia, and his look of annoyance was instantly replaced by a wide grin. He rushed over to her and hugged her. It was an interesting sensation to be hugged by a spirit. It gave Olivia a fizzy feeling across her skin, like stepping into a pool filled with club soda. Except nicer.

'I tried to contact you lots of times,' Olivia said.

'Sounds come in all garbled down here,' Branwell said. 'It's because of all the power lines, I think. But the funny thing is last Tuesday I was sure I could hear you. I even called out to you, but then you were gone.'

Joey stopped hopping and in one quick motion, he dropped his pants and mooned her.

'That's the thing he does,' Harriet said disgustedly.

'Pull your pants up, Joey,' Branwell said, and Joey pulled them up just as nonchalantly as he had dropped them.

Branwell told Joey and Harriet to go off and play, and then Olivia followed him into the ruined apartment, where they sat down at the table.

'What are you doing here anyway?' Olivia asked.

'Looking after them,' Branwell said, nodding towards the passage where the kids were spying on them. 'I heard about them from Mrs Babbish, when I was in the Spirit World. She's the woman who owns a pig farm next door to where I lived.'

'There are pig farms in the Spirit World?' Olivia asked.

'Oh, sure, there are all kinds of things there, you'd be amazed. Anyway, Mrs Babbish told me that when she was alive, she had once spotted little ghost children running wild and hooting and hollering in the subway tunnels, before they suddenly vanished. Well, I just kept thinking and worrying about those kids living down here, until Mrs Babbish said, "Well, honey, why don't you just pop in and pay them a visit." See, I didn't know you could do that kind of thing once you stopped being a ghost and moved on to the Spirit World. So I did. It was easy enough to find them. They were running around the tunnels like little savages covered in soot, yelling and whooping. When I suddenly appeared in front of them, they all stopped and stared with their mouths hanging open. They were so used to scaring other people they weren't used to being scared themselves.

'I didn't stay long that first time. It's easy to spy on people down here on earth, but it's a lot harder to actually appear in front of them when you're no longer a ghost. It made me so tired, I went home and slept for a whole day straight until Mrs Babbish came by to show me some baby weasels she'd found in her barn. After that, I'd visit the kids every chance I could, and each time I was able to stay a little longer. Now I'm with them all the time.'

'How much longer are you going to stay down here?' Olivia asked.

Branwell shrugged. 'As long as *they're* here, I guess. I've tried to get them to leave, to go to the Spirit World, but they flat out refuse. And I can't just abandon them. You understand, right?'

Olivia nodded. That was the way Branwell was. Always taking care of people.

'I try and teach them things,' Branwell said. 'Stuff like fractions and history. And I taught Sammy to play the piano. But mostly they hardly ever do what anyone tells them.'

As if to prove this point, Joey and the boy who had played the piano at Steenpister's station, came running into the apartment, and stood around Olivia to gape at her.

'Is she your *girlfriend*?' the piano player taunted Branwell.

'No, Sammy. Now both of you scram!'

They scattered quickly, but didn't go very far.

So much had happened in Olivia's life since she last saw Branwell that they spent the next hour just catching up, after which they played a rowdy game of Tag with the children. Finally, the smallest girl, named Mary, handed her a book to read to them. *Alice in Wonderland.*

'It's our favourite,' Harriet explained. 'The ladies in the church gave it to us one Christmas.'

Olivia read to them until a rat the size of a small raccoon slunk into the apartment.

Olivia screeched and the kids all jumped up to chase the animal out, then ran off to seek some other amusement.

'You should go,' Branwell said to Olivia. 'It's getting late.'

He walked with her through the passage. The crushing silence of the place was contagious and they didn't say a word to each other until they reached the grate.

'I won't blame you if you don't want to come back,' Branwell told her.

Olivia thought for a moment. 'According to William James,' she said, 'you should do two things that you hate every day. Well, I hate being around rats. And I hate noisy little kids.' She reached down, picked up a stone to wedge in the grating, and shoved it in her pocket. 'I'll see you tomorrow.'

CHAPTER THIRTY-TWO

'Good afternoon, Miss Kidney,' Cornwickle cheer-fully greeted her in the front hallway of the brownstone.

'Cornwickle, you're smiling.' Olivia stared up at him with amazement.

'Am I?' he said as though he knew perfectly well that he was. 'Well, I have good reason, Miss Kidney. *Help has arrived.*'

Cornwickle was such a competent person, that Olivia wondered who could possibly help *him*.

He opened the double white doors for her. Standing in the empty lagoon was a woman with tomato-red hair. She was holding a piece of paper and reciting to Ansel what appeared to be a list: 'Number two: I've arranged a meeting for you on Saturday with the Board of Exit Academies. Be there on time and no funny stuff. Number three: Go down to the hospital and apologize on bended knees to the man whose nose was bitten off. And I mean on *bended knees*, darling.'

'I don't see why, Mother,' Ansel said to Madame Brenda. 'It was his fault that he stuck his nose next to a snapping turtle's mouth. And anyway, they've reattached the thing, although it was such a large, lumpy nose to begin with that I'm surprised he wanted it back on his face.'

'Achh! You exasperate me!' Madame Brenda cried, flapping her hands in the air, each finger twinkling with rings. She turned then and when she saw Olivia she opened her arms wide.

'Darling!' Madame Brenda hurried to Olivia, her tower of red hair slipping to one side of her head. She pushed it back to centre before she threw her arms around Olivia and hugged her tightly. Then she stepped back and held Olivia by her shoulders, examining her carefully.

'You've been neglecting your pores again, I see. And take off that silly hat. What's this?' She frowned, and brushed off several streaks of subway soot on her shirt. 'Have you been playing in the sewers?'

'Sort of,' Olivia answered, smiling. She was wonderfully glad to see Madame Brenda again.

'I leave for a couple of months, and everything falls to pieces!' Madame Brenda exclaimed. 'My son is being evicted, people's noses are bitten off, children

315

are playing in the sewers! Tut-tut, I've come back just in time, I see.'

Dinner that evening was the best George had made in several days. He too seemed relieved that Madame Brenda was back. There was the general sense that she would put everything right again.

At the end of dinner, Madame Brenda sighed and patted her belly, which pooched quite a bit after the meal. 'That was delicious, George darling. And now I think I'll retire to my room.' She stood up. 'Come along, Olivia. You've got oodles of things to tell me.'

In fact, Olivia did. It occurred to her that Madame Brenda might be just the person to help Branwell. But before she could say anything, Madame Brenda sat down on the bed, unbuttoned the top button on her slacks to free her stomach, and said, 'So, cupcake. What do you think of Miss Monsoon?'

'Miss Monsoon? Do you know her?' Olivia asked, taken aback.

'Oh, I did a little job for her some years back. Chased away a pesky ghost who was stalking her. She's an eccentric old bird, isn't she?'

'Try *crazy* old bird,' Olivia said.

'Maybe. But once upon a time, she was a tremendously talented child, just like you, and she understands talented children better than most people.'

'Like me?' Olivia snorted. 'I'm the least talented person in the entire school.'

'Oh, you may have little artistic talent, cupcake. But you have tremendous talent nonetheless. The problem is, where can a Straddler learn her craft when there are so few Straddlers in the whole entire world? I agonized over this question all summer until I got a migraine, darling. Right here, between the eyes. Worst kind. And that's when I remembered the Malcolm Flavius School for the Arts. A school for *talented children*, darling! Oh, I know there are miles of difference between a painter and a Straddler, but all great talents need to learn the same things – patience and focus and, above all, how to fail gracefully. So I called in a favour from an old friend.'

'*Miss Monsoon* got me in the school?' Olivia cried.

'Let's just say she tipped the scales a bit. You had nearly made it in to begin with, according to Miss Monsoon. They felt you had "raw talent".'

'Really?' Olivia said, smiling, and remembering that her father had said the same thing.

'Yes, really. Now tell Madame Brenda what you were doing down in the sewer.'

It took Olivia quite a while to tell Madame Brenda the whole story, and when she came to the end, she said, 'So, what do you think?'

'I think, Miss Olivia Kidney, that if you were my daughter, I would clout you on the head with my shoe! Traipsing through New York City subway tunnels! Have you lost your mind?'

'I know, I know,' Olivia said impatiently, 'but can you make those kids leave the tunnel?'

'Of course not,' Madame Brenda said. 'I can't make ghosts do anything. I can only persuade them that it's in their best interests to stop being ghosts. Child ghosts, however, are notoriously hard to deal with. I've only been successful with them twice – once was with your friend Branwell, and that hardly counts since it was you who finally persuaded him to give up being a ghost. The problem with children is that they hate to follow rules, and as ghosts they can float about as they please and scare people and stay up all hours of the night. Plus, they tend to be stubborn, as do living children who refuse to clean out their pores!' She raised her eyebrows at Olivia.

'So you can't help them?' Olivia asked.

'I didn't say that, cupcake. Now, off to bed. I'll have a word with these children in the morning, but it's crucial that we do it before ten o'clock a.m. or things will get ugly.'

'Why? What happens to them after ten a.m.?' Olivia said.

'Nothing happens to *them*, darling. But I have a hair appointment at eleven o'clock that if I miss it . . . *oi gevalt*, things will definitely get ugly!'

CHAPTER THIRTY-THREE

For an old woman, Madame Brenda was pretty sure-footed. Even in a pair of lavender heels she managed to climb down the tunnel pipes lickety-split, landing with an admirably soft click compared to Olivia's scramble-and-thud technique.

'OK,' she said looking up and down the passage and readjusting her rhinestone-studded green glasses, 'which way? Ah! We have company already!'

Coming up the passage was Harriet, looking rather cautious, as though she smelt trouble.

'Hello, darling!' Madame Brenda hiked up her skirt and crouched down, careful not to touch the ground. She stretched her arms out and wiggled her fingers. 'Come let me have a look at you, such a pretty dress, and oh how clever you are to have such eyelashes, like a pair of dust brooms . . .' As she spoke, Madame Brenda was poking at Harriet here and there, like a doctor might poke at a patient.

Harriet's skin rippled in a rubbery way with each poke, until she finally grew so annoyed that she ducked under Madame Brenda's arm and backed away a few feet.

'Who is she?' Harriet asked Olivia.

'A friend of mine. Her name is Madame Brenda.'

'I don't like her,' Harriet said, and started back down the hall at a quick clip.

'They never do,' Madame Brenda murmured to Olivia as they followed Harriet.

'Well, maybe if you didn't poke them, they'd like you better,' Olivia suggested, hurrying along.

'Darling, how else am I supposed to find out what sort of ghost they are?'

'There are different kinds?' Olivia asked.

'Of course! Some feel very watery. They're easiest to deal with. Others are mostly watery with little clumpy bits here and there. They're a little more of a headache to deal with. But then you have the hard-core ghosts. They literally have a hard core that gets soft and rubbery closer to the skin. Those are the ones that give me indigestion.'

'What kind is she then?'

'Cupcake, if I swallowed a whole bottle of Mylanta, it wouldn't even touch the indigestion I have right now,' Madame Brenda said ominously.

'Well, can you do anything?' Olivia asked.

'I don't know. The first thing you try to do with a

hard-core ghost is to get it to leave its home – take a little outing, say. That would be a start. I'll try, but it's not going to be easy.'

They found Branwell in the apartment, scolding Sammy, the boy who had played the piano so well at Steenpister's station. Sammy was sitting cross-legged on the mattress, looking shamefaced and angry at the same time.

'What were you thinking, Sammy?' Branwell was saying. 'You nearly gave that poor man a heart attack. Not to mention the turtle.'

'Well, he doesn't have any business hanging around here,' Sammy said. 'And anyway, it wasn't so bad what I did.'

'Not so bad?! You ran around holding a turtle over your head, so the poor man thought the thing was flying all on its own, while screaming "I'm a killer turtle, I'm a killer turtle!"'

'Yeah, but I didn't let the turtle bite him or nothing.'

'Haunting people is bad manners, darling.' Madame Brenda stepped over the rubble carefully and entered the room.

'According to living people, maybe,' the boy snapped back.

'Oh my!' Madame Brenda said to Branwell, with great pity in her voice. 'You do have your hands full. I'm Madame Brenda.' She held out her hand, and Branwell stepped forward and shook it, smiling.

'I thought I recognized your voice,' Branwell said. The other kids had stealthily entered the room, tucking themselves away in the corners and behind furniture to catch a better glimpse of the strange red-haired woman.

'That's right,' Madame Brenda said, 'I spoke to you once, back when you were a ghost.'

'You were a ghost, Branwell?' Sammy said, obviously impressed.

'A ghost with *manners*,' Madame Brenda said, stepping forward and poking at Sammy.

'Get off! Quit that!' He squirmed, but she still managed to get a few good pokes in.

When Madame Brenda was finished, she shook her head at Olivia despondently. 'Indigestion, cupcake.' Madame Brenda tapped her stomach with her fist. 'Like fire the *kishkes*. 'All right.' Madame Brenda looked commandingly around at the kids peering at her curiously from the room's nooks and crannies. 'Which one of you is the leader of this wolf pack?' When no one stepped forward, she clarified, 'Who's the bossiest?'

Every finger pointed to Harriet.

'All right, darling,' Madame Brenda approached Harriet, 'how about we take a stroll and have a little chat?'

Harriet didn't move. She simply stared at Madame Brenda with squinty-eyed distrust.

'Tell you what. I'll let you wear my glasses while we talk,' Madame Brenda said, taking off her glasses and dangling them in front of Harriet. Olivia didn't think that was much of a deal, but to her surprise Harriet snatched the ugly green glasses and popped them on her nose. They covered half her face and made her eyes bulge a little, but she seemed tremendously happy with them.

'You look like a toad,' Joey said.

'Nonsense, she looks lovely,' Madame Brenda said.

Joey turned around, pulled down his pants, and mooned her.

'Oh, hold still a moment, darling,' Madame Brenda said as she walked up to Joey, 'there's a little speck of something . . .' And with one swift motion, she took off her shoe and smacked it hard on his behind.

'Hey!' Joey cried, pulling up his pants hurriedly.

'Best to keep your bits and pieces covered, darling,' Madame Brenda said, putting her shoe back on as Harriet watched her with fresh appreciation. 'Shall we?' Madame Brenda put her arm around Harriet and the two of them left the apartment and started down the passage.

'Do you really think she can help?' Branwell asked Olivia.

'If anybody can, she can,' Olivia replied.

Branwell smiled a small, hesitant smile.

'Hey, Branwell,' Olivia said as an idea occurred to her, 'how long has it been since you've been outside?'

Branwell shrugged. 'I don't know. Three months maybe. You sort of lose track of time down here.'

'Well, it's a beautiful day. Why don't you go out? I can look after the other kids while Madame Brenda's with Harriet.'

Branwell chewed at his lip for a moment. 'I don't know . . .'

'Go.' Olivia gave him a gentle push.

'OK, maybe just for a while. Thanks.' He smiled at Olivia and slowly the light in his body began to grow fainter. Right before he vanished altogether, he jabbed a blurry finger at each of the kids. 'Behave yourselves.'

While Madame Brenda was gone with Harriet, Olivia read from *Alice in Wonderland* while Sammy, Joey and Mary sat on the mattress, their mouths open as they listened. Madame Brenda returned nearly an hour after she'd left. Her shoes were covered with soot and her hair was leaning so far over to the right that it looked like it might pull her down. But Harriet was not with her.

'Where's Harriet?' Olivia asked.

'Gone,' Madame Brenda said.

'Gone? Really?' Olivia jumped up and rushed over. 'You did it!' she said. 'She left!'

'Oh, she left all right. Ran off and left me in the middle of some *fekakdah* tunnel. I've spent the last forty-five minutes trying to find my way back.' She flipped her hands backwards and cried, 'Feh! I'm done! It will be a miracle if I make it to my hair appointment on time.' And she started back up the passage towards the grate.

'Come on,' Olivia called after her, 'there must be *something* you can do.'

'Oh, absolutely, darling,' she said without stopping. 'I can buy a new pair of heels and have Andre shampoo the filth out of my hair. Apart from that, I'm afraid not. Toodle-oo, I've got to run!'

Olivia's heart sank as she listened to Madame Brenda's shoes click off down the passage. Poor Branwell. He was outside now, strolling under the morning sun, full of hope. And when he returned, she'd have to tell him that Madame Brenda had failed. That he was stuck down here, for years and years and years. Maybe forever.

'Is that lady gone?' Harriet had returned, still wearing the enormous green glasses, her magnified eyes scooting around the room slyly.

'Yes, she's gone,' Olivia said sharply. 'And that was a lousy thing you did to her!' Olivia said.

'She's pushy.' Harriet fingered her fringe.

'She's trying to help you,' Olivia said severely.

'Not interested.' Harriet squeezed in between her siblings on the mattress. 'What part are we up to?'

'Where Alice sees the cat in the tree,' said Mary.

'Oh good, I love this part,' Harriet said. The kids sat there, staring up at Olivia, waiting.

It was then that Miss Monsoon's Muse whispered to her. It was a very quiet, conspiratorial whisper. If Olivia wasn't so used to hearing voices in her head, she would never have taken notice of it. But she did, and in a flash she knew how to make the impossible possible.

'No more reading,' Olivia said.

Sammy said to Harriet, 'You ruin everything!' and punched her arm.

'I don't suppose you want to see the Cheshire Cat in person?' Olivia said.

'He's not real,' Sammy said.

'Want to bet?' Olivia said. 'He lives in Central Park.'

The kids were silent, eyeing her guardedly.

'He shows up at noon sharp, every Saturday,' Olivia said. 'He'll wink at you.' She checked her watch. 'If we leave now, we'll just be able to make it in time.'

They all looked at Harriet.

'You're lying,' Harriet said to Olivia coolly.

'Funny,' Olivia said, 'that's exactly what I said to

the girl who first told me about the Cheshire Cat. She also told me that there were ghost children who haunted the subway tunnels, but I didn't believe that either.'

There was a long pause and then Joey stood up. 'I'm going!'

'No, you're not!' Harriet tried to yank him back down again, but he squirmed free and ran down the passage towards the grating.

'I'm going too,' Sammy said, and in a minute all the kids were up and running down the passageway, except for Harriet.

Olivia tossed the copy of *Alice in Wonderland* on the bed beside Harriet. 'Here, you can look at the pictures while we're gone.'

As they started towards the grating, Olivia could hear a soft scurrying behind her every now and then. She resisted the urge to look, hoping that it was Harriet and not some huge rat. Olivia clambered up the pipes first and pushed open the grate, only to find the old Chinese woman was sitting in her chair with a Tupperware container full of shrimp. The old woman stared at her with a stunned look on her wizened face.

'Come on,' Olivia called down to the others.

The old woman leaned forward in her chair to see who would come out of the ground next. First came Sammy, then Joey, then Mary. The old lady didn't seem to see them, but kept her eyes on the grate while her fingers absently pulled the tails off the shrimp.

After a minute, Olivia saw a blonde head pop up and then a pair of huge green glasses. The old woman's eyes grew wide.

The glasses! Olivia realized. Quickly, she whipped them off Harriet's face.

'Hey! Give them back!' Harriet said and she scrambled out of the hole and lunged for them, snatching them back. A brief struggle followed, during which the old woman only saw a pair of green glasses darting about in the air like a confused bird. She laughed, showing a mouthful of brown teeth. Olivia finally managed to wrestle the glasses back from Harriet and she put them on top of her own head. The old woman clapped.

They rode the train uptown, a source of much amazement for the children. Although they'd seen trains rushing by in the tunnels, they'd never actually been in one. As soon as the train pulled out of the station, they darted around the car like monkeys, climbing across people's laps, scooching up the poles, all except Mary who stood between Olivia's legs and stared at everything with her huge, dark eyes.

Olivia breathed a sigh of relief when their stop finally came, and they followed her on to the platform, and then up the stairs and to the park.

The boat pond was teeming with tiny schooners and sailboats, and the children ran to the edge to see them better. Harriet dipped her fingers in the pond. To her delight, the water riffled around her hand.

'Look at that red one,' Joey said, pointing to a handsome sailboat. 'It's racing the yellow, see?' Indeed, the two boats were racing each other across the pond, navigated by two men standing a few feet from Olivia, holding radio remote controls. 'It's going to beat the yellow for sure.'

'Ya! You don't know nothing about ships,' Sammy said. 'The red's a fore-and-aft-rigged ship, so it's bound to be slower than the yellow.'

'What a lot of blabbedy-blab!' Joey said. 'Just open your eyes! The red's already sailing past the yellow!'

'Not for long!' Before Olivia could stop him, Sammy leaped into the pond, shoes and all, and ran pell-mell to the centre where the boats were racing. Hunkering down, he began to splash at the water by the red boat, making it teeter violently. The man who owned the red boat frantically worked his remote control, trying to steer the boat away from the minia-ture typhoon that had mysteriously erupted.

'No way, no way . . .' the man kept muttering. The other man, the owner of the yellow boat, took full advantage of the phenomenon to manoeuvre his boat in an arc around the faltering red boat, and then speed it on past.

But just as it appeared that the yellow boat would win the race without much trouble, Joey jumped in the pond too and, rushing in front of the yellow boat, began to push the water back with his hands. The yellow boat stalled, then reared up like a horse on the waves that Joey had created before it did a wobbly about-face. The yellow boat's owner now joined his adversary in a frenzied attempt to redirect his boat with his remote control.

'Ha!' Joey cried at his brother as his hands continued to push at the water.

'Ha, yourself!' Sammy ran to the yellow boat, picked it up, and tossed it to the winning end of the pond, where it missed the water and hit the cement edge, shattering into bits and splinters. 'Yellow won!'

The two men gawped at the ruined yellow boat, which to their eyes had magically risen out of the water and flown through the air of its own accord only to smash itself to pieces.

'It's almost noon!' Olivia cried out, because she could think of nothing else to do except to walk into the pond herself and try to drag the two of them out, which would have made her look completely crazy. As it was, people were staring at her for screaming to no one at the top of her lungs. But it worked. Joey and Sammy waded out of the pond on the instant, their clothes shedding the water like glass. They were both laughing so hard that Joey had a fit of hiccups. Though they had caused more trouble than a whole classroom full of second-graders, Olivia was somehow glad to see them laughing under the blue sky, like regular kids.

'Is he here?' Mary asked shyly, looking around the pond.

'Who?' Olivia asked.

'The Cheshire Cat,' Mary said.

'Oh. He's just over there,' Olivia said and led them towards the little enclave where the Alice in Wonderland statue was. They all stood there looking at it for a few seconds, awed by its size. But then Harriet snorted.

'It's just a statue. I knew she was lying.'

'It's not noon yet,' Olivia said, showing Harriet her watch. It was about a minute before. 'The cat's up there, right at the top. Watch him.'

The kids gathered around, staring up at the grinning cat. There were half a dozen other children climbing all over the statue, including one little boy who scaled up the statue to see the cat, blocking it from their view. Swiftly, Sammy climbed up after the boy and pinched his leg so hard that he yowled and lost his footing. Right before he tumbled off the statue, the boy miraculously regained his balance, as though an invisible hand had steadied him.

'Five, four, three . . .' Olivia stared at her watch, counting as quietly as she could. 'Keep watching, two, one. Noon!'

The children stared at the cat. So did Olivia. No one breathed.

Absolutely nothing happened.

Nothing at all.

A lump of disappointment clogged her throat. It was silly, she knew. Still, she couldn't help but feel a little disappointed herself. She had hoped that she hadn't been wrong all those years ago. At the time, she had been so sure that the cat had actually winked at her, despite what Christopher had said about it being a trick of sunlight.

Oh well, she thought now. I was just a little kid back then. Little kids have great imaginations. She hoped that little ghost kids did too.

'I told you she was a liar!' Harriet said, promptly dashing that hope.

'That was a cheap trick!' Sammy agreed.

Well, she had gotten the children to leave the tunnel, she told herself. That was the important thing. Now she would try and convince them to come back to the brownstone with her so Madame Brenda could have another try.

'He winked,' Mary said quietly.

'He did not!' Harriet replied.

'You looked away,' Mary said. 'That was when he winked.'

Olivia looked up at the cat. He was grinning, his eyes staring straight ahead.

Harriet made a snide *puh* sound.

The sky had been swiftly darkening, and now the sun was completely blotted out by angry purple clouds. A few drops of rain came down, plinking against the statue.

'He did wink at me,' Mary insisted. She suddenly scuttled up on to the statue with an unexpected burst of energy, climbed up to the Cheshire Cat, and stared right into the cat's face.

The rain was coming down harder now, sending the other children on the statue running to their parents, who hustled them to shelter.

'Come down, Mary,' Olivia called up. But Mary ignored her, throwing her bird-like arms around the cat's neck and pressing her ear against its mouth. She seemed to be listening to something, her solemn, thin face concentrating hard. She smiled and said something to the cat.

'Get down, Mary!' Sammy called to his sister. When she didn't budge, he started up after her.

The rain was falling in needle-drops, fast and numerous. It stung Olivia's eyes and created a filmy haze in the air, obscuring her vision. Consequently, when she saw Mary begin to rise into the air, above the statue, she thought she simply wasn't seeing things clearly.

'She's going!' Sammy yelled down at them through the hissing rain, a note of panic in his voice. He grabbed on to his sister's leg and held her, his legs braced against the cat's shoulder, but the wind picked up in a sudden, violent burst, and knocked him off balance, and then he too was in the air, still clutching Mary's leg.

'Come down, you two nitwits!' Harriet screamed at them.

They stopped for a second, their legs dangling, but then they started to rise again in a slow fashion, with sudden jerks and wobbles. It made Olivia slightly dizzy to watch them.

'Stop that! YOU TWO LOOK RIDICULOUS!' Harriet screamed.

That seemed to be enough incentive for Joey, who now began to rise too, sniggering like a person who is just about to tell the punchline to a really hilarious joke. Harriet made a grab for his legs, but he pulled them up quickly so she couldn't reach. In one final, magnificent gesture, he dropped his pants and mooned her – an impressive feat for someone who was floating in the air.

'I demand you all come back down here, RIGHT NOW!' Harriet pointed a severe finger up at them, but to no avail. Mary and Sammy were high above them, turning into mere wisps of colour in the sky, and Joey was quickly gaining on them, although his ascent was rather zigzaggy.

'It's OK, Harriet,' Olivia said. 'They're heading to the Spirit World. Go on. It's your turn.'

'Never!' Harriet said. She turned and ducked under the mushroom, passing through a veil of rainwater that was coursing over its edge. Olivia followed her.

'Then you'll be stuck here all alone,' Olivia said.

'No, I won't.' Harriet sat down cross-legged, looking as earthbound as possible. 'I'll have Branwell.'

'Well, that's the most selfish thing I ever heard of!' Olivia fumed. 'Did you ever for one moment think of poor Branwell, stuck down in that horrible place. Maybe *you* like it there, but he hates it!'

'I hate it too!' Harriet blurted out.

'Well, for Pete's sake, Harriet! If you hate it there, why don't you leave like the others?'

Harriet was silent, but beneath the steely little features, Olivia noticed something. It made Olivia stare so hard that Harriet began to suck nervously on her upper lip.

'Stop staring,' Harriet said.

'You already tried to leave,' Olivia said. She didn't ask. She just knew. She'd found that shameful secret, tucked in the cupboard behind the rusty can of corn niblets, in the back of Harriet's brain.

Harriet shifted her body uneasily. 'Once,' she admitted.

'What happened?' Olivia asked.

'I didn't like it.'

'Why not?'

'Because. Just because.' Harriet glared at Olivia.

'Oh, *that's* mature,' Olivia said.

'If you want to know,' Harriet said after a pause, 'I didn't like it because when I started to rise, I was afraid that people could look up my dress.'

Olivia had to fight to keep a straight face. 'So what did you do?'

'I started kicking my feet and waving my arms until I felt myself going back down again. When Sammy wanted to try next, I told him that it was awful, and that he'd hate it, and anyway we all should stay right where we were and do whatever we pleased forever after. So that's what we did.'

'But, Harriet,' Olivia said gently, 'living people can't see you, or your knickers. Didn't you notice that on the subway and by the boat pond?'

'Some living people can see me. *You* see me. And that pushy lady. And sometimes when we haunt the tunnels, someone will look right at us out of the window of a train, and you can tell they see us.'

'Look out there,' Olivia pointed out to the torrent of rain. 'Everyone's gone. No one will see up your dress.'

'*You* will,' Harriet said.

'I won't look,' Olivia said.

Harriet rolled on to her knees and peered outside, then looked back at Olivia.

'You promise?'

'Cross my heart.' Olivia crossed her heart.

'Can I have that lady's glasses?' Harriet asked.

'All right.' Olivia took Madame Brenda's glasses off the top of her head and handed them to Harriet, who put them on right away.

Harriet took a deep breath. 'OK. I'm ready,' she said, and she crawled out into the rain.

Olivia crouched under the mushroom and waited, listening in silence to the rapid *pink-pink-pink* of rain against the mushroom. The rain gradually slowed. The sheet of water falling off the mushroom's edge thinned to a trickle.

Finally, Olivia emerged from under the mushroom and looked up at the sky. The thick, dark storm clouds had slid to the east. A splinter of sun fought its way through, making the statue's wet bronze gleam.

Harriet was gone.

She looked up at the Cheshire Cat. It looked straight back at her, grinning madly at nothing at all.

CHAPTER THIRTY-FOUR

Olivia returned home in a jubilant mood, which was instantly squashed by Cornwickle's announcement as he opened the door for her.

'Good afternoon, Miss Kidney. Your mother arrived not an hour ago.'

'Oh?' Olivia said, and glanced past him, wondering if it wasn't too late to turn around and flee.

'Unfortunately, she couldn't wait any longer,' Cornwickle hastened to add.

'Oh,' Olivia brightened, then said, 'Too bad,' when Cornwickle's moustache twitched.

'She was sorry too.' Cornwickle plucked a little yellow bag off the hallway table and handed it to Olivia. 'She left this for you.'

Olivia pulled out a mound of silvery tissue paper from the bag, beneath which was a bra. It had no little pink ribbons or lacy cups or funny seams. It was just a plain white bra, the plainest white bra imaginable. She felt a pinprick of guilt. She shoved the tissue paper back over it so that Cornwickle couldn't see.

'What kind of bug was she today?' Olivia asked casually, trying to conceal her reaction.

'A ladybird, I believe,' Cornwickle said. 'An appropriate choice, since she is to "fly away home" today.'

'Oh, that's right, I forgot.' The pinprick of guilt blossomed into a full-on jab.

'She said she was heading back to her hotel room to pack. The Grand Blue Hotel. Eighty-ninth street and West End Avenue. I imagine it will take her some time to pack, what with all the wings and antennas and whatnot.'

Olivia put the bag back on the table.

'Thanks, Cornwickle,' she said and fled back out the door, down to West End Avenue, and five blocks uptown to The Grand Blue Hotel. Olivia walked by the hotel three times before she noticed it, a dingy brown building squashed between two apartment houses. She entered the dimly lit lobby with its scabby blue carpet, which appeared to be the 'grand blue' part of the hotel, and was directed to the second floor by a grizzled man at the front desk.

'Oh!' Monica was clearly surprised to see her when she opened her door, but she quickly added in a fake, high-pitched jolly tone, 'Well, here's a face I didn't expect to see again any time soon. *Entrez!*' She swept her arm back into a shabby little room whose floor was littered with a mess of clothing and three open suitcases.

'I just wanted to thank you. For the bra, I mean,' Olivia said. 'I really liked it.'

'I thought it would suit you,' Monica said, kneeling down and resuming her packing. 'It's very ordinary.'

Olivia clenched her fists and took a deep breath. It was so hard to like Monica, even when she was really trying to.

'A ladybird.' Olivia gestured to her mother's get-up – a black velvet catsuit with a black-spotted, red-velvet cape tied at her neck. 'Nice.'

'Huh? Oh, this?' Monica untied the cape, balled it up, and tossed it in a suitcase. 'The stores hated the insect idea. New York has been a dismal failure all around. I can't get out of this dump fast enough.' She seemed like she was about to cry. Olivia bit her lip and prayed that she wouldn't. She never knew what to do when people started crying, so she generally wound up standing around, looking like an idiot.

'It was nice to see you,' Olivia lied.

'Oh, please, let's not kid each other.' She flapped her hand at Olivia. 'It wasn't nice at all. You don't need me in your life. Not even for the girl-to-girl talks. You and George can talk about anything.' Monica wasn't even bothering to fold up her clothes, she was simply throwing them into the suitcases.

'That's not true,' Olivia said. 'There are certain things I can't tell Dad.'

'Really?' She stopped packing for a second to give Olivia a sceptical look. 'Like what?'

Olivia considered her mother for a moment. Yes, Monica was self-centred. And no, she wasn't the most stable person in the world. But what Monica did have was an open mind concerning things that were out of the ordinary. Like inner voices. And insect clothing.

'I can't tell Dad that I can talk to spirits.' Olivia spoke the words very quickly, then cringed. Even to her own ears, it sounded crazy.

'What do you talk to them about?' Monica asked. There wasn't a hint of sarcasm in her voice. In fact, she was waiting for an answer with a look of genuine interest on her face.

'I don't know.' Olivia shrugged, suddenly bashful. She wasn't used to discussing her secret so casually. 'The same kind of things I'd talk to living people about, I guess. Spirits and living people aren't all that different.'

After a few minutes of answering her mother's slew of questions – like if the spirits told her the future and did they wear clothes – Olivia actually felt relieved to be talking about the subject out loud with someone other than Madame Brenda.

Then Olivia ventured one step further. 'I talk to Christopher too,' she said.

Monica blinked and started, as though someone had suddenly reached out and snapped their fingers under her nose. She was silent for a few moments.

'How is he?' she asked finally.

'Good. Really good.'

'Honestly? You're not just saying that?' Her eyes were glassy with tears.

'Honestly,' Olivia assured her.

Monica nodded, smiling a little. The tears were slipping down her face now. 'I just can't think about him any more. It's too painful.'

Olivia sat down on the floor by her mother. 'He's tried to contact you, you know.'

'He has?' Monica looked at Olivia.

'Yes. Lots of times. But he says you've blocked him out. He can't get through at all.'

Monica nodded. She suddenly looked around the room. 'Is he here now?'

'No. But I can try and contact him. I haven't had much luck lately, but I can give it a shot.'

Monica stiffened up, frowning. 'I don't know.' Her fingers were nervously playing with her grasshopper hat. 'All right. Yes. Do it.'

'It'll just take a sec,' Olivia said, then closed her eyes. She thought of Christopher, and this time it took only moments before she felt him coming through – rushing through, really.

'Well, it's about time, kiddo!' she heard him say. 'Whenever I tried to visit you, I felt like someone was playing volleyball with my head. Remind me never to get you angry again.'

'I will,' Olivia said. She could feel his relief, the same as she could feel her own.

'Christopher, did you know that Mom never came to the hospital to visit you?'

'No,' he admitted. 'I guess that came as a bit of a shock.'

'Mom's here, you know.' She spoke to him out loud now, not just in her head. It felt incredibly free-ing, like the way she felt each spring when she finally was able to discard her winter jacket and feel the sun on her skin.

'I see her,' Christopher said.

'He sees you,' Olivia told Monica.

'Really?' Monica ran her hand through her hair. 'I look like a mess. My eyes are all swollen.'

'She's still so vain,' Christopher said laughing.

'He says you look fine,' Olivia told Monica.

'Tell him I'm sorry, Olivia,' Monica said.

'Tell him yourself,' Olivia said. 'He hears you.'

'Where is he? Where should I look?' Monica asked, gazing around.

'He's here.' Olivia patted her chest. 'You can look at me.'

'Really?' Monica looked into Olivia's eyes, as though she were trying to find him in there. It was disconcerting to have her mother look at her in that way. Monica's eyes looked different somehow, gentler maybe.

'Hi, Christopher . . .' Monica started uneasily. 'I want you to know . . . you see, when you got sick . . . it was so awful and everything. I mean, you were my little boy, my sweet, happy-go-lucky little boy, and the thought that you were going to . . . Oh, I know you were calling for me when you were in the hospital. George pleaded with me to come see you. But I'm not like George. Or Olivia. I just couldn't bear it. Not even for your sake, Christopher. You died feeling like I'd disappointed you. You died hating me, and I don't blame you.'

Olivia felt the urge to grab Monica's hand. It was Christopher's urge, not her own. But this time Christopher did not make Olivia's hand move. Olivia could feel him trying to keep still, out of respect for her.

'Thank you,' she said to Christopher.

'No problem,' he replied.

Then Olivia reached out and took Monica's hand of her own accord.

'Tell her that of course I don't hate her,' Christopher said. 'Tell her all I really wanted at the hospital was to say goodbye.'

Olivia told Monica, and Monica squeezed Olivia's hand. She was still crying, but she was smiling now too. 'Oh, wait!' Monica said suddenly, letting go of Olivia's hand. 'Shhh. I can hear him!'

'You can?' Olivia asked, amazed.

Christopher went silent in Olivia's head, and now appeared to be talking into Monica's. Monica tipped her head to the right, nodding and smiling every so often. 'I know,' Monica said, 'I feel the same.' And then, 'Well, I'll try but I'm not making any promises.'

It was a little disconcerting to see someone else talking to Christopher when she herself couldn't hear him, but Olivia waited as patiently as she could until they were through.

'Goodbye, Christopher,' Monica said. 'Come visit whenever you can. Do you need to know my address?' She listened, then laughed and held up her hands. 'All right, all right, I was just checking. I don't know how all this stuff works.' She waited for a second, frowning into space. 'He's gone,' she said finally.

'Oh.' Olivia couldn't help feeling a little hurt that he hadn't even said goodbye to her before going.

'Thank you, Olivia.'

'My pleasure,' she said, and she meant it. 'Well, I'll let you finish packing.' She moved to get up, but Monica leaned forward and grabbed her, then hugged her tightly.

'You've turned out to be a *very* interesting person,' Monica said. Olivia suppressed a smile. She knew it was silly, but she was flattered nevertheless.

Out in the hallway, a mote of dust flickered around her head.

'Christopher?' she said.

'Yup.'

'I thought you left already. Hey, what did you say to her?'

'Absolutely nothing,' Christopher replied with amusement.

'You mean she made all that stuff up?' Olivia asked as she headed back down the stairs.

'Let's just say Mom's got a great imagination. Anyway, whatever she heard seemed to make her happy. I don't mind taking the credit for it. Thanks for doing that, kiddo. You're a champ. I missed you, you know.'

'Yeah, me too. Are we on for a field trip next Saturday?'

'Don't think I can,' Christopher replied with a sigh.

'I've started a new assignment. And, by the way, I was right about them waiting for a real hard case to come along. And not just one of them, but four of the most unruly kids imaginable. The oldest one won't listen to a thing I say and the youngest one keeps mooning me!'

CHAPTER THIRTY-FIVE

They had company back at the brownstone. Olivia's mouth dropped open when she spotted the visitor through the living room's French doors, sitting very erectly on the divan in the garden. Ivan Simko was holding a saucer with a cup of tea and chatting amiably with Madame Brenda.

Olivia slipped past the doors and ran to the kitchen, where her father was busy piling several tiny little tarts on to a tray.

'Dad, what is that man doing here?' Olivia cried.

'Mister Simko, you mean? He lives across the street. Nice fellow –' then putting his hand over his mouth, added confidentially – 'but a little gloomy. Here, take this out for him.' He held out the tray of tarts filled with something greenish-brown. 'Liver tarts. They're for the wedding. I want to see if he thinks that they taste authentic. He's not Babatavian exactly but . . . Cazegornian, Kapastanian, something like that.'

'But, Dad, he's an assassin!'

'An assassin? No kidding?' George said, with exaggerated astonishment. 'Boy you never can tell about people. Go on.' He shoved the tray of tarts into Olivia's hands. 'Take this out to him. If he tries to kill you by hurling his dentures at your head, you can use the tray as a shield.'

'Ha, ha.'

Well, she thought, holding the tray in her hands, I'm not going to run from him. She went out through the kitchen door into the garden. Madame Brenda and Mr Simko stopped talking and looked over at her.

'Here she is now! We were just discussing you, darling!' Madame Brenda exclaimed. Her hair did look a lot better. It was still tomato-red, but the dark roots were gone and it was twirled tightly in a neat up-do. 'I'd like to introduce you to Ivan Simko.'

'I know who he is,' Olivia said coldly, putting the tray down on the little table.

'The littlin girlie seen me watching her window, I thinking,' Mr Simko said.

'That's right. What happened to your finger, Mister Simko?' Olivia demanded.

'Olivia, that's rude!' Madame Brenda cried, then looked at the tray. 'What are those things. They look awful.' Madame Brenda picked up one of the tarts and smelt it. 'Smell awful too.'

'Oh la! Liver tart!' Mr Simko took one and popped it in his mouth whole. His grey eyes rolled up in ecstasy. 'Perfectin! Bravo!' he cried after he swallowed, clapping towards the open kitchen door, where George was peering out anxiously. George smiled at Mr Simko's approval. When Mr Simko turned back to Madame Brenda, George tapped his teeth and widened his eyes at Olivia, then laughed and disappeared back in the kitchen.

'Mister Simko was *not* looking at you through your window,' Madame Brenda said to Olivia.

'Oh yes he was! He was staring right at me!' Olivia was incensed that no one believed her.

'I was looking in your window, this being true,' Mr Simko admitted. 'But not at you. No, I was looking for the other littlin girlie. The one who I . . . the one who I killed.'

Olivia stared at him in shock. 'You killed a girl?'

'He killed Abby, cupcake,' Madame Brenda said.

'Abby!' Olivia looked at them in confusion. 'But she said her sister killed her. That she pushed her out a window.'

'*I* did it!' Mr Simko pounded his chest. 'Me! Not sister! Me!'

Madame Brenda patted Mr Simko on the back. 'Now, now. No need to wallop yourself.' Madame

Brenda turned to Olivia and explained, 'Abby's sister and Mister Simko became very good friends when they were younger.'

'Good friends! Bah! I loved her!' Mr Simko interrupted passionately.

'Yes, but they were just young teenagers back then, and the situation was complicated. Anyway, Abby walked into a room and found Mr Simko kissing her sister. Abby has never been a particularly nice girl—'

'A jealous beast, she was!' Mr Simko cried.

'She flung open the window and threatened to tell the people on the street below that her sister had been kissing the famous Ivan Simko, whom they were all lined up to see perform that evening in that very theatre. He was dancing the role of the Nutcracker Prince while the part of Clara was to be performed by the even more famous and beloved Mona Monsoon – Abby's sister.'

'No kidding! Miss Monsoon?' Olivia was astonished.

'Oh yes, darling. And Abby's little announcement would have been the talk of all the gossip pages.'

'Mona was very modest girlie,' Mr Simko shook his head. 'She would have being depavaded.'

'Devastated, yes, darling.' Madame Brenda said. 'So in the *heat of the moment,*' Madame Brenda emphasized these last words for Mr Simko, 'Ivan gave Abby a shove just as she was leaning over the window sill, and out she tumbled. The horrified crowds looked up to see Mona, who had rushed to the window. They didn't see Ivan who had slumped to the floor, appalled by what he'd done. The Yurkistani Ballet Company hustled Ivan out of the country straight away. Mona never told the police that Ivan did it. She took the blame instead.'

'I live with suchin guilt for all my life,' Mr Simko shook his head. 'I am coward!' He started to pound on his chest again.

'Yes, perhaps you were, darling,' Madame Brenda put her hand on his to stop him from pummelling himself. 'But the fact is, now you have come to America to make it all right. Ivan tracked down Mona,' Madame Brenda explained to Olivia. 'He wanted to make an announcement to the newspapers about what had really happened to Abby. But Mona wouldn't hear of it. She said that the only thing she would like him to do was to tell Abby that he was the murderer, not her. Abby had been haunting poor Mona for years, until Mona came to me for help. I managed to make Abby leave Mona's apartment – and now, of course, we are plagued with the obnoxious girl – but Mona hates thinking that her sister blames her for her death. Mona told him where Abby was, and he took an apartment across the street and watched for her night after night. He promised Mona he wouldn't tell anyone the true story, so he was trying to speak with Abby in secret. But Abby's a wily one! Hard to find when you want her.'

'Not really,' Olivia said. 'She's always pestering me in my room.'

'Yes!' Mr Simko pointed a finger at Olivia. 'That's where-ing I seen her! That's why I always stare in your window.'

'A murderer can always see the ghost of the person he has murdered,' Madame Brenda explained just as Olivia was about to object.

'So finally, today,' Mr Simko continued, 'I come to knockin on your door and this plentiful great lady help me. I talk to Abby this afternoon. I tell her it was me. And that I'm sorry for what I been done. Guess what she say? She say she know it was me who killed her all along.'

'Of course she did, darling,' said Madame Brenda. 'Murdered ghosts always know who their real murderers are. Abby simply preferred the story about her sister being the killer – she knew it made poor Mona miserable.'

'Yeah, that sounds like Abby,' Olivia agreed.

Mr Simko slapped his knees and stood. 'I must shall tell Mona, yes. She will be so happy. Ah, but the little girlie, she wants to know about my finger.'

'No, no,' Olivia waved her hands, embarrassed. 'It's OK, really.'

'I don't mind telling you,' Mr Simko said affably. 'It

came from accident when I was boy. A tiger bit it off.'
He smiled. 'But I dance on toes, not on fingers, so I
not minding very much.'

After Mr Simko left, Olivia sat down on the divan
and smiled at Madame Brenda. 'Guess what?' she
said.

'Oh, darling, I hate the "guess what" game. I
always guess right and then you'll be disappointed.'

'You won't this time,' Olivia said.

'Oh, all right. Let's see . . . you talked those horrible children into leaving the tunnel. There! You see!'
Madame Brenda pointed at the disappointed expression on Olivia's face. 'But really, that's just
marvellous, darling! How did you manage it?'

So Olivia recounted the whole story about the children, and Madame Brenda listened to it all with such
absorption, occasionally shaking her head in wonder,
that it nearly made up for her guessing correctly. At
the end of the story, Madame Brenda asked her to
repeat the part about the Cheshire Cat winking and
Mary climbing up to talk to him.

'Crafty old devil!' Madame Brenda exclaimed,
smiling. 'Still hanging around that statue. I knew he'd
find a way.'

'Who are you talking about?' Olivia asked.

'Oh, many, many years ago, the commissioner of
Central Park hired me – in secret, of course – to get

rid of a ghost that had been haunting the Alice in Wonderland statue. He said that several people had spotted a morose-looking man lurking around the statue, then suddenly disappearing. Well, I went to have a chat with the ghost, and who do you think it was? Charles Lutwidge Dodgson!'

'*Who?*'

'The author of *Alice in Wonderland*. Lewis Carroll was only his pen name, darling. Anyway, long story short, he wasn't actually *haunting* the statue. On the contrary, he was watching over the little children who came to play there. The statue is treacherously slippery, he told me, and children were always losing their footing. He felt awfully responsible for them, since it was his statue, so he was sort of hanging around, catching the little ones who started to fall and setting them right again. I told him that while it was an admirable thing, he might try being a bit more discreet in the future. I guess he's hidden himself in the Cheshire Cat.'

Olivia smiled. So she hadn't been wrong about that cat after all.

'I bet Branwell will miss those kids,' Olivia said.

'Mark my words,' Madame Brenda said, 'Branwell will find someone else to look after. He's that type. Just like sneaky old Charles Lutwidge Dodgson.'

'I have a friend,' Olivia said slowly, the idea just forming in her head, 'who could use some sleep. Do you think Branwell would be willing to watch over an old lady at night?'

'Well, it wouldn't be nearly as exciting as chasing around a pack of under-aged monsters, but I'll bet he'd be happy to help. Ansel! Back from the meeting with the board already?'

Ansel had entered the garden through the living-room door, dressed in his sombre-looking suit, and looking exceptionally pleased with himself.

'I take it that things went well at the meeting?' Madame Brenda said, smiling back at her son.

'Gorgeously,' Ansel replied.

'And why not?' Madame Brenda addressed this to Olivia, clapping her hands together. 'My little boy can charm the stripes off a zebra.'

'Oh good Lord, they detest me, Mother,' Ansel said, pulling off his jacket and tossing in on to the privet hedge. 'We all have to leave the brownstone by next Friday, noon sharp.'

Both Madame Brenda and Olivia were shocked into silence.

'Come on, ladies, don't look so tragic!' Ansel said, squeezing in between them and putting an arm around each of them. 'Yes, I know I was feeling a little blue about all this myself, but at that meeting I realized something wonderful. In six days I'll be tossed to the gutter, stranded, with no place to go. Same with George and Olivia and even Cornwickle.'

'Ignore him, Olivia,' Madame Brenda said, looking very displeased. 'My son has obviously gone completely insane.'

'But I loved it here,' Olivia said. 'It was the first real home I've ever had.'

'Don't you see, Olivia, love,' Ansel said jubilantly. 'Deep down, in our heart of hearts, we are adventurers – you, your father and myself. Who knows where the wind will blow us? For myself, I do believe I will go to Italy – for a while at least, until the wind blows me elsewhere.'

'But I don't want to be blown anywhere!' Olivia insisted. 'I don't want adventure. I just want a normal life. One home, one school. Normal.'

'Really!' Ansel said in a shocked voice. 'What on earth would you do with a normal life? You'd be so bored you'd break out in hives. You wait and see, Olivia, my love.' Ansel squeezed her shoulder. 'We are all in for a splendid adventure!'

CHAPTER THIRTY-SIX

As was the custom in royal Babatavian weddings, the bride and the Royal Imposter were to ride down the aisle on a pair of black donkeys. The donkeys arrived twenty minutes before the wedding, in a tremendous truck on whose side was painted DIANA'S TRAVELLING BARNYARD. Below that, painted on as an afterthought it seemed was, & GIANT DONKEYS.

'Giant Donkeys?' Olivia looked at Frannie. Dressed in their gowns – Olivia in her wedding gown and Frannie in a bright orange bridesmaid gown with a strangely tattered-looking hem – they had peered out the window as the truck pulled up. 'I don't like the sound of that.'

But when the back door of the truck was lowered to form a ramp and the donkeys were led out, they were the tiniest donkeys imaginable. The two black animals, though very handsome, were no taller than Olivia's waist.

'How are we supposed to ride those things?' Olivia said. 'It must be a mistake. The Princepessa is going to have a fit.'

In a flash, Frannie lifted the hem of her gown and darted off, returning a few moments later with Arthur, dressed in a black morning jacket with tails, a white waistcoat and a grey tie.

'There they are,' Frannie told him, pointing out the window at a large-hipped, bleached-blonde woman pulling the donkeys around the front yard by leads attached to their halters. The halters seemed far too large for the little donkeys, hanging loosely around their delicate little faces.

Arthur turned pale and rushed outside, followed by Frannie and Olivia.

'No, no, no, my good woman,' he said to the blonde lady. 'Wrong donkeys! These beasts are way too small.'

'Shhh.' The woman shook her head sternly at him, although it was unclear why she was shushing him.

'Do you have any others in there?' He looked hopefully at the truck. It was large enough to hold half a dozen donkeys.

'Just these two.' Then she added in a loud voice directed at the donkeys, 'How on earth could I fit any *more* donkeys in that truck, sir, when these two are so *huge*!'

She smiled at Arthur and winked. He stared back at her as though she were mad.

After a moment he sighed loudly. 'All right. I guess they'll just have to do.' He returned to the house, muttering, 'She'll have my head . . .'

'Too bad the wedding isn't in a month from now,' the blonde woman said to Olivia and Frannie. 'By then these two should be big enough for a grown man to ride.'

'Are they babies?' Frannie asked, scratching at the muzzle of one of the donkeys.

'Adults. They're miniature donkeys. Or at least that's what everyone expects of them. They have the souls of bold, great big donkeys, of course, but the breeders expected them to be miniature donkeys, so that's what they became. I'm changing all that, however.' There was a hint of boastful pride in her voice.

'How?' Olivia asked.

'Pure common sense. I'm treating them as though they were gigantic donkeys, and eventually they'll grow into the idea.'

'Do you really think that will work?' Frannie asked doubtfully.

'Already has,' the woman said. 'They've each grown four inches in a week. Now come on, you big louts,' she said, fondly slapping the rump of one of the donkeys, 'go on and do your business. We don't want any accidents in these nice people's home.'

Olivia spotted him right then, walking up the street. He was dressed in a dark blue suit with a red tie, and his wild black curls were combed back off his face and tamed with gel.

'Who's that?' Frannie asked, noticing that Olivia was smiling in his direction.

'A friend of mine.' Olivia bit her upper lip to stop it from smiling.

'He's very dashing.'

'He's all right,' Olivia said, but the moment her teeth lost their hold on her lip, she found herself smiling again.

Ruben smiled back as he approached, slapping his hand at his hair as though to remind it to behave. When he reached her, his eyes passed over Olivia's gown with amused puzzlement.

'Isn't it illegal to get married when you're twelve?' he said.

'It's not *my* wedding, you dope,' Olivia said. 'This is Frannie.'

Ruben held out his hand and Frannie, blushing slightly, shook it.

'Some house!' Ruben said, taking in the Vondychomps' mansion. His eyes landed on the tiny donkeys, one of which was now urinating on a patch of grass. 'What's with the goats?'

'Donkeys. They're part of the wedding,' Olivia explained.

'Really?' Ruben looked at Olivia now with an expression of awe. 'Who would have guessed you have such an interesting life. What else haven't you told me?'

'That you have green sparkles in your hair,' Olivia replied.

'I do?' Ruben frowned, touching his hair.

'Did your mother get that hair gel on sale?' Olivia asked.

'Probably,' Ruben said glumly.

'Don't worry,' Olivia said. 'The lights are dim in the mansion. And anyway, I'm the one who's going to be riding on a donkey the size of a hamster. I doubt anyone's going to be looking at your hair.'

As it turned out, the Princepessa was a surprisingly good sport about the donkeys. The wedding was to be performed in the throne room. While the guests gathered, Olivia and the Princepessa waited outside the room's back door with their donkeys. Since they obviously couldn't ride them, they each simply stood with their legs on either side of their donkey, holding the jewel-encrusted reins.

Olivia could feel the Princepessa's eyes on her from behind her veil.

'What?' Olivia said.

'Are you wearing a *bra*?' the Princepessa asked, sounding appalled.

'So what if I am?' Olivia replied. 'You look very nice, by the way.'

'That's no compliment, since we look exactly the same,' the Princepessa responded sourly. Then added, 'But thank you.'

The music started to play – a sombre tune that sounded more like something you'd hear at a funeral. Olivia's donkey shifted his legs restlessly.

The Princepessa took a deep loud breath, and the doors were thrown open to a room festooned with flowers and packed with seated guests. The donkeys launched down the long blue carpet so fast that they scooted right out from between their legs. Olivia and the Princepessa had to scurry to catch them and then pretend to be riding them by walking in shuffling movements with the donkeys beneath them. It was all rather humiliating. As Olivia passed Ruben, who was sitting on the aisle next to her father, she carefully avoided his eyes. Still, she could hear his snorkelling laughter, along with a stifled chuckle that she was pretty sure came from her father. Finally they reached the front of the room and the donkeys were thankfully led away by two men in traditional Babatavian outfits – bright blue silk shirts with red sashes and billowy white trousers.

363

Standing near the throne, on which a crown and sceptre rested on a blue velvet pillow, were Frannie, Viola and Stacy. Dressed in their bright orange bridesmaids' gowns with the shredded hems, they looked like three goldfish with a case of fin rot.

The man performing the wedding gave a long speech in Babatavian, during which Olivia scoped the crowd for potential assassins. In the end, she decided that except for her father and Ruben, everyone looked like a potential assassin.

Finally, Arthur and the Princepessa exchanged vows, in English.

'Once upon a time, I fell in love with a beautiful Princepessa,' said Arthur. 'She was not sweet and kind like the Princepessas in fairy tales. She was stubborn and cranky and she stepped on me each morning like a doormat. But I was the happiest doormat that ever lived on this earth . . . and I still am! Christina Lilli, I love you with all my heart.'

'Doormat?' The Princepessa stared angrily at Arthur for a moment, before she gave her vow: 'In the entire history of Babatavia, no Princepessa has ever fallen in love with a lowly, mouldy-smelling caveboy. Chances are no Princepessa ever will again.' She stopped here, pinched her lips together, and blinked rapidly several times. 'Their loss.'

Arthur placed a large ring with a huge red stone on the Princepessa's finger and they were pronounced man and wife. A flock of doves were released into the air, and Arthur and the Princepessa kissed while everyone cheered.

It was right then that something whizzed through the air right by Olivia's head. It was so close she could feel the slight breeze tickle her cheek. There was a blood-curdling shriek and the sound of something thudding to the ground.

'Assassin!' someone screamed, and everyone scattered. The Princepessa had thrown herself on top of Olivia and Arthur threw himself on top of both of them and they all collapsed to the ground in a very unmajestic tumble.

After waiting a few minutes, during which Olivia had to endure the Princepessa's bony elbow wedged in her collarbone, Arthur rose, then the Princepessa, then Olivia. The room was nearly empty except for Frannie and Viola, who was splayed face down on the floor with Ruben sitting on her broad back. George was pacing around the whole scene, asking, 'Everyone all right? Anyone hurt?'

No one was. It took a few minutes of sorting things out before they realized what had happened. Apparently, at the sight of the flying birds, Viola had grabbed the royal sceptre and taken aim. Ruben had spotted Viola about to hurl the sceptre in the general direction of Olivia's head, and he jumped on her just as the sceptre left her hands.

'I warned you there would be birds in the ceremony,' Frannie scolded Viola, who was being helped to her feet by Ruben. After the Princepessa threatened to knock some sense into Viola with the very same sceptre, she and Arthur collected up the frightened guests and restored their good mood in the banquet room.

The table was heaped with the strange-looking food that George had prepared. None of it looked very appetizing. There were huge hunks of meat that might have come off the hide of a dinosaur, several heaps of some slippery pale green substance, doughy balls rolled in what looked like laundry lint, glutinous pink coils of some sea creature, and, of course, the liver tarts. Scattered about the room were bowls of red boomerang-shaped fruit and hairy black fruit the size of grapes. As per Babatavian tradition, there were no utensils at the table, and the royal-wedding guests plunged right in, scooping up the food with their hands and stuffing it into their mouths. It was all very barbaric. Viola and Mertha looked almost elegant in comparison, as they expertly pinched off bits of meat from the bones.

As the wedding cake was served – a five-tiered thing of beauty, dripping with sugar flowers and ribbons and topped with a sugar replica of the royal crest – the howling Babatavian singer began to serenade them. The guests rushed to the dance floor. Even

George was yanked out of his chair by a fleshy, dark-haired woman wearing a tiara, her neck and wrists and fingers flashing with jewels. Viola plucked Ruben from Olivia's side, much to his horror, and pulled him quite forcefully on to the dance floor.

'Let's get out of here!' Frannie screamed in Olivia's ear. 'This music is awful!'

Olivia checked to see if she could grab Ruben too, but he was already on the dance floor, being swung about mercilessly by Viola. Cake in hand, Olivia and Frannie ducked into the empty throne room, shutting the door to muffle the howling. Frannie ran up to the throne and smiled mischievously.

'I've always wanted to do this,' she said. Carefully, she picked up the crown and placed it on her head. Then she climbed the steps of the dais and hopped on to the throne.

'How do I look?'

'Very regal,' Olivia said. She really did too, Olivia thought.

'I've been thinking about what that woman with the donkeys said,' Frannie remarked as she took a bite of cake. 'About how the miniature donkeys have the souls of bold, great big donkeys? And that she's treating them as though they were gigantic donkeys, so that they'll eventually grow into the idea?'

'Yeah?'

'Do you think that might work for me as well?' Frannie asked.

'It might,' Olivia said. 'You could start by moving into a room with a higher ceiling. I get concussion every time I go in there. What would William James say?'

Frannie cinched her brow and stared up at the ceiling, deep in thought. Sitting on the throne, with the crown on her head, she looked exactly like a wise young queen with cake frosting on the corners of her lips.

'A human being can alter their life by altering their attitude.'

'Well, he hasn't been wrong yet,' Olivia said.

The throne room door opened suddenly, flooding the room with the Babatavian singer's howling. Frannie's mother and her husband, Claude, dashed in. They were holding champagne glasses and giggling while throwing the little hairy black fruits at each other.

'Oopsie!' Mimi cried when she saw that they weren't alone, then succumbed to another laughing fit.

'Maybe you'd better lay off the champagne, Mom,' Frannie said.

'Really? Who made *you* queen?' Mimi said, and began lobbing the fruits at Frannie. Claude joined in, the two of them laughing like hyenas, and Frannie removed her crown and abandoned the throne, crying, 'Oh for goodness sake, grow up!'

She grabbed Olivia and they ran back to the banquet room, dodging the fruits that were falling all around them like small hairy cannonballs.

'How about a spin, Sweetpea?' George came up behind Olivia and whisked her on to the dance floor, grinning wildly.

'You look happy,' Olivia said.

'Why shouldn't I be?' George said, as he waltzed her around. 'I just danced with the Empress of Blavatska.'

'You mean that fat woman?' Olivia asked.

'Stout,' George corrected. 'And what do you think? She loved my food so much, she offered me a job as a live-in cook.'

'In Blavatska?'

'In her *palace* in Blavatska!' George nodded, beaming. 'Wherever that is.' Then his face grew serious. 'Don't worry, I turned her down, of course. I told her that I was trying to keep my daughter's life as normal as possible these days.'

'Thanks, Dad,' Olivia said gratefully. As he spun her around, she saw that Ruben had been released by Viola and was catching his breath in the far corner of the room.

'Dad, do you mind?' She nodded towards Ruben.

'Oh, sure, go right ahead!' He gave her a final twirl

and she squeezed past the dancers and over to Ruben.

'Having fun?' Olivia asked him. His face was pink and shiny with sweat.

'You'd never guess it,' Ruben said, blowing a flopped curl out of his eye, 'but that Viola is a pretty good dancer. Light on her feet and all. I bet she wouldn't be half-bad on a skateboard.'

'Well, she's right over there, sticking her finger in the wedding cake,' Olivia said a little huffily. 'Go ask her to dance again.'

'Nah.' Ruben stood up and took Olivia by the hand. 'I'd rather dance with you.'

At first it felt very strange to dance with Ruben. His hand rested lightly on her back and she put her hand on his shoulder. She'd never stood so close to him. She wondered if her breath smelt OK. Then she realized that his breath didn't smell too great anyway – apparently he had sampled one of George's liver tarts – but she found that she didn't mind at all. She didn't even mind the music that much either. In fact, she was starting to see why the Princepessa liked it. As she danced, the wailing began to sound very much like a wild, wind-whipped ocean, which made her think of faraway places and of ancient stone castles under a brooding purple sky.

Quite suddenly, a prickly heat spread across her

neck where the veil was touching it. She took the veil off her head and draped it over her arm, but the skin on her neck still tingled uncomfortably. Then it began to itch.

'Fleas?' Ruben asked when Olivia began to scratch at the back of her neck.

'Ha, ha.' The itch grew worse, and she scratched even harder.

'Let me have a look,' Ruben said. He turned her around and lifted her hair to see her neck. 'Hmm. Looks like you just broke out in hives,' he said.

'Hives?' Olivia said. She frowned as Ansel's words came back to her: *What on earth would you do with a normal life? You'd be so bored you'd break out in hives.*

'Hey, Ruben,' Olivia said, when they started dancing again. 'Have you ever heard of Blavatska?'

'Is it a disease?' he asked, eyeing her neck.

'No! It's a country, you dope.'

'Can't be much of one if I've never even heard of it.'

'Enough of a country to have an empress,' she retorted as Ruben dipped her. 'And a palace.'

The singer made a strange high-pitched noise in his throat. It sounded like the wind whistling through craggy, white-tipped mountains. A wild wind that was strong enough to lift Olivia and her father high above New York City and blow them clear across the

Atlantic Ocean. A wind that would blow them far, far away from a normal life, and closer to a splendid adventure.

GOT A MIND-BLOWING MYSTERY TO SOLVE?
CALL OLIVIA KIDNEY!

Have you read Olivia's first two crazy adventures?

AND

Enter Olivia's world and meet a weird and wonderful cast of characters. There's an exiled princess, a ghostly friend, talking lizards, snapping turtles – and more!

**A hilarious helter-skelter adventure
from the creator of the OLIVIA KIDNEY series!**

Clara Frankofile is only eleven and she already has her own apartment – complete with roller coaster and bumper cars! Each night at her parents' hip Pish Posh restaurant, stylish Clara watches the glittery movie actors and rock stars and decides who is important enough to stay – and who is not. But Clara's world is turned upside down when she discovers that a mystery is happening right under her nose. With the help of her new friend Annabelle, a whip-smart jewel thief, Clara embarks on a spectacular mission through the streets of New York City to uncover a 200-year-old secret.

A selected list of titles available from Macmillan Children's Books

The prices shown below are correct at the time of going to press.
However, Macmillan Publishers reserves the right to show new retail prices
on covers, which may differ from those previously advertised.

Ellen Potter

Olivia Kidney	978-0330-42079-2	£4.99
Olivia Kidney Stops for No One	978-0330-42080-8	£4.99
Pish Posh	978-0330-44631-0	£7.99

All Pan Macmillan titles can be ordered from our website,
www.panmacmillan.com, or from your local bookshop
and are also available by post from:

Bookpost, PO Box 29, Douglas, Isle of Man IM99 IBQ
Credit cards accepted. For details:
Telephone: 01624 677237
Fax: 01624 670923
Email: bookshop@enterprise.net
www.bookpost.co.uk

Free postage and packing in the United Kingdom